Water and Blood

WATER
and
BLOOD

Rik Lonsdale

NP
Nordor Press

For JIS.

Chapter 1

On a grey, autumn afternoon in October, an ebbing tide tugged at the few remaining slates clinging to the spire of St Oswald's church. The click-clack of the slates easing from their nails carried across the water, through the open window of the jeep, and into the ears of Lucy Marchand.

'At least we've got the cockerel,' she said, turning her attention from the slow demolition of Barfleet's parish church to the makeshift willow cage on her lap.

'It cost us the last of the diesel. We've just about enough to get us home,' said her father. 'Can you see the roof of the nave yet?'

Lucy peered across the estuary at the receding water. 'Yes, it's clearing the tide, look.' James followed her outstretched finger.

'Good. We can cross the bridge now.' He started the engine and edged the jeep onto the empty road.

The Old Barr Bridge now served as a ford, passable only at low tide. Crossing at a crawl, the jeep slushed a wake at the ramparts, steam coming from the bonnet as it climbed from

1

the water and turned away from the sunken town.

A few miles from home James pulled up in the middle of the road.

'Why are we stopping here?' said Lucy.

'Look.' He pointed at a twist of smoke climbing above the trees ahead. 'That wasn't there when we left. It's on the road too. Put the cage behind the seat.'

Around the corner, men were building a barricade, piling rubbish around the wreck of a smouldering saloon. When they heard the engine two of the men stepped from the barricade into the road, signalling the jeep to stop; their nonchalance buttressed by a shotgun.

'I'm pulling over, be ready to leave, and smile.'

As the jeep slowed the men shared a look and a grin. From the corner of her eye, Lucy saw another man jump from the growing blockade and approach the other side of the jeep.

'We've got to get out of here, they're surrounding us.'

'I know,' said James, riding the clutch, 'hold tight.' He floored the accelerator and they sped forward. One man jumped to avoid them; the others yelled. The jeep found the last gap, shouts pursued them as they crashed through, sending trash cartwheeling skyward. Then the blast, the pounding, wounding blast.

The cabin filled with shot, automotive glass, and Lucy's screams. The blast threw her against her father. His hold on the wheel slipped when he turned and saw Lucy's blood covered face.

The jeep jinked, hit the kerb, swerved across the road, and took the bark from the edge of a tree. James forced his attention to his driving and wrestled the jeep from its mad meander back onto the narrow strip of tarmac; his daughter slumped against him.

'Lucy, Lucy!' he called. The answer was another blast.

James heard shot peppering the back of the jeep. He snatched a look in the blood spattered rear-view. A black pickup truck pulled up by the barricade, men jumped aboard. Determination joined his hands gripping the wheel.

James drove as fast as he dared. He took corners at angles which would have killed him with oncoming traffic, a few weeks ago. Now the fuel was gone, and the roads deserted.

While he drove, he kept calling. 'Lucy, wake up, are you all right?' A moan rewarded his efforts as the old oak tree came into view. Around the next bend, The Lane to Cleeve House offered sanctuary.

He stomped on the brakes and swung the jeep towards what looked like a hedge. The bushes parted. James bumped the jeep into The Lane, killed the engine, and turned to Lucy.

A bearded face appeared at the blown-out window.

'Christ she's a mess, what happened?'

'Rob, thank God. There's a barricade. They wanted us to stop. They're following, can you...'

'It's secure. They can't get in. We need to get her to the house; she needs help.'

Lucy moaned. Blood ran from her face and arm.

'It looks bad,' said Rob.

'Have they gone past yet?'

The roar of an engine passing gave James his answer.

'Do you want me to drive?' said Rob.

'I'm okay, but can you take her weight?'

Rob climbed into the cab, ignoring the shards of glass, and squeezed in beside his sister, hugging her bloody form towards him.

Lucy moaned again when Rob moved her.

'Hush, it's okay, we'll have you home soon.' He cradled Lucy in his arms, trying to avoid her injuries.

James began the slow descent along the gloomy tree lined

track, fast becoming slippery now trees were shedding. The mile to the narrow bridge over the River Wast took an age.

'What happened?' moaned Lucy as the jeep bumped over the bridge and began the steep ascent. 'Ow! My eye hurts.' She began to raise her arm to her face, but Rob took hold of her wrist.

'You've been shot, Lucy. Best not rub your eye in case there's some damage there. Now hush, there's nothing we can do until we get home.'

'Don't "hush" me,' Lucy flared and shrugged his arm off. 'I want to see what's happened.'

She stretched her hand out and turned the bloody rear-view so she could see herself. 'Christ, I can only see out of one eye.' She lifted her hand to her face again.

'Careful, if there's glass in there, you'll do more damage,' said Rob.

The jeep lurched over a rut as her hand approached her face, jolting her arm. 'Okay, I'll wait until we get home.'

In the yard behind Cleeve House, Lucy climbed from the jeep, blood dripping from her fingers, leaving smears on the door handle and upholstery. As her feet touched the ground her mother rushed from the house.

'What's happened? You're hurt.' Her face creased with worry, Connie took in her daughter's bloody face and pushed past James to her side.

'There was a barricade, it was horrible, they shot me.'

Lucy swayed. 'We've got the rooster, Mum, haven't we, Dad?' As she turned to look at her father, the car, the house, the yard, all began to spin. She opened her mouth to speak again, but no words came. A whirling black tornado overwhelmed her. She fell.

Rob caught his sister and lowered her to the ground as Ben

came running into the yard.

'What's happened, Dad?' said Ben.

'There was a barricade your sis—'

'There isn't time now,' said Connie. 'Ben, you and Rob carry her into the house. Lay her on the couch; I'll get some water.' Connie hurried off to the kitchen while the brothers carried their unconscious sister into Cleeve House.

When Connie returned the three men stood watching her wring a cloth in the cold water and begin to clean Lucy's face. Tending her daughter's wounds, Connie felt her eyes stab with oncoming tears. She stopped and stood. 'Shouldn't you three be doing something useful?'

There were sheepish looks and mumbles as the brothers left the room.

'I need to know she's okay,' said James, brow furrowed.

'Of course you do, Jim. Leave me to look after her. I'll let you know as soon as I can.'

James turned to leave. 'I should never…' James began. But Connie had already turned her attention back to Lucy, wrapping a blanket around her in the cold room. She didn't notice him slip out of the door, pulling it closed behind him.

Connie dipped the cloth in water, already turning crimson from Lucy's blood, and dabbed at the wounds again. Her vision misted as she worked. Her spirits had soared when Lucy returned from the USA; now she lay injured. She had no skill except that gained being a mother, and no facilities. They had some first aid supplies, but they could only help with minor injuries. Her concern was tinged with outrage; who dared put her daughter's life at risk? She pulled strands of Lucy's strawberry blonde hair away from her bloody face. The same colour and wilfulness as Connie's own hair once was. Now she was grey, and still nursing her children.

* * *

She remembered cleaning the skinned knees of seven-year-old Lucy, the child's mouth clamped shut, eyes bright, her determination already strong. That determination had tugged Connie's heart.

These wounds were different. They were malicious. Connie prised a shard of glass from Lucy's cheek and used the cloth to stem oozing blood. She's going to have scars, thought Connie, moving on to another remnant of the shooting, avoiding the eye until Lucy awoke.

Seven-year-old Lucy wore the scar on her knee like a badge of honour. Connie couldn't persuade her to wear trousers or long skirts until deep into autumn. She covered it only after a school friend had a broken arm.

Connie used a sleeve to wipe the tears from her eyes as Lucy stirred. Her heart sang with relief as she watched her daughter's eyelids flutter, and the faces of the seven-year-old and the twenty-five-year-old Lucy merged.

Lucy moaned and began to turn over. A gentle hand on her shoulder stopped her.

'Stay still a moment, Lucy. Take your time. It's best if you stay lying down just now.'

'Ow, my eye hurts. What happened?'

'You fainted. Probably shock.'

'I remember the car, the barricade, it was awful. Is my eye all right?'

'I haven't looked at your eye yet. And there's bits of shot and glass I need to take out of your cheek before I can clean you up properly.' She paused and examined the eye. 'This might hurt, I'll have to clean away some dried blood before I can look. Stay still now.'

Peering at the eye Connie saw a piece of glass caught on the inside of the bottom lid, pressing against the sclera, the eye bloodshot. She picked up a pair of tweezers and aimed for the shard. Lucy blinked and yelled.

'You have to stay still. I know it's hard, but if you scratch the cornea, it will be permanent damage. I need to get it out.'

'Okay, Mum, sorry,' said Lucy, her hands squeezing the cushions of the couch.

Connie tried once more, this time gripping the glass in the tweezers and pulling it free. A fresh wound opened in Lucy's eyelid.

'Will my eye be all right now?'

'Maybe, I don't know. Can you see out if it?' Connie covered Lucy's right eye with her hand.

'It just looks red.'

'That's blood, but there's something else in there. Maybe a piece of shot. It's buried in your eyeball. I'm not sure I can get it without causing more damage.'

'What do you mean? Are you going to leave it there?'

'If you can put up with it. I'll see to the rest of your face while I think about it. Your hand's okay. It looks worse than it is. Just a few scratches.'

Lucy gave herself over to the ministrations of her mother; wincing as remnants of the shooting were persuaded from her face.

'Aw Mum, my youthful good looks, what'll happen to them?'

Connie smiled. 'You're young enough for most of these to heal soon. There are one or two could do with a stitch. You'll probably have a couple of small scars. Now stay still, unless you want big scars.'

'Where is everybody?' said Lucy.

'Emily and Lottie are seeing to the chickens. Everyone else is making sure no one came up The Lane after you. Now let's have another look at the eye.'

After a close inspection Connie drew a breath. 'There's definitely something in there, it probably hurts. It's too deep for me to get a hold of. Your body might just push it out. We'll cover it and leave it bandaged for a few days, see if that helps. I'll have a look every day and clean it.'

Lucy saw hidden worry behind her mother's calmness. She saw the damp stains on front of Connie's jacket, below her chin, and knew them to be the remnants of Connie's tears.

Chapter 2

'What's wrong with Auntie Lucy, Mum?' said Lottie.

'She's just had an accident but don't worry, she has Gran looking after her,' Emily told her six-year-old.

'I want to look after her, but she's all... horrid.'

'It did look scary, but she'll be fine once Gran has cleaned her up.'

'I bet Daddy could mend her.'

'I expect you're right.'

'He can do anything, my daddy.'

Emily hid her sigh. How had Ben become Lottie's favourite parent? 'He is very clever, but Gran can do lots too and I'm sure Auntie Lucy will be fine with her.'

'Are you really, really sure?'

'You'll see when we get back. Now those chickens will be getting hungry.'

'Yay, I like the chickens.'

'Here's the grain bucket and here's the kitchen scraps, which would you like to carry?'

'The grain bucket is soooo heavy, and the scrap bucket is yucky.'

Emily smiled at her daughter's dilemma. 'Never mind, I'll carry them both and you can open the gates for me.'

As they trudged up the path to the chicken run Lottie asked, 'When are we going home, Mummy?'

An image of their house in London, awash with fetid water, swam into Emily's head. The home they had saved hard for, the nursery where Lottie slept, the kitchen extension with its bright atrium, all gone, swamped by the rising sea. And gone with it all the hopes and dreams of the future of their family. 'Don't you like it here at Gran's?' she asked.

'Yes, it's just…'

They arrived at the run. A chorus of clucks welcomed the springing of the corn bucket lid.

'Just what, poppet? That one over there looks hungry.'

Lottie threw a fistful of corn at the chicken.

'Just, I want to play with Michaela.'

'Michaela won't be at school anymore, none of the children will be.'

'Why? We're best friends.'

'The school will be under the big water I told you about.'

'Gran's isn't under the big water.'

'No, poppet, it isn't. Like I told you, Gran's house is higher than the big water.'

'Is the big water very high? I'm big, is it higher than me?'

'It's much higher than you, Lottie.'

'Is it higher than Daddy?'

'Yes, it's higher than Daddy. If I stood on Daddy's head, and you stood on my head, it would still be higher than all three of us.' She watched Lottie try to fathom the image. How else could she explain an eight-metre increase in sea levels?

A frown crossed Lottie's face. 'Is it bigger than Michaela?' she said.

'It's bigger than everyone.'

'Does that mean Michaela is under the big water?'

Emily heard the distress in Lottie's voice. 'I expect Michaela has gone to her gran's, just like you.' She loaded her voice with false conviction. She didn't know the fate of the millions in the city. Her imagination baulked at creating the scenes of panic flooding the city as swiftly as the water.

Emily watched Lottie weigh her words and saw another question begin to form. 'And besides, Gran needs us here to help with the chickens. You like the chickens, don't you?'

The first time Lottie asked these questions, Emily had tried to explain about the West Antarctic glacier falling into the sea, and the wave circling the globe causing more ice to cascade from Greenland. But the questions kept coming and now Emily resorted to distraction.

Within her, another new life made itself felt. What sort of world would she be bringing her second child into? Already Emily was always hungry. The stock room was piled high with cans and packets but when Ben showed her how much they used in a day she could see it wouldn't last long unless there were other sources of food. The dozen birds they had wouldn't be enough.

Thanks to his post in the Climate Research Institute, Ben had given his family time to get to Cleeve House. Now Lucy lay injured. A tug at her sleeve pulled her from her thoughts.

'Mum, are you thinking about Auntie Lucy?'

'No, poppet, I'm thinking about chickens. Which is your favourite today?'

'I like that one best, the one with the black feather,' said Lottie, pointing to one of the flock of Welsummers. Ben had thought of everything, there were extra sacks of grain and oyster shell for them.

'What's her name?' said Emily.

'Bobby,' said Lottie, throwing a handful of corn.

Emily closed the latch on the corn bin. 'Come on, let's see how many eggs we get today.'

'Can I carry them?'

'Yes, but you must be careful, they are very precious.'

Chapter 3

Ben paused at the door of the lounge to listen to Lucy playing the piano.

'That's lovely, though a bit downbeat,' he said.

Lucy startled to a stop. She turned her good eye on Ben. 'I didn't hear you come in. It's Einaudi's "Elegy for the Arctic". I needed to take my mind off...' she paused then shut the lid and leaned on her folded arms.

'At least your hands are okay,' said Ben. 'I should never have let you go; this is all my fault.'

'I wanted to go. Besides, I went with Dad.' Her voice muffled by her arms.

'And what did he do to help? This wouldn't have happened if I'd gone.'

Lucy sat up. 'You don't know that. And it had nothing to do with Dad; he didn't shoot me.'

'I should have been there to protect you.'

'It wouldn't have made any difference. There were more men than even you could have managed, and they were armed.'

'You know what Dad's like. He'd cave at the first threat,

wouldn't stand his ground.'

'It wasn't like that. He was great. If he'd rushed the barricade, they would have shot the windscreen out; neither of us would have got home. He cut them just enough slack to believe they had us before legging it.'

'You still got shot.'

'I know; it hurts like hell and you're not helping.'

'I'm sorry, Lucy, I came to make sure you were okay, not to argue with you.'

'It doesn't feel that way. And I'm not okay. It was horrible and scary, and I keep thinking about what would have happened if…' She stopped. Lucy sniffed and lifted a hand to wipe her eye, met the bandage as she did.

Ben went to hug her as he used to. She stopped him with her raised hand.

'I'm all right. I'm not going to give in to this; there's too much to do.'

'Okay, but look at you, you look like a pirate with the eye patch. You should have got a parrot not a cockerel, matey.' Ben's pirate imitation raised a smile from Lucy. 'And the bandages, how bad is your face?'

'Mum says they're minor, they'll heal with just a couple of scars at worst. It's the eye that's the real worry. She'll have another look tomorrow.'

'It's started though, hasn't it?'

'Yes, it's started. The barricade on the road is only the beginning. It's going to get more dangerous out there.'

'It's going to get dangerous here, too. They followed you, didn't they?'

'They didn't see us turn into The Lane.'

'They'll know you turned off somewhere. It's only a matter of time before they start looking and find us. We need to prepare.'

'I thought we were already well prepared. I guess we could do with a goat.'

'Not that sort of preparation, Lucy. If they come up The Lane, they'll be armed. We're going to have to fight. Apart from Dad's old shotgun all we have are some crossbows.'

'Have we? I didn't know.'

'If you're feeling fit enough, I'll show you.'

'Anything to distract me from this bloody eye will help,' said Lucy

Ben led the way out through the yard to an old cellar entrance. Down the steep wooden steps, past the food supplies stored on shelves at the back, a dozen or so cardboard parcels were stacked.

He slid a knife along the seam of the top box and took out the crossbow laying inside. 'We need to assemble them, what do you think?' He handed the black body of the bow to Lucy.

'It's not as heavy as I thought.'

'This is one of the lighter bows. Range won't be so great. There's a variety of strengths. Try this one.' He handed her another.

'This is heavy, too heavy for me.'

'It's one-eighty pounds pull to cock. A range of over sixty metres if you've practised enough; further than a shotgun can do damage.'

'Ben, you're talking about killing people.'

'If we don't defend ourselves, what will happen? Look at your face, you never even spoke to them, and they shot you. They could have killed you.'

Lucy paused, then said, 'Okay, what sort of preparation do you mean?'

'We need to learn to use these weapons effectively. I've done some archery; I can teach a few skills. We'll set some targets up.'

'What about Dad's shotgun?'

'Knowing Dad there's a couple of dozen cartridges. And no more once they're gone. Arrows and bolts we can reuse or make our own if we must.'

'You've already thought this through, haven't you?'

'You'll need to train too.'

'Me! I don't think I could shoot someone.'

'Even the guy who shot you. Imagine they were threatening Mum or Lottie. You couldn't sit back and watch it happen. So best get prepared.'

'And I've only got one eye.' She pointed at the eye patch.

'You'll be a useless shot, but it's not just about you. If Rob sees you, he'll practise too. If he doesn't, he'll only argue with me.'

'Okay, I'll join in the training if it will help persuade Rob. What about Faye? Will she be training too?'

'Fey Faye? I'm not sure she could manage the reality. God knows why he brought her here. I guess she keeps him warm at night.'

'You're being unfair. She's only nineteen. I like her.'

'She's high as a kite most days. I don't know where she gets the stuff.'

'Come on, she has a joint or two occasionally. Which of us hasn't at her age, and older? She'll run out soon.'

'I still think she's flaky. The latest in a long line of flaky bed-warmers, I can't trust her with a weapon,' said Ben.

'If you don't, how do you think Rob will react? He'll take it personally.'

Ben thought for a moment. 'I'll find something lightweight for her; it'll match her personality. What about your hand? Will it stop you holding a bow?'

'No, it only got scratched. When do you want to start the practice?'

'Tomorrow.'

'Okay, Rob is bound to come and see me; I'll mention this to him; smooth the way.'

'Good idea, I'll assemble all these today and we'll see who can manage which.'

Chapter 4

When the electricity went off and didn't return it took a full day to move the woodburning stove stored in the barn and install it in the kitchen. When lit, the stove created the only warm room in the house.

The family now sat around the large kitchen table while Ben told them about the crossbows and his plans for practice.

'I'm not convinced we need to do this,' said James.

'It will be too late if we wait for them to arrive. It's not a simple point and shoot thing. There's a bit more to it. We need to practise,' said Ben.

'It can't be so hard we have to have lessons,' said Rob.

'Despite what my brother thinks, we need to get used to these weapons,' said Ben, glancing around the room. 'All except Emily.' He looked at her. 'You shouldn't do this with the baby.'

'You mean I should be a defenceless pregnant woman? No, I'll join you. I've got two people to defend.'

'I shan't be doing this,' said Connie. 'I couldn't contemplate ending another person's life, and that's what this is about isn't it?'

'Suppose we are attacked.'

'Suppose we are? I still couldn't do anything to hurt them.'

'It's not the answer anyway,' said James. 'The best thing would be to negotiate, come to an agreement.'

'You can't bargain in the face of violence. Unless we defend ourselves, they'll take everything we have,' said Ben.

'Or they'll become allies and share what they have,' said James. 'You couch everything negatively. It doesn't have to be that way. It could be the beginning of rebuilding a community.'

'If you think they'll come unarmed you're a fool. They will be armed and desperate. If we're not ready for them, we'll die.'

'What do you think, Lucy?' said James.

'I wish it weren't true, I wish things could be peaceful. I wish it could be a new beginning. But after the barricade, the... shooting. I think Ben's right. We need to be prepared.'

'I think we should vote on it,' said James.

'Vote! If we're attacked there won't be time to vote,' said Ben.

'The rest of the world maybe falling apart, but civilisation can't just disappear. Here in this house, this family, we can be civilised. We shall have a vote. All those who support Ben's idea of practising with crossbows, raise a hand.'

James looked around the table. Faye, Lucy, and Ben had their hands raised.

'Now all those against Ben's idea.' James put his own hand up soon followed by Rob's, but neither Connie nor Emily raised their arms.

'Aren't you going to vote, Connie?'

'No, James, I shan't be fighting, so I shan't be voting.'

'What about you Emily?' said James.

'I want to be able to defend myself, but I shan't be fighting in any battles. Not while I'm pregnant.'

James conceded. 'Okay, Ben, you've got your way. We'll start practising with these weapons. But I don't like it.'

James, turned to Connie. 'I'll take a walk down to Dunster Cottage and make sure everything's okay there.'

'You mean the Reevers? What's it got to do with them?' said Ben.

'If whoever followed us is looking for where we went, their house is on the road, they're going to be a prime target.'

'Your father's right,' said Connie. 'The Reevers are our nearest neighbours, it's the least we can do.'

'If you're going down to the road we'll come along and block The Lane permanently. If anyone does find it, they'll have to come on foot,' said Ben.

Chapter 5

'Fuck you,' yelled Marcus, running from Dunster Cottage, Stuart's laughter pursuing him.

Ignoring his stepbrother's laugh and his mother's call, Marcus sped across the garden, behind the shed, and over the crumbling wall into the woodland gorge between Dunster Cottage and Cleeve House.

'I am not a Reever. I'm a Tennant,' he repeated as he stumbled down the steep path towards the river.

When his mum and Andy moved into Dunster Cottage seven years ago, Marcus had to share a room with his older stepbrother. It was fine to start with. To the ten-year-old Marcus, twelve-year-old Stuart seemed sophisticated and worldly, but soon became bossy and belligerent. Now, at seventeen, Marcus could find no solitude in Dunster Cottage.

Half a mile downstream a submerged rock functioned as a steppingstone. Crossing the river involved getting at least one wet foot, and usually two. Autumn meant freezing water and muddy banks. On the other side the wood rose to a clearing with a view over the river.

Approaching the clearing Marcus heard a match striking

and froze. He edged forward. There, on a log, a girl sat smoking. He smelt a hint of cannabis float through the air.

He stood watching, hands stuffed in his pockets, eyes flicking over the clearing, he couldn't see anyone else. Only this girl, occupying "his" spot, and not much older than him. Her pale face framed by dark hair seemed fragile compared to the jeans and DMs she wore, with a parka about three sizes too big. She hugged her knees, holding the joint in one hand, looking out over the river. She lifted the joint to her mouth and Marcus watched her lips pucker around the tip. Her cheeks hollowed as she sucked smoke into her lungs and held her breath. Her other hand flipped her long hair away from her mouth; her arms went back to her knees, and she exhaled a plume of smoke.

He made a couple of noisy pretend steps where he stood, and walked into the clearing, feigning surprise.

'Oh, I didn't know there was anyone here,' he said.

'Didn't you?' said the girl. 'I felt like I was being watched.'

Marcus shuffled his feet, his eyes flicked away from the girl and looked across the river. 'It's beautiful, isn't it?' He waved his arm over the view.

'Yes. Were you?'

'Was I what?'

'Watching me.'

Marcus looked at her, at the ground, at the trees. 'No, not really, only for a minute, I was surprised, I didn't expect anyone, I'm usually alone, I'm sorry, I...'

The girl laughed. 'You're from the house by the road, aren't you?' She took another drag on the joint.

'Yeah, Dunster Cottage; are you up at Cleeve House?'

'Have you got a name then? And do you want some of this?' She held the joint out towards him.

'Marcus, I'm Marcus,' he said. 'Who are you?'

'I'm...'

Marcus didn't hear her answer, he was busy coughing. The girl laughed again while he recovered.

She held her hand out; fingers splayed. 'Better give it back if you're not used to it. I'm Faye. Are you okay?'

'Yeah, I'm fine, I just didn't expect to find anyone here.'

Faye raised her eyebrows and tilted her head, 'You've found me; is it a problem?'

'No, no, not at all, company can be nice sometimes.'

'I'm company now, am I?'

'No, I didn't mean, I...'

'Do you want to sit down?' Faye shuffled along the log to make room for Marcus.

'Do you like it here?' said Marcus.

'Yeah, it's kind of peaceful. The sound of running water and all that stuff.'

'No, I mean here, at Cleeve House.'

Marcus watched her as she looked over the river and beyond. Up close her hair wasn't quite black and had hints of what may have been purple. Old streaks, he guessed. Her long hair, hiding her ears and pushed forward by the bulk of the parka, fell like a black waterfall across her neck, disappearing beneath the coat. He looked away as Faye turned to answer him.

'It's a bit strange. It's okay for a holiday, I guess. You live here all the time, don't you?'

'Yeah, I live with Andy and Mum.'

'Don't you get bored?'

'No, there's always something to see; deer, foxes, badgers, all sorts of wildlife.'

'But no people.'

'I don't mind being alone. What made you come here?'

'I came with Rob. I met him at uni. He said he had to get

out of the city and would I like to come. Made it sound like it would be a week or something. I didn't realise it would be months, maybe years.'

'You got here just in time. They closed all the petrol stations that night. Cancelled all public transport.'

'Yeah, I saw on the TV before the power went off. Panic everywhere. Only four weeks ago I was chatting with my mates, now I don't even know if they're alive. My phone died the day after we got here. Rob says they turned the net off.'

'Is he your tutor, like, or something?'

Faye laughed. 'No, he's… a friend.'

'Only I thought…'

'Thought what?'

'Nothing, just it's all horrible. But nature won't care. Nature will recover.'

'How can you tell?'

'It's always been like this for wild animals, living on the edge of survival. They won't even know there's been a flood. It can't be any worse than having a road built over them, or an airport.'

'You're a bit of a tree hugger, aren't you, Marcus?'

'What if I am? Someone's got to care about the planet.'

'Do you like living here?'

'I like the woods, the animals. Here I can be alone.'

'I'd better leave then.'

'No, no, I didn't mean you. It's good to have someone to talk to who's…'

'A girl?' said Faye.

'No, yes, well, not family.'

'You mean you'd rather I was a boy?'

'No, I don't mean that. You're teasing me.' He began to get up.

Faye took hold of his sleeve and gave it a tug.

'Don't go, I was only joking. It's good for me to have someone to talk to too, who's not so—'

'Shh, look?' A kingfisher paused on a branch over the river. Electric blue flashed into the river then away.

'I saw it!' Faye said, grabbing Marcus's pointing hand.

Marcus felt the warmth of her hand on his skin. He froze, not wanting to break this contact. Just a kingfisher and here she was, holding his hand. What should he say? He couldn't think of anything. Stuart would have, Stuart always knew what to say to girls.

'Mmm,' he said.

'What?'

'They, er, they're cute aren't they.'

'Cute? They're beautiful, such a blue. I've never seen one before. The flash as it flew by. I loved it.'

Marcus watched her mouth move as she spoke, saw her tongue between her lips, heard the sounds she made, but heard no words.

She looked sideways at him. 'Are you all right?'

'Yes, yes, fine, I'm okay,' said Marcus, startled by the change in tone.

'You looked a bit vacant, like you weren't here.'

'I'm okay, really, I'm very okay.' He said feeling the pressure of her hand diminish as she lifted it and returned it to her pocket.

'Time I went,' she said, standing. 'Thanks for the nature lesson. Maybe see you around.'

Marcus couldn't speak as he watched Faye leave.

Chapter 6

'It's getting worse,' said Connie, after uncovering Lucy's eye.

'I know, it feels worse every day. It pounds away at my head all the time. I barely sleep,' said Lucy.

Lucy gritted her teeth while Connie washed the eye.

'You could have some of the paracetamol,' said Connie.

'Save it until it's unbearable, who knows when we'll get anymore.'

'Can you see anything out of it?'

Lucy held her hand over her good eye for a few seconds. 'Only a grey mistiness. And it hurts if I try to move it.'

Connie was silent for a moment before putting her hand on Lucy's. 'Lucy, I think...'

'It's going to have to come out, isn't it?' said Lucy.

'I think it is. It looks angry and swollen. I'm worried it might infect other parts of you. Your brain. And that would be worse. If you can't see from it...'

'It's just a useless source of pain? I know, Mum. It's been four days of pointless agony.'

'I've never done anything like this before, and I doubt your brothers have. I've seen it done to a cat when I worked at the vets, years ago. Even if we take it out you might be ill.'

'You're filling me with confidence,' said Lucy.

'Oh, Lucy, I'm sorry. I'm only being honest with you. I'll do everything I can to be quick and clean, but it's going to be horrible.'

'When?'

'It will take me a little while to organise things. I'll get your father and brothers to help.'

'What, to pin me down?'

'Pretty much. The stiller you are, the quicker I can be and the sooner it will all be over.'

'Okay, let's do this.'

'Do you want to leave it another day to think about it?'

'No. It will be worse. Do it while I've got the courage.'

'You wait here in your room. I'll come and get you when we're ready.

For Lucy it was an age yet only a moment before Connie reappeared at her door carrying a bottle and a glass.

'I've got everything ready,' said Connie.

'I'm scared, Mum.'

'Here, drink this, it's your dad's whisky.' Connie poured a large measure from the bottle. 'And have a couple of these.' Connie handed Lucy a couple of the precious paracetamol tablets.

Lucy didn't hesitate and gulped them down with the whisky. She held the glass out for another, and her mother poured.

'I feel like a child at the dentist, only worse.'

'Maybe it won't be any worse than having a tooth out. Here, have some more.'

'I'm feeling pretty woozy now, Mum.'

'Let's go downstairs.'

'Will there be music, like in hospital theatres? Will there be a handsome junior doctor who'll fall in love with me, who I'll spurn for the rugged delinquent who comes good but dies at the end of the movie?'

'I've ordered them in especially for you,' said Connie. 'Come on, let's go through to the OR.'

Heat from the stove welcomed them into the kitchen. An old sheet covered the kitchen table. On this were a collection of cushions from other rooms in the house for Lucy to lie on. A blanket sat on a nearby chair to cover her. Her father and brothers were waiting, all nervous smiles and quick glances.

'Let's get you on the table,' said James.

'I'm scared, Dad.'

'Of course. But we'll do this quickly. It will soon be over. Come on, up you get.' He helped her onto the table while Ben and Rob tucked cushions around her.

'This won't take long,' said Connie, pouring boiling water into a bowl containing a small pair of scissors and a teaspoon.

Lucy took a deep breath and another one. She could feel her pulse racing, throbbing in her temple, pounding in her chest. She let out a whimper.

'Would you like something to bite on?' said James. 'I've got this clean piece of leather; it would protect your teeth. You can scream if you like, but you mustn't move your head. I'll be holding it but try and keep still.'

Lucy nodded. 'Yeah, I'll have the leather. I don't want this.'

'None of us do. Now lie down. Your brothers are going to take your arms. You know we all love you, so relax.'

'I'll pop this patch over your other eye,' said Connie. 'You won't be able to see for a few minutes. I'll take it off as soon as it's over.'

'Okay, Mum,' said Lucy, her lip quivering despite the alcohol in her system. But when the darkness enclosed her, she began to tremble, her head shaking, tiny movements between her father's grip.

'You must try and be still,' said Connie. 'I don't want to damage anything else.

The brothers took an arm each, gripping the wrist and above the elbow, and pinned them to her sides, then leaned onto her shoulders.

Connie murmured to Lucy laying on the table, whispering nothings, inconsequential childhood memories, while she unwrapped the useless festering remains of the left eye. It bulged from the socket, swollen and raw, pushing the eyelids apart. Connie kept murmuring to Lucy as she lifted the teaspoon from the bowl of hot water. One side of the spoon ground to as sharp an edge as the whetstone allowed. In her left hand she picked up the small scissors, inserting thumb and index finger into the loops. Still talking to Lucy, she looked at her sons and husband, all watching her, all ready, all clamping Lucy's body to the table. She gave a nod.

Lucy moaned through the leather in her mouth as if she could see the preparations. Rob glanced away towards Lucy's feet as the spoon approached her eye, but Ben's gaze was fixed on his mother's hand.

As Connie slipped the spoon into the eye Lucy struggled, but it was too late to stop. The spoon slipped behind the eyeball, pulling it forward. Connie used the scissors to snip the muscle first on one side of the eyeball, then the other. Lucy's teeth ground down on the leather and she grunted her pain, her legs flailing. Her brothers now leaned heavily on her torso, struggling to keep her still; her father panting with the effort of restraining her head. Connie blinked back tears which threatened her vision as she sawed at the optic nerve with the spoon. The festering eyeball spilled from Lucy's face and rolled down her cheek onto the sheet beside her.

Blood oozed from the socket. Connie let go her breath and the tears she'd been holding, dropped her implements, and covered the wound with clean cloth. She took the eyeball and dropped it into an empty pot.

'We're done, Lucy. I only need to bandage you. I'm going to uncover your good eye now,' said Connie, unfastening the patch.

Lucy's scream was more relief it was over than pain as her family relaxed their holds on her.

'Let's get you sitting up. It will slow the blood loss.' Connie nodded at James and her sons, who levered Lucy into a sitting position.

As Connie began to bandage her empty socket Lucy shook her head. She spat the chewed piece of leather from her mouth. 'Wait, I want to see it.'

'Are you sure?' said Connie.

'Yes. I want to see it at its worst, so I can tell myself what it might have been like.'

Connie nodded at James who brought a small mirror and held it before Lucy's face.

'Oh God, it's hideous.'

'It won't be so bad when the blood has been cleaned away,' said Connie.

'Yes, it will. Where's the eye? I want to see that too.'

Connie passed her the pot with the festering carbuncle of an eyeball sitting in the bottom.

'Christ, no wonder it hurt so much. Those bastards.'

'Can I bandage you now?' said Connie. 'I don't want you to catch an infection in the wound.'

After she'd finished Connie said, 'Now I think you should go to bed for the rest of the day. I'll come up with you to get you settled in.'

'That was fucking horrible,' said Lucy. 'And it still fucking hurts.'

James drained the last of the bottle of whisky into a glass and handed it to Lucy. 'Drink this. It's the last.'

She swallowed it in a single gulp.

Chapter 7

In the pitch black of the night Marcus heard the clank of chains against the tall gates protecting Dunster Cottage. The sound drew his attention like a magnet. 'Shit, it's happening,' he muttered under his breath, his heart pounding in his ears. Old man Marchand had been right. And now a flash of torchlight.

Through the window he heard a muffled voice. The torch illuminated a hand, the chains, and a pair of bolt cutters. Marcus gently pulled the window closed, locked it, and rushed upstairs.

'Mum, Andy, wake up.' It wasn't a whisper, not quite a yell.

'What is it?' growled Andy as he rolled out of his slumber.

'It's happening,' said Marcus. 'There are people trying to get in. They've got bolt cutters.'

Andy heard Marcus's words through the fog of awakening. He sat up and put his feet on the floor.

'Fuck. Are you sure? How many? Where are they? Did you see?' he said, scrabbling for his jeans and pulling them on.

'I couldn't tell, more than one at least.'

'Sue.' Andy prodded her.

'Okay, I'm awake, I heard,' said Sue.

'Get ready to leave. If we have to, we'll go up The Lane; use the back gate.'

'Up to Cleeve House?' said Sue.

'Yes. Marcus, wake your brother.'

'He's not my brother,' hissed Marcus.

'We haven't time for this, go and get Stuart.'

Watching from windows at either end of the lounge Marcus and Stuart heard the last of the chains clank their way to the ground. Two shadows of men tried to push the gates open, but a ton of rock had been piled behind them. A voice called out, an engine started, and a large 4x4 drove slowly up to the gates. When Andy appeared, he carried two crossbows. He gave one to Stuart and rested the other on the windowsill.

'Sue's by the back gate. How many of them are there?'

'I've only seen two,' said Stuart.

'There's at least three, the guy driving the truck, and the two blokes who cut and pulled the chains away,' said Marcus.

'If there's more than three, we'll leave,' said Andy.

'Leave? Where would we go, up to Cleeve? They hate us there,' said Stuart.

'There isn't anywhere else, and they don't hate us. James is a good bloke,' said Andy.

The truck eased against the gates, made contact, and pushed. The large boulders stacked behind the gates began to grind through the gravel driveway, toppling and rolling as they were pushed aside. The wrought iron of the gates drew screeches from the thin panels of the truck as it forced itself between them. Andy crouched behind the open window taking aim with the crossbow.

'You going to shoot one of them, Dad?' said Stuart, sighting down his own bow.

'If you shoot one, they'll think we have something worth stealing,' said Marcus.

'If we shoot one of them it'll slow them down, give us time to escape,' said Andy.

The 4x4 was almost through the gates. It was a short and easy shot. The crossbow bolt shattered the windscreen and hit the driver in the chest. The car lurched to a stop. A flashlight shone into the cab and voices shouted warnings.

Andy, still holding his loaded crossbow, looked over at his son, watching as Stuart re-tensioned his bow and slipped another bolt into place.

'We'd better leave,' said Andy, 'there will be more of them, and they'll want revenge.' His voice flat, calm, steady. His eyes watching his son, the killer of a man. Now it was decided. They would be coming for them. 'Come on, out the back before they overrun us.' He looked again at Stuart, watching him weigh the words, deciding whether to comply or not.

'I guess you're right, Dad, look.'

Outside another vehicle had arrived, reversing up to the gate, sheltering the men trying to get in. Andy fired blindly beneath the truck and was rewarded by a shout of caution. He turned to leave, Marcus and Stuart followed. As they ran from their home, they heard a shotgun and the sound of glass breaking.

James woke when Manuka barked. He pulled trousers over his pyjamas and hurried down to the kitchen. The Labrador had her nose pressed against the back door, woofing warnings. In movements smooth with recent practice, James slipped on the Barbour jacket hanging nearby; his right hand felt the shelf above the door and found the wooden stock of his "over and under" while his left dipped into the jacket pocket, feeling for the plastic roundness of cartridges. He slipped two into the broken shotgun and gently clicked the gun closed before stepping out into the cold, autumn night. Voices spoke in urgent whispers. Walking towards them, the figures coalesced into the recognisable shapes of the Reever family.

James flicked on a torch. 'Andy, what's the problem?'

'James! I'm glad it's you. We've been attacked, at least half a dozen armed men, shotguns. Can we stay here? Just for the night?' said Andy.

'Of course. I don't have room in the house. We're bursting with the whole family here. Come with me.' James led the family to the stone barn at the edge of the yard. 'You can stay in here for the night. It's dry at least. I'll see what I can find in the way of spare blankets. Take this torch, I'll pick up another in the house.'

James found Connie in the kitchen when he got back. Together they took what spare bedding they had to the barn.

'I'll get Ben or Rob to keep watch for the rest of the night,' said Connie.

'Don't disturb them, we're already awake,' said Andy. 'We've been keeping watch at night anyway. Stuart and Marcus can keep guard, can't you?'

'Yeah, we'll go up to the cairn and keep watch there,' said Stuart.

'James, we must help them,' said Connie when they were back in the kitchen.

'Yes, of course we must. There's four of them. It's a lot.'

'They can stay in the barn. It's only used as a garage.'

'It's not that, they'll need to eat.'

35

'We'll have to share,' said Connie.

'You're right, it's just...'

'They're neighbours, we can't let them starve.'

'Look, it's late. You go back to bed and get a bit more sleep, it's going to be busy tomorrow. I'll stay up a while. Make sure they're settled in.'

He broke his shotgun, removed the cartridges, and sat down to wait.

James woke with a start, his head on the kitchen table, his eldest son standing over him.

'Are you okay, Dad? This is early for you.'

'I'm glad it's you, Ben, we need to talk.'

'Okay, but I'm on my way to check the gates. Can't it wait?'

'It won't take long, sit a minute.'

Ben let out a sigh and sat at the table.

'You know I appreciate all the planning and effort you've put into this; making sure we have all the stores we need,' said James.

'I don't know if we've got all we need. We have Faye with us. An extra mouth to feed. She wasn't in my calculations. And Emily's pregnant, she'll need extra.'

'But we have enough?'

'Should have. Is this all you wanted to tell me?'

'No, there's something else. It's about the Reevers.'

'They'll be struggling, I guess. We can let them have the eggs we've been giving them up to now. I don't think we can give them anything else. Not without compromising ourselves.'

'They're not only struggling,' said James, 'they've been attacked, in the night. They came here.'

'They came here! Why?'

'They had nowhere else to go, Ben. The attackers were armed. They would have been killed. They have nothing.'

'What's it got to do with us?' Ben forced the words through a stiffened jaw.

'They're our closest neighbours. I've given them the barn to use, they'll need to eat.'

'There won't be enough.'

'We'll have to share with them, otherwise they'll starve.'

'There won't be enough,' repeated Ben.

'If we cut our ration, we should be okay.'

'There won't be enough, we'll all starve.'

'Ben, you're not listening to me. We can't let them starve; we must share.'

'There's four of them, all adults. It's too many extra stomachs to fill. We can't survive on less than what we have now.'

'Maybe the stores won't last quite as long, something will turn up. We'll be all right.'

'It won't work,' said Ben.

'It has to. They're staying. I've decided.'

'If it's already decided you didn't need to speak to me, did you,' said Ben standing up. He slammed the door behind him.

Chapter 8

Relief accompanied the grey of dawn filtering between Lucy's curtains; signalling the end of a sleepless night caused by throbbing pain from the socket her eye once occupied. The faint murmur of voices swelling up the stairs and creeping under her door kept her from the kitchen. The voices grew until cut short by the slam of a door.

She waited a few minutes, hearing only silence, then found her father in the kitchen alone and sombre.

'You okay, Dad?' she got in first.

'Yes, I'm fine.' His insincere smile said otherwise. 'How's the eye?'

'It hurts, kept me awake. It's subsiding a bit. What about you really? You're up early.'

'I haven't slept, and I've just been arguing with your brother.'

Lucy sat opposite him. 'Tell me about it, Dad. Sometimes it helps to talk.'

'I guess it's no worse than many of the other arguments we've had, but...' and James told his daughter about the events of the night and the sanctuary he'd given the Reevers.

'Ben thinks I was wrong, thinks it puts us all at risk.'

'I don't. It's what I would have done. Ben's a good organiser, we'd be floundering without him, but I think you've done the right thing.'

'I blame myself you know,' said James, nodding at Lucy's eye patch.

'It wasn't your fault. You know that really.'

'My head does, not my heart.'

'Aww Dad.' Lucy gave him a hug over the table.

Sounds of the rest of the household stirring wafted in. Lucy heard Lottie talking to Emily, then their tread on the stair.

'I don't feel much like company, Dad. I'm going out to the potting shed. I'll try and do something useful there. I don't want people fussing around me.'

Ben found her and burst through the door. Startled, Lucy spilled seed all over the floor.

'Look what you made me do.' Lucy knelt to gather the spillage.

Ben stooped to help. 'I didn't mean to surprise you, sorry. Have you heard the Reevers are here?' He swept the seeds into his hands in a swift, smooth movement.

'It's terrible what's happened to them. They must have been petrified,' she said.

'They might have been, but why did they come here? We've nothing for them.'

Lucy wiped compost from her hands. 'Where else could they go?'

'They could have gone anywhere, now they're here. And Dad says they can stay.'

'Of course they can. Should they leave and be murdered?'

'It wouldn't make any difference, they'll die here anyway,

we all will. Starvation. There isn't enough to go round now, and with them here it will be worse. Just think about it, Lucy.'

'They came here in need; we can't turn them away. You might have already left when the Reevers moved into Dunster Cottage, but I was still at uni. I saw how honest and friendly they were. I saw how easily Dad took to them, and Mum. They may be a couple of miles away, but that's next door here. Dad would always help a neighbour, it's his nature, and I, for one, am glad he's got a generous heart. It may be a bit harder for us, but we'll manage somehow.'

'I'm disappointed, I thought you'd understand. Use your brain. You know what we have and how long it will last. With them here it won't make any difference how many seeds you sow, we won't be around to eat them.'

'You're only seeing the negative. They need to eat, of course they do. They can also help. Work in the paddock, we'll need to turn it all to veg anyway, the more hands we have the quicker it will become productive.'

'I think I see it clearly, Lucy. They are a risk to our future. I need you onside with this. If you aren't part of the solution here, you know what that means.'

Lucy paused, turned her good eye on him. 'Ben, are you threatening me?'

He took a breath. 'Look, I don't want to argue with you. I've done so much to make sure we'll get through this and it's all going to waste.'

'I know, and everybody is grateful. We'd already be starving if you hadn't organised things. But this isn't only about us. There's a world of people out there, thousands will be starving. If we can get through the winter, into May, June, there'll be some respite, we'll be producing much more.'

'It's not just the food. It won't be long before they're

followed, then we'll have an invasion on our hands.'

'You're being unfair, Ben. They didn't want to be attacked. Dad and I might have caused it. Anyway, if people do come up The Lane looking for us, the Reevers will help. Can't you do something to prepare?'

'I think we might,' said Ben. 'They say attack is the best form of defence. The Reevers came up here, they can help deal with whoever's in their place. Maybe they could go back. You're brilliant, Lucy.'

'I don't know what you mean?'

'It's simple. If the Reevers go back to Dunster Cottage, they won't be a problem anymore.'

Chapter 9

At midnight, under a cold and gibbous moon, Ben led them along The Lane to Dunster Cottage. He had said yes to Faye's offer to come along. It might encourage Rob into some bravery. Andy, Stuart, and Marcus padded behind.

'Tell me again why this is such a great idea,' said Rob, as they crossed the narrow bridge.

'It's simple. They know the Reevers came up The Lane. Either they surprise us, or we surprise them. I prefer to do the surprising myself.'

'So, we're doing this because Ben thinks it's a good idea?'

Ben stopped and turned to his brother, his voice a harsh hiss. 'Listen, you can fuck off back to Mum and Dad if you're shitting yourself, this isn't some sort of game, mate. This is life and death. You need to man-up.'

'If you have to fight, it makes sense to get in the first blow,' said Faye.

'Half a working brain cell at least. Maybe I've underestimated you,' said Ben, catching and holding Faye's eye.

'I never knew you were estimating,' said Faye, returning

his gaze. 'You should have asked; I'd have given you precision.'

'I might do. Now, if there are no more stupid questions, we'll go and sort these bastards out.' Ben led them up The Lane.

Marcus caught Ben's attention as they approached the gate to Dunster Cottage.

'If they've set a guard he'll be behind the gate,' whispered Marcus. 'There's an easy way in along the wall here.'

Ben signalled him to lead the way, and Marcus took the party to the crumbled wall behind the shed. Ben nodded for Marcus to go over first and saw the fear spread through his face. Marcus placed a hesitant hand on the wall to hoist himself over. He paused to check his crossbow, made sure his knife was secure, and began to climb over.

Stuart gave a sneer of contempt, pushed past Marcus and climbed the wall, crossbow held aloft in one hand, ready to aim. He disappeared for a couple of minutes. 'There's no one by the gate. They must be in the house,' he said when he returned.

'Right,' Ben said, 'we'll all go over and spread out. Keep under cover until I give the say so, okay?' He looked around the group, there were nods and a shrug from Stuart.

Ben peered from behind the shed. There was no one to be seen. No sign of life in the garden at all. The house was about thirty metres away. He saw a figure in a ground floor window. He pulled back behind the shed and told the group.

'I'll have a pop at him,' said Stuart.

'Not until we're all spread out, we need to take cover before we try anything. We can pick them off from this distance if we need to.'

They heard voices calling to each other and engines starting. Stuart looked around the end of the shed.

'They've set fire to it,' he said.

'The house?' said Andy.

Voices yelled and car doors slammed as the flames took hold.

'Shit,' said Ben to himself.

'Let me look,' said Andy, pushing past Ben. 'No!' he yelled and took a step towards the house.

Ben stepped out, grabbed his arm and pulled him back behind the shed, holding him fast.

'Be quiet, you idiot,' he hissed in Andy's ear. 'Do you want to get us all killed?'

The fire soon took hold of the thatched cottage. Smoke billowed and the flames grew, and so did Andy's distress.

'No! My house, all my work...' Andy covered his grief-stricken face with his hands and peered between the fingers; appalled and horrified at the destruction of years of hard labour.

A breeze fanned the flames and spread smoke over the garden. They stood helplessly in the smoke while flames licked the roof, reflecting off their eyes and weapons. The heat of the fire grew with its hunger, driving them back behind the shed and onto The Lane, where Andy slumped to the ground.

'It was Mum's house too,' said Marcus to Andy. 'We'd better go and tell her.'

Chapter 10

'I'm furious with him, he's such an arrogant bastard,' said Rob.

Lucy closed the lid of the piano and swivelled on the seat to look at him. She listened to his diatribe against Ben for a couple of minutes before interrupting.

'Rob, he was right. It was serious, it was the right thing to do, nobody got hurt, except your pride, and he didn't set off to embarrass you in front of Faye, you brought it on yourself.'

'How can you say this. He could see her standing there, and she sided with him.'

'Because he was right, like I said. You could have gone along and said nothing, and everything would have turned out the same.'

'Now Faye thinks I'm a coward and won't...' Rob's voice faded away.

'Won't what?'

'Nothing, she's just gone off me a bit, probably her period or something.'

'Now you're behaving like an idiot. You don't have to

make an enemy of people because they don't agree with you. Cut her some slack, she's only young.'

'You're right, she'll be okay in a day or two. But it doesn't alter what Ben's done.'

'I know Ben isn't the most subtle of people, and he can be bossy, but he gets like that when he's under stress. Think about it, there he is, leading a rag tag mob into danger, risking everyone's life. He's got a daughter and a pregnant wife to think about too. Maybe Ben could do with a bit of slack from you too.'

She watched Rob struggle not to bite back; struggle to understand her point of view. She heard his teeth grind as he grimaced. Watched his hands clench into fists.

'This isn't the first time, or the hundredth, he's been like this to me. None of those other times had anything to do with stress, why should this. I think he enjoyed putting me down, and he enjoyed Faye watching, it meant he could cut deeper. I hate him.'

'I understand,' said Lucy, 'but we're stuck here, and we need each other. The more of us there are, the easier life will be, the more likely we'll get through this. We need to pull together. It may be hard to cover how you feel, but do you want to spend the next months, maybe years, with Ben at you all the time? Don't give him the excuses to bully you and he won't.'

'You're saying I should give in to my big brother all the time, even when he's being a total arse? Please tell me you aren't serious, Lucy. What would it say about me?'

'It would make you the more mature man, the sensible one, the guy who has an eye on the long game, the real outcomes which are important to our lives and our survival. We need Ben and his way of doing things now, today, when there is danger from outside. It won't always be like this,

Rob. Things will calm down and your strengths, your humour, your innate goodness and creativity, will be important, essential. Just hang on in there. This can't go on forever.'

'I swear you should have been a politician, Lucy. You do this every time. Okay, I'll bite my tongue, I'll hear what he has to say and not tell him he's an idiot. I don't know how long I can keep it up.'

'Good, now fetch your guitar. Let's play together a while.'

Chapter 11

Marcus glanced about him. Everyone seemed busy. He lay down his fork. He'd had enough of toiling in the mud and headed for the clearing by the river.

He'd sat on the log several times over the last few days, always alone. He sat staring over the river, then heard footsteps and turned to see Faye strolling towards him, smiling.

'Shouldn't you be working?' she said, sitting next to him, forcing him to shift up the log.

'I… er… as much as you should be, I think,' said Marcus.

'That's better, I like a bit of banter. How come you're here?'

'I always come here when I need to think.'

'I'm sorry about your house.'

'It's a shame for Mum, she loved the place. I didn't like living there but now it's even worse.'

'How can it be worse than a burnt-out shell?'

'We're sleeping in that crappy barn. There's even less space than before.'

'At least you don't have to sleep with Rob Marchand.'

'I thought you liked him, you said he was clever.'

Faye glowered. 'I came here for a bit of peace and quiet away from the crap. If you're going to insult me, maybe you should fuck off.'

'I'm sorry, Faye, I didn't mean to upset you. I was really pleased when I saw you. I've been wanting to talk to you.'

'You've a strange way of showing it. It sounds like you want to score points.'

'I don't. I'm just sick of this whole shitty business. I hate it here. Stuart throws his weight about whenever he can, and everyone seems to be bossing me about. No matter how hard I work it's not hard enough. The old barn is even less private than the house was, and it's draughty and it's got mice, might even have rats. All we get to sleep on are a few old hay bales. It's awful.'

'Yeah, tell me about it. I feel the same, but you don't have the expectations laid on you that I have.'

'What do you mean?'

'Oh, come on, Marcus. Don't be naive.'

'I'm sorry, I don't know what you're getting at.'

When Faye looked at him, he saw the disbelief in her eyes.

'I'm really going to have to spell it out for you, aren't I?' she said. 'It's like this, Marcus. In exchange for staying in a house with no water, no electricity, no bleeding toilets even; I'm expected to fulfil the sexual fantasies of an unimaginative bloke in his thirties who thinks I enjoy my orifices being probed by his fetid smelly body. That he imagines he's doing me a favour is the icing on the cake.'

As Faye spoke Marcus coloured. His neck, his face, turning red. He looked at the ground, at his hands, at his feet, at Faye's feet. Anywhere but Faye's face.

'I never realised,' he mumbled when she stopped.

'No, men don't,' said Faye.

Marcus couldn't help but raise his head and straighten his

back on being included as a man. 'Why don't you leave?' he said. 'Come and stay in the barn with us.'

'After how you've described it? You must be joking.'

'You wouldn't have Rob pestering you all the time.'

'It's true, it wouldn't be Rob pestering me.'

'I don't think you need worry about Stuart. He's got the hots for Lucy.'

'That's flying way over his ceiling, I'd say. Besides, it wasn't Stuart who I thought would be doing the pestering.'

'There isn't anyone else who... oh! I wouldn't pester you, Faye, honest.'

'Not much you wouldn't, I know you fancy me.' Faye pulled a crumpled joint from the inside pocket of her parka. 'This is the last, do you want to have another go?' she said as she put a match to the tip and drew deep.

Marcus didn't deny her observation but did accept her offer of the joint. His hand briefly touched hers as he took it, and as he placed it between his lips, he felt the slight dampness on the tip from her mouth. He was sitting close enough to feel her limbs move as she uncrossed her legs. Marcus drew on the joint and handed it back, again rewarded by a brief contact.

'Do you get the munchies?' said Faye.

'All the time, I could eat anything.'

'No, I mean when you smoke dope, do you get the munchies. I know I do.'

'Yeah, I guess I do,' said Marcus, querying his body.

'There's only one thing to eat around here.'

'What?' said Marcus, looking round and finding nothing edible.

Faye waited until his eyes returned to hers. 'Me,' she said, holding his gaze, smoke drifting between them.

Marcus, confused, watched her lips part, a slick of saliva

linking them, a hint of ivory between. The pink of her tongue as it toured her lips, and the slight lean of her body left him in no doubt.

Heart hammering, Marcus leant into the kiss and tasted her, tasted the smoke of her, the smell, the flavour of her mouth. He felt the soft giving of her lips, the dart of Faye's tongue touching his, sending currents racing through his blood. His arms found her and surrounded her.

She pushed him off her as she broke the kiss and backed away. 'There, see, I know who would be pestering me in the barn.' Her mischievous smile broke the spell on him. She stood. 'Now I think I'd better be getting back to work. I don't want anyone to think I'm not pulling my weight.'

'Faye, wait, wait, when will I see you again?'

'I'm not going anywhere, am I? You'll see me soon enough, around and about.'

'But will I see you here I mean, on your own?'

Faye laughed. 'Maybe,' she said over her shoulder as she left.

Chapter 12

Faye woke to find Rob's hand stroking her stomach. His usual prelude to sex.

'No, Rob, I don't want to,' she said, brushing his arm away.

'What do you mean, no? Why not?'

'I'm not in the mood, okay.'

'Come on, it's been ages, you're never in the mood, what's the matter with you?'

'Nothing's the matter with me, I just don't want to, is it a problem for you?'

'You always used to be up for it, what's wrong?' said Rob.

'There's nothing wrong, just leave me alone. You don't own me.'

'If it wasn't for me, you'd still be stuck in Manchester, starving, maybe even dead, or worse.'

'What's that supposed to mean? Is it some kind of threat? Does it mean you get to fuck me whenever you feel like it? I work as hard as anyone here, so don't give me crap.'

'If that's how you feel maybe you should sleep somewhere else. It's comfortable here in this room in a proper bed, but if you don't want to sleep here, that's up to you.'

'It's getting late, I'm hungry, I'm not going to miss breakfast.' Faye swung her legs out of the bed and stood. She dressed with quick efficiency, her back to Rob, then left.

Connie divided the breakfast porridge into two pots. One for the Marchands, the other Ben took to the barn for the Reevers.

'It makes sense if I have my breakfast with them,' said Ben. 'They'll know it's fair, and it won't be so crowded in here first thing in the morning.'

'I think Ben finally understands the importance of working together,' James had told Connie after this regime had begun.

Ben had no bowl. 'Too much to carry,' he'd explained, 'easier to eat my share left in the bottom of the pot.' That each portion measured out into the Reevers' bowls didn't quite make a fifth of what was in the pot would have gone unnoticed in times of plenty. When Andy questioned the measures, Ben suggested he eat elsewhere if he was dissatisfied. Andy's bowl felt light for the next three days until he apologised to Ben for his stupidity.

The jar of jam Ben tucked in his inside pocket when he carried the steaming pot across the yard remained there throughout the meagre breakfast. Ben ate five teaspoons of jam, one for each of the Reevers and one for himself, before locking the jar in the storeroom.

Faye took a bowl and spoon and joined the queue. Connie and James oversaw the serving of breakfast, porridge with a scant scattering of dried fruit and a teaspoon of jam added.

'I don't get it,' said Faye. 'It's been weeks, I know we have no milk and still you make this creamy porridge every day.

How do you do it?'

Connie laughed. Compliments about her food used to be commonplace; now, her culinary expertise redundant, they were rare. There were not the ingredients to spare nor the fuel available for anything other than simple fare. 'It's dried milk, dear. We have a supply and use a little each day. It will last a few weeks yet.'

'The jam comes from our stores,' said James as he spooned the teaspoonful allowed into Faye's porridge. 'This is blackcurrant from last year. We have a few jars in reserve, but they won't last long.'

Faye took her now full bowl and sat hunched in a corner; relief relaxed her shoulders when Lucy sat beside her.

'D'you mind me sitting here? Or are you saving it for Rob?'

'No, yes, I mean I'm glad it's you, Lucy. Are you okay? I'm sorry about your eye. You're braver than I am.'

Lucy snorted a laugh. 'Bravery had nothing to do with it. It had to come out, it hurt and was useless. It's still sore now, maybe it'll feel better in a few days. What about you? Are you okay?'

'I'm fine, it's just... nothing, never mind.' Faye focused on spooning her breakfast into her complaining stomach.

'If you eat it slowly it will take away the hunger for longer,' said Lucy. She took a quarter spoonful at a time, savouring each mouthful before swallowing. Faye looked sceptical. 'Try it,' said Lucy deliberately pausing before spooning more porridge from the bowl.

Despite her ever-present hunger, Faye only half filled her spoon and paused before letting herself put it in her mouth, forced herself to allow her mouth to taste the porridge, the sweetness of the jam, before swallowing. Even so, Lucy still had almost half a bowl left by the time Faye had finished. Across the table, despite arriving last, Rob had finished his bowl. He looked at her. 'Come on,' he said, 'let's get going, work to do.'

'I'm having a word with Lucy, you go ahead.' Faye watched him leave.

'So, what's wrong?' said Lucy. 'Is it Rob?'

'No, yes, maybe. It's time I had my own space. He can be a bit full on sometimes.'

'I don't know where you'd find it. We're full up here. There aren't any spare rooms. Have you and Rob been arguing?'

'No, not really. Thanks for asking. I just sometimes feel a bit trapped.'

'I guess we all are in a way. If you're serious about your own space, you could try and ask Ben. He's done most of the organising; he may have some ideas.'

'I don't think Ben likes me.'

'It's up to you, you don't have to talk to him. You can't set up anywhere else without him knowing about it and his temper is worse than Rob's if he thinks someone's put one over on him. He's just eaten, he'll be in the best mood he's going to be all day, why don't you catch him?'

They watched Ben come in with the pot from the barn and leave again.

'I will, thanks,' said Faye.

'What do you want?' said Ben when Faye caught up with him on his way to the cairn.

'Why should I want anything? Maybe I want some company.'

Ben glanced round at her and shook his head. 'I'm not Rob. Don't treat me like an idiot. What do you want?'

'You're right, I do want something.'

'There isn't any more to eat, don't even think of asking.'

'I'm not looking for food. I was wondering if there was a

small room I could have, it doesn't have to be big, as tiny as you like,' said Faye.

'No, there isn't. Why, are you fed up with lover boy already?'

'I can tell you don't like me, I've no idea why. It wasn't my idea to come here, and I'm pulling my weight, working my ass off in the bloody field. Don't I deserve at least a bit of courtesy?'

Ben turned his head to her again but didn't slow his pace. 'There's a bit of fire in you. Find me after the evening meal and I might have something to show you. Don't tell anyone. Now you'd better get back to work.'

Chapter 13

Ben ran his thumbnail around the skin of an apple, gave it a sharp twist between his hands, and handed half to Emily.

'Here, have this,' he said, joining her on an old bench in the vegetable garden.

'I guess this is what passes for lunch these days,' said Emily, brushing soil from her hands.

'You'd better not get used to it. It's only going to get worse as winter draws in.'

'To start with, but we're doing the right thing, preparing for next year. Things will get better, surely. It's why we're doing all this prep and planting isn't it?'

'Yes, that's why I want you to swap with Lucy in the potting shed.'

'Why? Don't you think I'm capable of working in the garden?'

'I'm thinking about our baby. You're about six months now, it must be getting hard for you.'

'Don't you think I know what my body can do?'

'We need to be careful. There aren't any emergency services anymore. You'd both be in danger if something went wrong.'

'When I was having Lottie, I decorated the house, have you forgotten?'

'It's different now. I want you in the shed.'

He watched her staring at him, felt his jaw clench and ground his teeth. Emily might not like it, but she'd have to put up with what he'd decided. He didn't have time for yet another blazing row with her. Pregnancy made her argumentative. And she's pregnant now, at the worst possible time. He'd found out when he got back from Greenland. The row had been long, loud, and hurtful. He wanted her to get rid of it. She wouldn't. He told her what would happen, no doctors, no healthcare. But she was pregnant, she knew best. Sometimes he hated her, and this was shaping up to be one of those times.

'What about what I want?' said Emily. 'I like working in the garden, it's good for my muscles and keeps me supple.'

'But is it good for the baby?'

'I haven't had any complaints. No, I think I'll stay in the garden for now. I'll let you know when I want to do something lighter,' Emily said. 'And besides, I'll hardly see anyone out there. Maybe you're trying to get me out of the way.'

'You're being stupid now, there's nothing I can do here. We're all stuck, and we all have to put up with it. And right now, I need you in the potting shed, you'll be able to work there for longer than you can here.'

'You need me in the potting shed. But you don't need me in our bed, do you?'

'What's that supposed to mean?'

'You know damn well what it means. This happened last time I was pregnant.'

Ben almost denied any knowledge of what Emily was

talking about. They'd had the argument many times, and he'd lost it when Emily had found out about his affair with the girl at work. He struggled to remember her name now, Tamsin, that was it.

'I'm only being careful, I don't want anything to happen to the baby, or you.'

'Don't I get a say? It's my body,' said Emily.

'I'm worried about the baby. It doesn't mean I don't love you, or that things won't be back to normal later. Look, I just want everything to go well for us.'

'You said that last time, then you started with that Yasmin or whatever her name was. If you do that to me again, I'll never forgive you.'

Ben sat stony faced. He didn't have time for this nonsense. 'Things are different now. This is what's going to happen. Tomorrow, you take over from Lucy in the shed and she works in the garden. I've decided. If you don't like it, tough. The safety of our daughter depends on me getting this right. There isn't any help for us out here, we're on our own. I'll do everything in my power to protect Lottie, and our new baby, whether you like it or not.'

Ben spat apple pips towards the hedge and stomped off.

Chapter 14

Sitting at the table with her bowl before her, Faye paused before dipping her spoon into the meagre meal. She let herself hear the staccato of desperate consumption; bowls being scraped, spoons licked, chewing, swallowing; before putting the spoon to her own mouth. She rolled the broth of beans and vegetables around her mouth, allowing herself to taste the individual elements; the salty tang of the last continental sausage in the broth was a rare treat, a couple of thin rounds to each bowl.

She caught sight of Lucy across the table, watching her, and gave a nod of acknowledgement. She also tolerated Rob sitting with her while she ate.

'I'm sorry about this morning, okay?' said Rob, scraping the last remnants from his bowl.

'Fine,' said Faye.

'We're good, then?'

'I know I'm okay, you have to decide about yourself.'

'I'm okay too. It's bloody cold. Why don't we go and warm up?'

'You go on, I haven't finished eating.'

'I'll wait for you.'

'I may be a while. There's something else I want to do too.'

'What?' said Rob.

Faye glared at him. 'You should go; you're putting me off my food.'

'Okay, you need a bit of time by yourself. You only had to say,' said Rob standing up, almost bumping into Ben as he left.

Faye watched as Ben returned the pot he'd used to feed the Reevers to the kitchen and left again. She hurried the last of her meal, threw the parka around her shoulders and followed him. Outside a half moon tried to push through scudding clouds, occasionally throwing buildings into silhouette.

It took a while for her eyes to become accustomed to the darkness, then she saw Ben emerging from the storeroom, locking it behind him.

'I'd love to see what's in there,' she said to his back.

He whipped round. 'What are you doing here, what do you want?'

'I've come to find you, like you said this morning. You hinted you might have somewhere to show me.'

'Are you sure you want somewhere away from my loving brother?'

'Yes, I do. I've never spent so much time in someone else's company, I need my own space.'

'Come on.' Ben strode away towards the orchard. Faye scurried after him.

'Where are we going? The house is the other way.'

'I didn't say it was in the house, did I? And you said it only needed to be small.'

As they walked Ben pulled a torch from his pocket to light the path. They walked past the orchard and beyond. The path grew narrower. They crossed a stile into a field, Ben ignoring Faye's trip when she clambered over, Faye getting up and hurrying after him.

'Here we are,' he said. He shone the torch over a small stone-built shelter, roofed with corrugated iron. At one time it may have housed a farm labourer in its one room, centuries before. The door leant against the wall by the side of the opening, and the single window was open to the night sky.

'Is this it?' said Faye, stepping inside. The hovel was empty save for a couple of hay bales in the middle of the small room.

'What's wrong with it?' said Ben. 'It keeps the elements out, mostly, and it's private. It might need a bit of work. It could be yours if you really want it.'

In the darkness, Ben's voice struck Faye, so like Rob's but a couple of tones deeper, a darker, more mysterious sound. She turned towards the voice. The shadow that was Ben was taller than Rob, and broader. 'Not very comfy though, is it?'

'Those hay bales look comfortable to me,' said Ben. He turned to face Faye, switching off and pocketing the torch. 'I think you should try them.'

Ben stepped towards her. Faye took a step backwards and Ben followed until the backs of her knees were against the hay bale. Ben kept coming, she put her arm out, hand raised; it met his chest.

'What are you doing?' she asked. She heard a hint of breathlessness in her own voice. She knew what he was doing, she wanted him to carry on, she knew he would. He took another step closer, and her arm bent at the elbow trapping her hand between their two bodies.

'Don't pretend you don't know,' he said.

Faye felt a hand around her head, felt it pull her towards him. She knew Ben was going to kiss her. Should she reject him here, out in the middle of nowhere? She didn't think he would do anything if she did. But this wasn't Marcus, poor innocent Marcus. She couldn't play tease with this man, nor did she want to. He was so much more confident than Rob, taller, heavier, stronger. When he leaned in and placed his mouth on hers, she opened her lips to the kiss. He even tasted like Rob, but with something else, some flavour of darkness. Then she was falling over as Ben pushed against her, falling on to the hay bales, and Ben followed, pushing her down, kissing her deep and urgent.

She wore jeans, Ben combat trousers. It should have been clumsy; it should have been awkward. Somehow it wasn't. The chill of the October night went unnoticed as the rhythm of their bodies began to move the hay bales. Her legs circled him, jeans hanging from one ankle, and pulled him tight to her as she began to gasp. He was so much more than Rob.

Chapter 15

Everyone who could wield a crossbow was in the yard, firing at targets set twenty metres away.

'I don't think we need to do this,' said James.

'We've discussed this before, Dad. They know where we are, they've destroyed the Reevers' place. They'll be coming for us next.'

'That was two weeks ago, I don't think they'll be coming now.'

'They'll come. Every day they wait means we get better with the crossbows. But they'll come, and if we're not prepared, we'll die.' Ben took aim and placed the bolt in the heart drawn in the human figure chalked on the old door.

'Remember what I said about the drop of the bolt over this distance. It will fall more when we go to thirty and forty metres.'

Lucy's attempt flew wide of the mark by several metres. 'You're still not aiming well, Lucy. Maybe you'd better sit this out,' said Ben.

'I need to do this,' said Lucy. 'If they come and I can't fire the damn thing I'll be useless. I'm having another go.'

Lucy reloaded the bow, shouldered it, and took aim again. This time she missed the door by only half a metre.

'Okay, you carry on if you want to,' said Ben, 'but you'll have to get better. Right now, you're not good enough to fight. And you're holding your head at the wrong angle.'

'It's so I can see. I'm trying to get my eye over where the bolt is so I can sight along it. Every time I fire, I get closer. It's the distance I'm struggling with. I was fine at ten metres then it all went haywire. I suppose it'll be the same when we move further out.'

'Right now, you'll be a liability in a fight. I intend to push the target out to forty and fifty metres eventually. When you can hit those, you'll be good enough.'

Lucy winced as she let fly another bolt which missed the target. 'I feel every shot judder in my missing eye,' said Lucy, 'and it hurts like hell.' She stepped aside.

Stuart slotted his bolt alongside Ben's and was rewarded by an approving grunt. Faye grazed the edge of the heart. Even James hit the target on the lower leg.

'I'll relieve Marcus so he can have a go, you all keep at it, get to know your weapon.' Ben retrieved his bolt from the target.

Marcus, binoculars to his eyes, balanced precariously on the cairn's peak.

'What's going on, Marcus?' said Ben.

Marcus lowered the bins to glance at him. A couple of stones rattled down the cairn as he adjusted his stance.

'I'm not sure, I think I saw the movement over there. It's a long way, I can't be certain.'

'Let me look,' said Ben, holding his hand out for the binoculars.

Marcus was right, something was going on at the entrance

to The Lane, it was too far to see what. It could only be people. The felled trees preventing vehicles coming up the track would not stop an attack on foot.

'I'm going to the bridge. You go and get everyone else who can carry a crossbow and tell them to join me as quick as they can. Run.'

Even if this wasn't an attack it would be a good drill. Ben vaulted the gate as Marcus sped down to the yard.

Halfway to the bridge he paused. In the distance he heard the shouts and yelps of men. Men without fear, men determined. There were many voices. He looked behind him to see Stuart running down The Lane.

Ben reached the bridge first and stopped. They would have to cross the river at this pinch point and would be vulnerable. He could hear them clearly now. Stuart joined him.

'The others are on their way,' said Stuart.

'Sounds like there's quite a few of them. You take the other side, I'll stay here.' He crouched behind a rock just off the track, Stuart crossed The Lane and sheltered behind the trunk of a large oak. Ben knelt and cradled his crossbow as he squinted up the track.

Connie, Lucy, and Emily with Lottie stayed at Cleeve House, the rest made their way to the bridge, ducking in to shelter as they arrived. By the time James had brought up the rear, the invaders had rounded a corner in the track and were in view of the bridge. A hundred metres was too far to be certain. Ben saw at least fifteen, maybe twenty or even more.

'We're outnumbered,' he whispered to his father, kneeling beside him.

'Maybe we won't need to fight,' said James.

The marauders had stopped. Ben watched as someone

gauged their strength and spoke to a couple of bandits. Heads nodded and two of them peeled away from the main group and headed east through the trees. Ben signalled Rob, who slid down the edge of the track to join him behind the boulder.

'We're outnumbered here, and a couple of them have gone off through the trees. They're probably heading for the swing. Can you take them?'

Ben watched his brother and waited for an answer. It had to be Ben or Rob who went to the swing, no one else would find their childhood haunt, and it would be easy to cross the river there. Rob just stared at him, what was he waiting for?

'You should be able to pick them off as they cross if you get there quick,' said Ben. 'If you wait much longer, they'll be over the river.'

'Right,' said Rob and disappeared into the trees.

Ben didn't know if they'd sent anyone to the west. He signalled Faye.

'Go to the clearing. Kill anyone who tries to cross there,' said Ben.

'Me?'

'Yes, you, now.'

Faye crept through the trees to the west.

A cry rent the air and the marauders began their charge to the bridge. Ben scanned the group, a hundred metres away, beyond the range of their weapons. He recognised no one in the band, if any of them had been old school friends from way back, they were now hidden in beards, filth, and murderous intent. They held aloft makeshift spears, carried axes, cleavers, knives. Some carried crossbows, a few shotguns. His eyes scanned them again, counting. Not too bad, maybe fifteen, he thought. Although they were only six, Ben could sense a lack of discipline in the enemy, they crowded together, making easy targets, their bravado fed by encouragement not training.

They were at eighty metres now, still beyond the range of his crossbow. He selected his first target. Not the big guy at the front leading the charge, a steel helmet on his head and a torn leather jerkin which wouldn't stop his crossbow bolt. He'd be good to bring down, but he wasn't the commander. This guy would get his second shot if he had time.

At sixty metres they were just in range. It would need an accurate shot to bring down a moving target. Ben signalled his small group to wait. He could see them all individually now. Some were only kids, maybe fifteen, sixteen, pushed to the vanguard by the commander, himself hanging back a little, waiting to rush forward and claim a victory, no doubt. He seemed unconcerned by any possibility of losing, knew his band outnumbered the opposition. He wasn't looking at Ben, his head swung from side to side, encouraging his troops forward, into battle. There were no insignia of rank, only a posture, an assumption of obedience reflected by the actions of those he commanded. He became Ben's primary target, Ben's eyes fixed on him, measuring the range of movement of his arms, legs, head; watching the pace and rhythm of his stride, preparing for the single shot he would get.

They were at forty metres now, and those with firearms or loaded bows had futilely let fly at Ben and his band, crossbow bolts landing short, shot spreading too wide to cause damage. The yelling redoubled as hand weapons were lofted. Feet thumped on the track; occasional arrows whizzed through the air. Ben the rock to support his crossbow, sighted along its length at the commander. Watched as his head turned aside, encouraging his troops to greater efforts, smelling a victory. Ben's finger squeezed the crossbow trigger, and the bolt flew. His sight telescoped along the trajectory, the noise of the battle dimmed, his peripheral vision blurred, time slowed. He saw the target's head begin to turn back, saw a scar on his cheek, a smile on his mouth, saw the bolt strike in his throat. Saw the blood. The target's hands dropped his weapons, grabbed at his throat; his mouth opened as he stared down the hill towards Ben, met his eyes, then he fell.

They were at thirty metres when Ben saw the big guy, his next target, fall to a bolt from Stuart. No one else had found a target and they were all reloading. The enemy were still yelling, still charging.

While reloading, Ben glanced at his father. He was watching Ben, crossbow still unfired.

'If we don't deal with these bastards, they'll kill us all, Dad. Get one of them before he gets you.'

Ben watched his father turn to the melee before him. It would be hand to hand fighting soon.

'There must be another way,' said James. Ben watched in disbelief as James walked onto the bridge and raised his hands. He called across to the invaders, 'Stop, stop, let's talk about…' His call for peace was broken when an arrow struck him in the shoulder, turned him round with the force of the blow and sat him heavily on the deck of the bridge.

Ben took aim at the archer who had shot his father and killed him. If James wasn't already dead, he would be an easy target. He drew his knife and charged for the bridge, urging the rest of the band to follow him.

Ten metres from the bridge the kids in the van faltered, turned towards their leader for encouragement, but he lay dead or dying up The Lane.

Stuart had a bolt in his crossbow. He raised it and took out another of the enemy, they faltered again. Kneeling by his father, Ben hoisted the fallen crossbow. His eyes met those of a target. He must only be fifteen, thought Ben. He saw the fear in the boy before he turned to flee. But next year he'll be sixteen, and Ben let the bolt fly, hitting the boy between the shoulders, knocking him to the ground.

Reduced to half their men the invaders turned to flee.

'Stuart, take your family and chase these bastards all the way to the end of The Lane. I need to see to my dad.'

After the Reevers had rounded the bend and disappeared, Ben turned to look at his father, sitting on the bridge.

'What the fuck do you think you're playing at, Dad,' he said, contempt twisting the shape of his mouth.

'This isn't right, we should be working together, not fighting each other,' said James, wincing with pain. The arrow had struck beneath his right collar bone, it would have to be removed with care.

'You could have been killed. And we've talked about this. There isn't enough to go around now, yet you'd let these bastards take everything we have and slaughter us.' Ben helped his father to his feet.

'They're people just like you and me, they're capable of being reasonable,' said James.

'You're an old man living in the past. That might have been the way before. Now it's every man for himself. Kill or be killed.'

His father met Ben's eyes. 'I saw. You enjoyed it, didn't you? Enjoyed killing those poor men.'

'Poor men! They would have taken great delight in killing me, and you, if they had the chance. You've got to toughen up if you're going to survive.'

'What happened to "we", son? I thought we were all in this together.'

'We may be right now, and it might continue, if everyone pulls their weight and does as they're told.'

'And who's going to be doing the telling? I expect you think it's you.'

'You've shown how incapable you are of leading us. I have no choice if we're to survive.'

'This is my house and property. You're not in charge here. Just because you're...' James raised his arm, forgetting the arrow in his shoulder, and gasped in pain.

Ben watched him as the pain subsided.

'Just because I'm what, Father? Just because I'm the strongest, the fittest, the best shot. Just because I can see what's happening and what's needed to survive. Just because I have a brain and use it. You may have been the big fella once, now you're a weak old man. Your pissing about with the crossbow could have got us all killed.'

'Don't you talk to me like that. I'll—'

'You'll what? Look at you. Others listening to what you say doesn't make you right. You're wrong most of the time. We've got to toughen up, get selfish, keep what's ours to ourselves. You're already risking our survival giving to those losers, the Reevers.'

'Those are our friends and neighbours you're talking about. What's happened to you? I don't recognise you as my son anymore. Where did this selfish so-and-so come from?'

'He's always been here, Dad, always. It's just now he's woken up. I think you need to do the same. Get real or get out.'

'Is that a threat? Are you threatening your own father? I don't believe I'm hearing this. Let's be clear, while I am here what I say goes as far as Cleeve House and all its resources are concerned. If I think we should share what we have, that's what will happen. Maybe it's you who needs to get real. Now, help me back up to the house, I need to get this shoulder seen to.'

Ben stood quietly looking at his father, watching as rain began to drip down his face, off his nose, his chin. He looked at the slow trickle of blood from the arrow running down his father's arm, staining his jacket. He looked at his steely grey eyes. Ben reached out and gripped the arrow shaft buried in the wound.

'This shoulder, Father?' he said, twisting the shaft in his grip. His father groaned. 'It looks like you've been lucky, it's missed the artery. Now if it struck a little more to the left, we wouldn't be having this conversation.'

Ben rocked the arrow shaft back and forth, forcing the head to move in James's body, scraping it against bone. James staggered backwards in shock and pain until he came to a stop against the low wall of the bridge.

'Don't, what are you doing? Stop!' he cried, his face creasing, his body hunching.

Ben pushed and twisted the arrow in a single vicious movement. The bright red of arterial blood spat from the wound. Ignoring the blood splattering his face, Ben stepped in close to his father, still holding the arrow shaft, and gave a final push. James toppled backwards over the wall of the bridge. He called out as he fell the twelve feet into the river, his cry cut short as he hit the water.

Ben glanced around him; he was alone. He called out for help as he scrambled down the steep rocks of the gorge to the river below. He found his father still alive, his lifeblood turning the water about him pink, his face ashen. Ben took a firm grip on a rock, leaned over and placed a foot on James's chest. James half raised an arm in protest but couldn't hold its weight. Ben met his father's eyes for a last time as they blinked open, leaned all his weight onto his chest and pushed him beneath the surface. He watched his father under the water, barely able to struggle, and soon the tell-tale stream of bubbles from his last breath escaped from James's lungs. Still Ben waited. When he heard voices calling through the trees. He jumped into the waist deep river, took his father's dead body in his arms, and called out again for help.

Chapter 16

Faye kept close watch on the river crossing she'd been sent to. She saw nobody. No one tried to cross, no one approached, no one called her. She heard shouts and cries of pain from the battle raging by the bridge but remained watching the river.

Although her eyes kept their vigil her mind was elsewhere. How did Ben know about her and the clearing? Had he been spying on her? Had he seen her with Marcus? Not that there was anything to see, one kiss, that was all. Nothing like what Rob might have seen between her and Ben if he'd seen them that night in the old hovel, and every night since. Ben ignored her most of the time, only catching her eye and nodding in the direction of the shelter. She'd wait there for him. He'd brought her a blanket when he came, a plank of wood to cover the window. They'd christened the blanket immediately. Faye was bored with Rob, resisted all his approaches, and now slept in the hovel every night.

The sounds of the battle began to die away. She was wasting her time waiting for nothing to happen and began to make her way back to the bridge. She was sure the raiders had been beaten; she'd heard Ben's voice, and Stuart's.

Through the branches she could see down to the bridge and there was Ben and his father talking. Faye almost set off to join them, but something in the way they stood held her back. She couldn't make out what they were saying to each other, it didn't look friendly.

She saw Ben grab his father, and there was blood spurting, and she was sure Ben pushed him over the bridge. Faye heard James cry out, her hand went to her mouth, as if to stop a return cry. Ben looked around but she didn't want to be seen and slipped behind a trunk as his eyes swept past where she stood. She heard Ben call for help. Again, she almost went down, but again something held her back. Then Ben climbed down into the gorge and out of view.

She waited. It felt like hours. Should she go and help? But Ben would know. Faye could sense what it would be like, his eyes seeing through her, he would look at her and know she had seen him. She waited, her eyes flicking up and down the track, back to the bridge, and up and down again. Where was everyone, why didn't someone come?

Rob appeared on the track by the bridge. She heard Ben call again, and a splash of water. Then Rob was there, going over the bridge to help, and the Reevers arrived, and everyone was there except her.

She ran through the trees onto The Lane to join what she knew was the already failed attempt to save James Marchand's life.

Chapter 17

They used fallen branches and clothing stripped from the dead to fashion a stretcher; belts to tie the body in place. Hoisted on their shoulders, Ben and Rob at the front, Stuart and Marcus behind, they made the slow way up The Lane towards Cleeve House. Faye hid her relief when told to run ahead with the news.

Connie and Lucy were standing at the gate, waiting, when Faye ran towards them.

'What's happened? Is one of them hurt?' said Connie, reading Faye's expression.

'It's James,' gasped Faye.

'He's injured?'

'No, I'm sorry, he's dead.'

A groan began in the depths of Connie's soul and became manifest in the mewling escaping her lips as her hand clutched at her chest. 'No.'

'Oh, Mum,' said Lucy, then to Faye, 'Are you sure? There's no mistake?'

'I'm sure. He was wounded, fell in the river. They're carrying him back.'

Connie took a breath, stifled her voice, climbed the gate.

Lucy followed her. 'Mum, I'm so sorry, I can't believe this.' Her disbelief in every expression.

Connie said nothing, shed no tears, just hurried as fast as she could to meet the dread she had feared.

They stopped and lowered the stretcher to the ground. Connie knelt beside the still soaking body and took hold of his arm, held it to her face, kissed it, and laid it back on the stretcher. Nobody spoke.

When Connie stood Lucy wrapped her arms around her and sobbed onto her shoulder. Connie patted her back and suffered the hug for a few moments before slowly pushing Lucy away.

Her chin trembling, Connie turned to Ben and said, 'Take him to the lounge.' She turned and walked away, hiding her tears from her children.

They laid him on the same couch she had nursed Lucy on only weeks before.

'I'd like to be alone with him now, could you all leave me,' said Connie. Her three children each hugged her and shared what words of comfort they could. Connie called Ben back when he got to the door.

'Close the door and sit with me a minute, Ben. Now, tell me exactly what happened.'

'Oh, Mum. I know you're upset; it will only make it worse.'

'Tell me; I need to know. I have a right to know.'

'It's not pleasant,' said Ben.

'Of course it's not.' Connie's exasperation spat her words. 'Just get on with it and tell me it all, every last detail.'

Ben took a breath and looked at the floor before telling her about the battle. 'Dad didn't want to fight. He wanted to talk to them, negotiate.'

'Go on, what happened next?'

'He stood up, out of cover, he didn't seem to care about the danger. He started calling at them, asking them to talk. Then he got hit. You saw where the arrow got him. The fight was still going on and he didn't look too bad, there wasn't much blood.' Ben stopped and glanced up at Connie.

'Tell me about after they ran away. How did he die?'

Ben's head bent again. 'I sent the others after them, to chase them from The Lane. It needed everyone who could go. I didn't want them to be attacking again. And Dad looked okay, I mean he was breathing, looking around him. I told them to chase them all the way to the road and I would look after Dad, bring him home.'

Ben raised his head and met his mother's look. 'I helped him stand up and something must have happened because the wound started spurting blood, it hit me in my face. I let go of his arm for a second, automatically, I had to wipe my eyes. It was only a second, and he fell, tumbled over the wall, off the bridge, into the river. I yelled for help and rushed down the rocks, he was dead when I got there. I'm sorry, Mum, there was nothing I could do.'

Connie sat looking at her hands in her lap, one clutching the other. Only the sound of breathing broke the silence. She again looked up at Ben and said, 'You can leave now.'

Ben's eyes burned with the vision of his mother's face as he left. His frowning face found Lucy waiting for him outside the room. She hugged him.

'She wanted to hear all the details,' said Ben.

'Poor Mum. So do I,' said Lucy.

'Not here, let's find somewhere private.'

The small room had once been a pantry. One small, frosted window facing north, the only lighting, cast its shiver across the narrow space onto two upright chairs. Lucy listened to Ben as he retold his account of their father's death.

When he'd finished Lucy said, 'That's so like him, he was always a peace maker.'

'The way Mum looked at me, I felt like a child again. Like a seven-year-old caught with his hand in the cookie jar.'

'She's upset, Ben. We all are.'

'I know, I felt guilty, as if it was my fault, as if I'd killed him.'

'She wouldn't have meant anything by it. Dad's dead, they've been together for ages. How do you think she's feeling? Give her some time.'

'You're right, I'm being paranoid. But in a way it was my fault. I was there, I should have stopped him running out, held him back.'

'You couldn't have, you know what he was like. If he believed something was right, there was no stopping him.'

'That's the tragedy. If I could have I would, you know that don't you Lucy?'

'Yes, I know Ben. It wasn't your fault. What are we going to do now? Without him.'

'I don't know, I guess we'll have to muddle on.'

'We'll have to have some sort of funeral, but it won't be how Mum would have wanted,' said Ben, the morning after the battle at the bridge. 'We can't have the body in the house any longer.'

'Yes, of course,' said Lucy, 'but I don't know if Mum's ready, or me.'

'We can't have disease in the house, or we might be burying more. I've dug a grave, up by the cairn.'

'What about Mum, does she know?

'They may come back; we need to be ready. We have to

deal with this now.'

'You're being heartless, Ben. What's the matter with you? It's our father you're talking about.'

'I'm only being practical. I'm as upset as everyone, but it's the living that count.'

'What do you want from me?'

'Will you tell Mum? I think she'd take it better from you. You see more of her every day than me or Rob.'

'Okay, I can tell her. I think she'll understand.'

'And you'll have to give the eulogy.'

'Me? You're the eldest. It should be you.'

'I'm the eldest, it should be me,' he echoed. 'I'm the strong one, the one who always looks after everything. It's always been like this. What about me? How I feel? What I want? Does it never count? Do I always have to be the strong one?'

'I'm sure Rob will stand in, he'll make a good stab at it,' said Lucy.

'Rob!' Ben's eyes flashed up at her. 'He'll start talking about his experiment growing weed, or how he freed the chickens to live in the wild. Stuff Mum won't want to hear. She was upset then and will be again. It can't be Rob.'

They sat in silence for a moment, then Ben said, 'After all, you were always his favourite.'

Words never spoken before, but Lucy knew them to be true. Despite all the outward fairness, the equal shares, she knew she'd been favoured in ways which could not be measured, the intensity of a gaze, the gentleness of a hug, the openness of a smile. Her gaze fell from Ben's face as she realised Ben knew it too.

'And you'll make a better job of it than I would,' said Ben. 'You'll say all the touchy-feely stuff I'd forget about. I'd spout some nonsense about a father figure which I wouldn't really believe, and Mum would know. It would spoil it for her. Do it for Mum, not for me.'

In Lucy's head scenes of her childhood and her father played on a screen filled with happy memories. Each one almost brought her to tears, she recognised in them parts of her father, his character, things her mother would respond to. Ben was right. He could make the speech, but it would be full of camping trips and mechanics. She would talk about love and tenderness. It would mean much more to Mum.

'Alright,' said Lucy, 'only if it's okay with Mum.'

'It will be okay with Mum if you tell her you want to do it,' said Ben.

Chapter 18

A week after burying his father, Ben sat atop the five-bar gate on look-out duty. A task he'd rostered himself for, since he'd been elected leader of the community following the funeral. Only Rob and his mother had put up any resistance.

Ben lowered his binoculars and slid from his perch when he heard the scrape of footsteps behind him.

'What are you doing here, brother?' said Ben. 'Shouldn't you be tilling the fields or something.'

'You bastard,' said Rob.

'We've had this conversation. It isn't my fault Dad's dead.'

'That's not why you're a bastard.'

'What is it? Didn't you get enough glory for defending that kid's swing against those two teenagers last week? I think you should have killed them both, not let one run away.'

Rob shook his head at his brother and ground his teeth. His fists clenched against his thighs. 'No, you know what you've done. You utter shite.'

'Something I've done? You mean everyone chose me to be leader in Dad's place and not you? You make me laugh,' said Ben.

'It's not that, you arsehole.' Rob raised an arm to poke Ben in the chest. Ben grabbed his wrist before he could make contact.

'How am I supposed to know what you're angry about? I'm not a bloody mind reader. Whatever it is why don't you get it off your chest and get back to doing something useful.' He gave Rob's wrist a twist and pushed him away.

'All my fucking life you've been doing this to me. When we were kids, you always took my toys, right out of my hands. And not because you wanted them, you just didn't want them to be mine.'

'You haven't come all the way up here to complain about your old dinky cars, have you? You're wasting your time; I haven't got them with me.'

Rob's eyes narrowed; his hands balled into fists. Ben watched the same signals of an imminent attack he'd been seeing since he was a child. Ben remained still as he assessed his brother's next move, preparing himself. Rob was on the edge, just one more little push would send him over.

'You're not jealous about the bed-warmer you brought here finding a decent shag, are—'

Ben didn't finish the sentence. Rob rushed at him, throwing a fist. His telegraphed punch never connected. Ben side stepped and Rob's fist whistled past his head. Before Rob could turn, Ben thumped him on his ear and took a step backwards.

'It's not me has the problem here, mate. If you can't keep your women in order why the hell should I care,' he said as Rob rounded on him.

Rob roared and charged him again, fists flailing. Ben stepped in close and took a weakened punch to his chest, then grabbed and twisted the arm, tripped Rob with his booted foot, and threw him to the floor. Ben hung on to his brother's arm as he fell, put a further twist on the arm and shoved his boot in Rob's armpit.

'It would only take a little turn like this…' he put pressure on Rob's arm, 'to dislocate your shoulder. Not life threatening, but disabling, and painful. Are you going to behave, or do I need to make you?'

Rob tried to wriggle free. Ben scorned an ineffectual attempt to hit him and leaned into his arm a little more. At every move of Rob's, Ben increased the pressure on his shoulder. Rob stopped struggling and lay still, his face pressed into the dirt.

'That's better,' said Ben, 'now are you going to be a good little boy or are you going to be naughty again?' After a pause, 'I'm sorry, I didn't hear you,' he said, leaning on the arm he held and raising a curse from Rob.

Ben lifted his boot from Rob's armpit and kicked him in the ribs. 'Tell me you're going to behave, or it won't be a tap from my boot, and it won't be your ribs that get kicked.'

'Okay, okay,' said Rob.

'Okay what, little brother?'

'Okay, I won't hit you.'

Ben laughed. 'Come on, little brother, you know you have to say the words, save yourself some pain and say them now.' He kicked his brother again in the same spot.

Rob grunted when the boot met his ribs. 'Okay, I'll behave,' he spat through gritted teeth.

'That's better,' said Ben, releasing his arm and lifting his boot from his brother's armpit. 'Now let's get you dusted off and stood up.' With apparent care Ben leaned down and helped his brother to his knees and then his feet.

'And before you go,' said Ben, 'I don't want you to forget what's happened here today.' Ben lashed a sudden fist at Rob's unsuspecting face. It was a hard punch on Rob's mouth, his lip split, and blood began to run. 'I'm in charge now, remember? Things are different. Now fuck off back to work and don't come to me again with your pathetic complaints.'

Chapter 19

Three weeks later, Rob appeared at Lucy's door.

'Oh, Rob, not again. Sit down and let me look at you,' she said.

Rob tilted his bloody face at her.

'Is it the same lip?'

Rob nodded. Lucy poured a tiny amount of water into a small bowl, took a rag, and began to clean his face.

'I've tried to talk to him, you know?' said Lucy wringing out the cloth and dabbing his face again.

Rob winced in reply.

'He says it's always you who starts these fights.'

Rob shook his head.

'No, I don't think it's you either. He says you throw the first punch. Just like when you were kids. You haven't said anything, what's wrong?'

Rob opened his mouth. Lucy cried out in dismay when she saw the blackening mass of coagulated blood where a front tooth should have been.

'This is serious, I'm going to see him now.' Lucy got up to leave but Rob grabbed her hand and shook his head.

'It won't do any good. He'll do it anyway, even if I don't lose my temper first.' His voice stilted, breathy through the gap, not quite a lisp. Enough of a defect to attract Ben's sarcastic attention. 'It's not only my mouth that hurts.'

'Has he kicked you again?' Rob nodded. 'In the same place?' He nodded again.

'Let me have a look,' said Lucy. She began to pull up his filthy shirt. The dark blue of the bruise overlay the yellow streaks of the older injuries. The area bruised had grown since Lucy last looked. Always at the same place, on Rob's ribs. Lucy couldn't tell if Rob had cracked ribs or not, either from this injury or the last. Rob was getting thinner, and the kicks were getting harder.

'I have a little arnica, let me rub some on.' Rob allowing her told Lucy how serious these injuries were.

Rob winced again despite Lucy's gentle application of the ointment.

'You'll end up with a serious injury. If he kicked you in your stomach like this, or kidneys, it could be...' Lucy stopped herself, shook her head to cast away the oncoming tears of frustration.

'It's every week since Dad died. Every fucking week. Sometimes more than once. He finds me, riles me, and beats me. I hate him.'

'I don't understand why he won't listen to me. He insists it's all your fault, but I know that can't be true. Can you keep out of his way?'

'I try, but I've got to eat, and I've got to work. He comes looking for me if he hasn't beaten me for a few days. It's pathetic.'

'It would be if it wasn't dangerous.'

'I don't think I can stay here any longer, Lucy.'

'Wait, I'll be finished soon.'

'No, I mean here at Cleeve House.'

'Where will you go? What about Mum?'

'I'll have to take my chances; it can't be any worse out there than it is here. And Mum will understand.'

'Rob, it's almost December, where will you go?'

'I've thought about it. I'm going to need your help. If I'm careful I've got about half a week before he has another go at me. I want to be gone in four days max. I'll need a stockpile of food. There's loads of stuff in the storeroom.'

'Only Ben has the key.'

'You go in there every day to help Mum with dinner. If you could get me some tins of stuff it would help. Enough to keep me going for a few days.'

'It'll be hard. It would be easier if Mum knew. I'm sure she'd help. She's not stupid. She knows what it's like between you and Ben.'

'Tell her then. I expect she'll be upset.'

'You must talk to her before you go. She's your mother.'

'I will, but not today. When I'm looking less beaten.'

He left Lucy alone wringing out the cloth. Her eye caught the photos of her and her brothers on the shelf. She swung out her hand and knocked Ben's image to the floor, shattering the glass in the frame.

Lucy handed the bag to Rob. It held everything she and her mother had stolen during the few days since Rob's beating. 'You're taking your guitar?' she said.

'It's the only thing I'd miss, apart from you and Mum,' said Rob slinging the bag over his shoulder with his guitar before easing open the door onto the pre-dawn winter.

'How will you get past the lookout?' said Lucy.

'I'm not going that way. I'm going north, along the old back path to Histon. Ben will probably guess which way I've gone when he realises, but I doubt he'll be bothered to follow. He'll be too busy being the big boss here.'

'Have you seen Mum?'

'Yes, I've just said goodbye. I told her not to come down.'

'Will I see you again?' said Lucy.

'You remember Goff's Cove? We went there when we were kids. Go there on Sundays, find an excuse, maybe do some fishing. I'll try and get there. Sometimes I will, sometimes I won't. I can't promise. If you're alone leave a rag on the post at the top of the path. I'll try and see you, Lucy. Thank you for everything, the torch, the knife. Everything.'

Lucy hugged him to her, holding him for a few precious seconds, capturing the feel of him, then he was gone.

Chapter 20

A couple of days after Rob's departure, Lucy found Emily sitting in a corner of the lounge. 'Emily, what's the matter?'

Emily's fearful glance relaxed when she recognised Lucy.

'I thought I was alone here.'

'Do you want me to go? Is there nothing I can do?'

'You're probably the only person I could stand being with right now. I'd like you to stay,' said Emily, wiping her eyes.

'What's wrong, Em?'

'It's happened, like I knew it would.' She nodded at a packed bag on the floor.

'I don't understand, what's happened?'

'It's your brother's doing, he's told me to leave.'

'Leave the house! He can't, there isn't anywhere to go, what about Lottie?'

'No, he says I have to leave our room. He's got another room for me. I don't know what's going on. It's because I'm pregnant, I know it.'

'What do you mean?'

'He did this when I was pregnant with Lottie. He went to sleep in the spare room in my third trimester. And now I'm twenty-seven weeks. Almost the same to the day.'

'Why?'

'He said he couldn't sleep with me being restless in the night. I think he lied. I never noticed him awake during the night. Now he's using it as an excuse to get me out of the room.'

'Couldn't he have moved out? Wouldn't that be easier?'

'Ours is the most private room in the house. I think he wants his privacy. I don't trust him.'

'Do you want me to talk to him? I might be able to get him to change his mind.'

'You'd be wasting your time. And he'd go berserk if he thought I'd been talking to you about our private life.'

'He wouldn't hurt you.'

'Maybe not.'

'You think he might? You're pregnant, for Christ's sake.'

'He wouldn't do anything to harm the baby. But there are ways he could hurt me.'

'Where does he think you're going to sleep?'

'In Rob's room. He's gone to sort it out, he'll be back soon.'

'Rob only left a few days ago. He might come back.'

'Not if he's got any sense. Ben hates him, he's constantly told me how stupid he is. He's not though, is he? He's the sensible one, he got out.'

'I'm sorry, Emily. Maybe you'll be more comfortable on your own.'

'And I will be on my own,' said Emily. 'He says Lottie has to stay with him. She sleeps in a little alcove off the room, and he won't let her come with me.' These last words struggled from the now sobbing mother.

'But that will only be until you've had your baby,' said Lucy.

'Maybe. He's probably having it off with Faye and that's

why he wants me out of the way.'

'Faye's sleeping up in the old shelter, isn't she?' said Lucy.

Emily flashed at Lucy, 'I'm pretending I don't know, otherwise I might go and kill her.'

'Emily, you wouldn't.'

'No, of course not, but I might do something terrible, even though it's not really her fault, is it?'

'Em, you don't know for sure he's sleeping with her. He might just be tired like he says. He does work hard.'

'Yes, I do work hard,' said Ben from the doorway. He strode in as the women shared a look.

'Em told me you want her to sleep somewhere else. What's going on?' said Lucy.

'Emily and I agreed it would be the best for both of us right now, didn't we?' Ben's pointed look at her received a 'Yes, Ben,' from Emily.

'Couldn't you have moved out?' said Lucy.

Lucy's words soaked into the walls, the floor, the ceiling, but bounced off her brother. Ben inhaled through his nostrils. 'It makes more sense for Emily to be where she can be heard if anything happens later. We don't want to keep changing rooms. Not that this is any of your business, Lucy.'

'No, of course not, but... Rob might come back, and he'll need his room again. I miss him I guess; I can't believe he just disappeared.'

Ben's face softened, his jaw unclenched, his shoulders relaxed. 'I'm sure he had his reasons, whatever they were. He's his own man and makes his own decisions. If he comes back, he'll be welcome; we'll find somewhere for him to stay. I want to get Emily settled and I'll be back. Wait for me, Lucy.'

Ben took Emily's bag and led her away. At the door Emily glanced over her shoulder at Lucy, her eyes had a hunted look, and her head gave a quick shake before she turned and left.

Lucy thought about leaving, even stood to go. Before she could, Ben hurried back into the room, insisted they sat.

'I don't know what Emily has been telling you, whatever it is you can take it with a large dose of salt,' said Ben.

'What do you mean? She's always been upfront and honest with me.'

'I'm going to share something with you, you mustn't let on, especially to Emily, it would destroy her. I can trust you, can't I?'

'Do you really need to ask?'

'Okay. Emily's first pregnancy, with Lottie, wasn't a happy time for us. She had a terrible time with perinatal anxiety. It took over her whole life, and mine. She couldn't function properly, couldn't sleep, couldn't plan. She worried about everything. She even started accusing me of having an affair. It was horrible. She said I didn't care about her. I couldn't get her to listen to me. Eventually, I came home early one day and saw the midwife. I told her what had been happening. She recognised it immediately. She got the doctor to prescribe something for Emily. Things weren't too bad afterwards, but she didn't have as much energy as she had before.'

'I never knew,' said Lucy. 'It must have been terrible.'

'You wouldn't know, we didn't exactly advertise it. Anyway, it's happening again. She's worrying all the time, especially at night. She wakes me up at least half a dozen times every night to make sure she's okay. Now she's accusing me again, who with I've no idea. I can't stand it anymore, I'm getting tired, and there's so much to do. And this time there's no doctor and no medicine for her. We have to tough it out until the child is born. She recovered quickly once she had Lottie in her arms. I'm hoping it will be the same this time.'

'Oh, Ben.' Lucy's hand went out to touch him, but she withdrew it before it reached him, putting her hands together in her lap, looking down at them for a moment. Her instinct confounded by the hurt and fear in Emily's parting expression. 'Poor Emily. What can I do to help her?' she spoke her thoughts aloud, not expecting a response.

'Keep an eye on her for me, make sure she's all right. She's always liked you, Lucy, and she trusts you. If you tell her something, she'll believe you.'

Chapter 21

Faye had ignored the nausea she'd felt, pushed it to the back of her mind, blamed the unpredictable and shrinking diet, wished it away. When she began to empty her stomach at random intervals, despite her constant hunger, she had to accept what she already knew. When alone at the hovel, she could hide around the back and throw her guts into the brambles. Nobody would know, or care. When Ben chose to visit, she had to be careful, control and contain her body somehow, prevent it from betraying her. During mealtimes, she couldn't feign lack of appetite. Everyone was hungry and if she left her meagre bowl someone else would have it.

Maybe Ben wouldn't reject her in the same way he rejected Emily. Or maybe she'd lose the baby, maybe the starvation would get rid of it for her. Around her head the thoughts flew and always came to the same conclusion. She was alone. Alone and in thrall to a murderer. She could tell no one, they wouldn't believe her. She couldn't let Ben know she'd seen him; he would deal with her in the same ruthless fashion. There was no one she could trust. Lucy was kind, but also Ben's sister, and friendly with Emily. Only one other person had shown her any kindness.

It took a single glance from Faye for Marcus to become distracted from the grinding labour of the field. When she caught his eye, she stood and walked away. She threw a glance over her shoulder when she got to the edge of the field and caught him watching her. She turned past the hedge out of view, knowing he would follow.

Faye didn't look back again, and walked directly to the clearing by the river, a place which had become "their" spot. Where they met occasionally to share their troubles and to flirt.

She sat on the log and waited. Marcus soon appeared through the trees.

'I thought you'd be coming here,' he said, sitting next to her.

'I'm getting predictable am I, Sherlock?' said Faye.

'No, I hoped you were, I wanted to see you,' said Marcus.

'And here I am. What do you want to see me for?'

'Just because… I like you. You're teasing me, aren't you?'

Faye laughed. Poor Marcus, he was so transparent. 'You like me? Are you sure, or is it lust?'

Marcus looked at the ground, at the mud around his feet. 'You're beautiful, of course I fancy you. I like you too.'

'And I like you, Marcus.' She stopped short of declaring any physical attraction she felt for him. Faye had brought him here with a singular purpose, but part of her silently screamed at him to run away, escape from the bind she would throw around him. But she didn't. She looked at the future and saw herself lost and desperate. Marcus may be her only help.

'I'm glad,' said Marcus, 'I hoped it might be more than "like".' He didn't look up at her. He kept his head looking at the mud he found himself swirling with his foot, his shoulders slumped.

Faye put an arm around him. She could feel the bones of his shoulder through his coat. He was getting thinner, losing weight. She reached up to his cheek, to the soft downy growth, and turned his head towards her. She met his eyes as his head turned and then kissed him. She felt him hesitate, then surrender to her.

'It is more than "like", Marcus,' she said when they broke. 'But in this god-awful place at this god-awful time, it's hard to find the words and mean them.'

Marcus took a breath to reply, then lightning flashed across the clearing and rain began to pour.

'Come on, let's run,' said Marcus taking her hand and pulling her towards the path.

'No, not that way,' said Faye. 'Come with me.'

Faye led Marcus through dripping trees, away from the house. She found her deer track and the way out of the wood to the west of Cleeve House.

'Where are we going? We'll get soaked,' said Marcus.

'I've something to show you. Not afraid of a bit of water, are you?'

The rain soaked their hair, seeped into their clothes, the wet grass drenched their trousers. It didn't take long for the water wicking up their legs to join that draining down from above.

Faye found the gate. They splashed through the mud surrounding it and climbed over into a field.

'Over there, look,' said Faye pointing through the rain to the hovel in the opposite corner of the field.

'I'm soaked!' said Marcus as they burst through the door. He looked around. 'What's going on in here?'

'I didn't tell you; I've moved out of the house. I'm staying here now.'

Marcus took in the blankets and hay bales, the sheet of wood nailed to where the window would have been, the old wooden box serving as a table, another as a stool.

'It looks great, but we could have got out of the rain sooner going to the house.'

'We haven't come here to get out of the rain,' said Faye, removing her sodden coat.

Marcus took his coat off. He found nowhere to hang it so lay it on the floor.

'You can't get in my bed,' said Faye, her arm sweeping over the hay bales covered with blankets, 'with those soggy pants on, you'd better take them off.' She took off her boots and her own pants while she watched Marcus, his eyes tracing the tattooed serpent that wound around her thigh. She did the sums again in her head, five or six weeks since she was first with Ben, not too long a gap for this to be believable. She climbed under the blankets while Marcus stood, mouth open, eyes wide. 'You going to get in, or just stand there shivering?'

Chapter 22

A five-mile hike along a neglected path from Cleeve House led to Goff's Cove. Lucy had wanted to go alone. Ben had insisted someone go with her. 'We don't know if there's anyone out there or not. You could be attacked,' he'd said. Stuart's skill with the crossbow got him the job. No one at Cleeve had been to the coast since the flood. Fish might help their dwindling food stores, so Lucy agreed to the company on this first trip.

'I know the way,' said Lucy, 'I grew up here.'

For a moment she thought he would snap at her. But Stuart said, 'Okay, I thought you might have forgotten, sorry.'

'And I'm perfectly capable of carrying a couple of fishing rods, stop patronising me.'

'Okay, okay, I said I'm sorry. I'm only trying to help.'

Lucy led, and at every step she felt Stuart's eyes watching her.

'Maybe we could collect mussels too,' said Stuart to Lucy's back.

She glanced behind to find him grinning at her. 'They

would only be tiny if we found any. The mature ones will be twenty feet underwater,' Lucy said, shaking her head.

The summit of the path allowed a first glimpse of the sea. From a mile away the coastline seemed unchanged. Lucy gave way to Stuart and let him take the lead. She'd had enough of feeling his eyes on her.

The isolation of Goff's Cove, inaccessible by road, encouraged the childhood Lucy to make the long walk with parents or brothers, when summer days would be spent in rockpool and sand dune adventures. The cove held equal appeal for her as a young teenager, meeting late night assignations with torches and swimming costumes.

Shards of splintered timber, splashes of broken plastic, and occasional shreds of torn fabric, marched across the salt grasses marking the high point of the flood tide on the day the world changed. The detritus, thrown there by the tidal wave, lay high above the new high tide level, itself twenty-five feet above what Lucy remembered. Lower down, recognisable remnants of the wooden steps to the beach, and the old beach hut someone built many years before, were dotted here and there. The hills of Lucy's childhood adventures were now small islands poking from the sea. The famous coastal path had disappeared, and the track they were following ended abruptly with a steep incline into angry water. They headed westward to where a gentler slope led to the new coastline.

'I see what you mean about the mussels,' said Stuart. 'Stupid of me not to have realised. If we use those rocks for a base, we should be able to cast into the water easy enough.'

Lucy followed Stuart's pointing arm. It made sense. 'Okay, we'll set up there.'

'Have you done this before?'

'I've done a little, mainly from boats during the summer,

when I was a kid,' said Lucy.

'There's a bit more to it, casting from the shore.' Stuart set up the two tripods they had to hold the rods and explained about casting into the sea. How you needed to judge the waves and make a long cast, letting the line out as you came back to the tripod to set the rod. 'You should try a couple of practice casts.'

Lucy watched Stuart timing the waves before casting to throw the line as far out as he could. He ran backwards, line spinning out, before he got wet feet. Lucy picked up the other rod and mimicked his footwork.

'Hey, that's good,' said Stuart, 'you're a natural.'

They baited the hooks and cast again.

'What now?' said Lucy after the rods were secured.

'Now we wait. If there's a bite the top of the rod will start to bend. If there isn't a bite some little bugger will have nibbled off the bait and then we do it again. Can you watch them for a bit?' said Stuart.

'Where are you going?'

'I'll be back in a few minutes.'

Stuart was out of sight when one of the rods began to bend. Lucy ignored an urge to call him back, she needed to do this herself. She took the rod and felt the tug against her pull. Line began to spin out when she dislodged the ratchet on the reel. She almost dropped the rod in surprise but managed to grab the reel winder and held it fast. She reeled it in feeling like she had a whale on the hook. Then it was there before her, a silver bellied mackerel with its distinct dark stripes, hanging from the line. She unhooked it, baited the line, and cast again.

Driftwood clattering onto rocks announced Stuart's return as Lucy reeled in another fish.

'Fantastic, I'm starving,' he said, arranging stones into a

makeshift fireplace and arranging the driftwood in the centre. From his pocket he took some dry newspaper and a box of matches.

'Where did you get those?' said Lucy.

'Never mind, here, take the heads off those two and skewer them.' He handed her a couple of sticks.

Lucy's mouth opened as objections formed in her head. The fish were for everyone. They should take them back. But no words came out. Her hand went to the well-honed knife in its sheath in her boot. She picked up the two fish and walked away a few paces.

'Where are you going?' said Stuart.

It was her turn not to answer. She stopped by a large rock, and using it as a table expertly beheaded, gutted, and skewered the fish.

'Where did you learn that?' asked Stuart as she handed him the fish.

'Spent a summer working in the kitchen of a fish restaurant. Once you've learned you never forget.'

As the fish were toasting against the flames a rod again bent. 'There'll be plenty to take back,' said Stuart. 'The others haven't had to walk ten miles, have they?' The line was empty. Stuart shrugged and used some of the fish gut for bait before casting again.

'Only one each though,' she said, a little respect for Stuart's resourcefulness in her voice. Stuart nodded and grinned as he passed her one of the cooked fish.

'That was so good,' said Lucy licking her fingers. 'We should have done this weeks ago.'

'Don't tell your brother I've pinched the matches, will you. You know how touchy he is about stuff.'

'He is, it's for all our welfare. We'd be starving if it weren't for him.'

'Some of us are, but he looks okay, doesn't he?'

'What do you mean?'

'Nothing, I guess it affects people in different ways. My dad's really hungry all the time. I expect it's because he misses his beer. I think he's been living off his beer belly since we got here. Sue says he's not half as cuddly as he used to be.'

Lucy laughed. 'I could have done with a bit extra round me. I'm hungry most of the time.'

'I think you're fine just as you are,' said Stuart, his gaze steady on her single eye for a moment before he turned away to deal with one of the lines.

Lucy frowned as she watched him bait the hook and recast. He spoke again, without looking at her.

'Did you come home on your own?'

'Sorry?'

'You didn't bring a boyfriend, or a girlfriend if that's what you're into.'

'That's a bit personal,' said Lucy.

'We're here for a few hours yet, and fish aren't too interesting. What do you want to talk about?'

Lucy laughed and relented. 'Okay, no I didn't bring a boyfriend, and no I'm not really into girls. What about you, you didn't bring anyone either.'

'I've got an excuse. I've not long finished school, all the girls I know are at home with their mums and dads. There are a couple who would have come if they could have got here, but I'm glad they couldn't. Good company for a party, but I wouldn't want to live with them. If you know what I mean.'

Lucy threw her mind back to when she was nineteen. 'Yes, I know what you mean, I knew a couple of boys like that.'

'Is that why you're by yourself here? You didn't want to

bring him?'

'I didn't say that, and what even makes you think there is a "him"?'

'Because you're good looking, even with the eye patch. I bet men are always sniffing around you.'

He stared right at her as he spoke. Lucy turned her head away, glanced down at her hands. Despite her hair, unwashed for weeks, despite her filthy clothes, despite not having a proper shower for months, he said that. Her memory zapped back over the Atlantic, over the US to Palo Alto. A flush began to creep up Lucy's neck, something which hadn't happened since she'd been a schoolchild. Now she used baiting an empty line to disguise her feelings.

'There is a man, or there was,' said Lucy after casting. 'I came here from the States and he's still over there. I don't expect I'll ever see him again. We were close, but not close enough to be together, if you know what I mean. We might have been, in time. I liked him. Now I'll never know.'

One of the rods bent and caught their attention. Stuart reeled it in, this time with a fish attached. 'Don't worry, look,' he said, tossing the catch onto the bag they'd brought, 'plenty more fish in the sea.'

Lucy's laugh was stifled by Stuart's mouth as he leapt on her, pushing her to the ground, kissing her. She felt his tongue pushing into her mouth. She clamped her teeth together, his tongue escaped. She shook her head and forced his mouth off hers.

'Stop! Get off! What do you think you're doing?' she said, anger rising in her voice.

Stuart raised his head and looked at her. 'Come on, Lucy, you must be gagging for it by now. And there's only me isn't there? There's no one else in the whole place who isn't either your brother or a wimp. Let's not mess about, there isn't time in this new world. Let's just get on with it.'

She turned her head away as he leant down to try and kiss her again. It might have been a long time for her, but she had no intention of sharing herself with Stuart Reever.

'Stop it! I don't want this.' Her anger finding a voice.

'Don't play games with me. I've had prick teasers before, and I know how to deal with them.'

Lucy glared at him. 'I'm not —' she began but he kissed her again. His legs now straddling her, his hands holding her wrists.

She struggled but he pulled her arms together above her head and clasped her wrists in one hand. The other began to open the buttons on her coat.

Lucy brought a knee up hard against him, aiming between his legs, intent on dislodging him. He smothered the blow with a twist of his hips, worked his legs between hers, forcing them apart.

'Come on, Lucy, stop playing games with me. Things could be worse; if a gang caught you, they'd all have you. I'll protect you.'

The arrogant little shite, she thought, and he believes himself. His hand, rough and cruel, pushed underneath her clothes, rubbing and squeezing her breast, hurting her. She twisted and turned and pulled and pushed with arms and legs but couldn't break free. Her wrists burning in his grip, her heart pounding. Inside the fear and disgust, the futility of her struggle dawned. Her strength waning, she stopped and lay still.

'That's better, relax, it'll be more fun for you.'

Lucy brought her leg up as high as she could, spreading her legs wider, as if inviting him. She felt the grip on her wrists relax a little. Then his hand slid down her body to the belt on her trousers to unbuckle it. His weight all on the hand holding her wrists, pushing them into the ground. He hoisted himself to get access to her belt. The confusion of her belt, fastened in the opposite direction to his own, made him glance down between their bodies.

Lucy grabbed the chance and heaved her arms apart, breaking the hold on her wrist. Stuart collapsed onto her, his other hand trapped between them, his head striking the side of her face. She pushed her foot into the ground and twisted, rolling him off her downhill.

His arms came back up, hands searching for her wrists and finding one, grabbed it hard. Her other hand had gone to her boot and drawn the knife. She jabbed the point into Stuart's leg. She felt the blade hard against his skin before it gave way and sank into his flesh. He leaped off her.

'You've cut me, you bitch.'

Lucy scrambled to her feet, brandishing the knife. Stuart moved in on her.

'Keep away from me. Next time it won't be just a scratch.'

'I don't think so, stop playing hard to get.' He stepped forward again, trying to edge to her blind side.

'I'm not playing, this isn't a game; Ben will kill you when he hears about this.'

Stuart paused. Lucy watched him considering the likelihood of her threat. 'What are you going to tell him? I kissed you and squeezed your tit? He's not going to kill me for that.'

'You were going to rape me.'

'No, I wasn't. We'd eaten the fish we should have taken back. I tried to kiss you and my hand brushed your tits. That's all, and that's why there's only one fish, you ate them.'

Lucy measured the lies rolling off his tongue against her brother. Ben had spoken positively about Stuart, his strength, his value to the community, his ruthlessness. If she'd been fifteen Ben would have given Stuart a beating. But things were different now.

'Let's get those lines reeled in and go home,' said Stuart, 'one fish will have to do.'

Lucy, standing stock still, her eye fixed on Stuart, knife at the ready, paused, then said, 'Okay, I'll stand here and watch you pack up, and I'll walk behind you.'

'And you'll forget any of this happened?' said Stuart, meeting her eye.

Lucy took a breath. 'And I'll forget this happened,' she said, knowing she would never forget.

Chapter 23

A week later, Lucy knocked on Emily's door. 'Hi Emily, I've brought you something. Can I come in?'

Emily lay on her bed, her hands stroking her swollen stomach. The streaks on her face told Lucy she'd been crying.

'What is it?' said Lucy.

'Nothing, just everything,' said Emily, pushing herself into a sitting position.

Lucy sat on the bed and proffered the small package she'd wrapped in some old wrapping paper, tied with a scrap of garden string. 'I thought this would be more useful now than after the birth.'

Emily weighed it in her hand. A quizzical smile spread across her face. 'I can tell it's a bottle. It's not vodka, is it? Now that I could do with.'

Lucy laughed, 'Sorry, no. If it were, I'd have drunk it by now.'

Emily tugged at the bow of rough string and opened the parcel. Inside was a small bottle of olive oil.

'It's for the bump,' said Lucy. 'I found it in the pantry when we first got here and hid it away.'

'But…'

'No buts, this is for you, and the bump. It wouldn't go far between us all, and there's no way you'll get any belly butter now.'

'I don't know what to say,' said Emily, turning the bottle over and over. 'I think I'll rub some on now. Close the door will you.'

Lucy clicked the door shut while Emily began to lift her top and expose her thirty-week pregnancy.

'Let me do it for you. You lie down and get comfortable.'

'Ha, comfortable, I think I remember that ages ago; now it's just varying degrees of discomfort,' said Emily, as she shucked down on the bed and exposed her belly.

'I've never done this before. You'll have to let me know if I'm being too heavy handed.' Lucy warmed a few drops of the precious oil in her hands.

'He's pretty tough is junior, so don't worry. I think he's asleep now. He may wake up and give you a kick.'

'He's definitely a he?' said Lucy, spreading oil over the mound of Emily's stomach, smoothing it into the skin.

'I don't know, really. I know it's what Ben wants. I don't care as long as it's a healthy baby.'

Lucy poured more oil into her cupped hand and spread it on her lower belly. Emily's body relaxed under Lucy's attention, her arms stilled beside her, her breathing slowed.

Lucy concentrated on the sweep of her hands around the contours of the pregnancy. She felt what might have been a foot beneath her fingers, but she didn't know, it could have been a knee, elbow, head. It didn't matter, she marvelled at another human being inside her sister-in-law, not something Lucy had ever experienced and now doubted she ever would. She felt, rather than heard, a big sigh escape from Emily, who began to shake as if laughing. Lucy's smile vanished when she saw Emily's face with tears streaming from her eyes as she sobbed silently.

'Em, what's wrong? Have I hurt you?' said Lucy, concern crossing her brow, her hands lifting from Emily's body.

Emily sniffed; the back of her hand brushing tears away from her eyes. 'No, you haven't hurt me, or young junior, it's just...' another sob, '... it's been so long since anyone else has touched me like this, with care and attention. It's been months.'

Lucy leaned over Emily and gave her a half-hug as she lay there sobbing. After a minute Emily quietened.

'Doesn't Ben...'

'No, he doesn't. He doesn't come near me. I don't want him to. He hardly even speaks to me, only if it's about Lottie or "his" baby. I know he's been seeing...' Emily didn't finish the sentence.

'I know. I'm furious at him. He won't talk to me about it. He just says he needs to see her. He—'

'Don't tell me. If he's afraid to tell me himself I don't want to know, the bastard.' She paused. 'I'm sorry, Lucy, I know he's your brother, I shouldn't have mentioned it. You can leave if you want, I won't be offended.'

'I'd like to stay, do you mind?'

'I might cry again. I do it a lot.'

'Oh, Em.'

'It's not only Ben, but the baby too. Not only am I pumped full of hormones, but I'm also scared as fuck.'

Lucy had never heard Emily swear before. She looked at her oily hands, none of her thoughts coalescing into anything she could say. She placed her hands back on Emily's belly and stroked her gently, smoothing round the bump. As her strokes circled the unborn child Lucy felt Emily begin to relax again.

'This is lovely, Lucy, it really is. I'm sorry...'

'Hush, it's okay. Just enjoy, you deserve it.'

Lucy gently kneaded the oil into her skin. Emily's breathing slowed.

'Can I ask you a big favour, Lucy?'

'Sure.' Lucy hands again circumnavigated Emily's unborn baby.

'When he or she, whoever it is, decides it's time to join us in this wreck of a world, will you be there with me?'

'Oh, Em, of course I will. Mum might be more use. She's at least got experience.'

'Her too, I have an ulterior motive I feel a bit guilty about. I want you there mainly because you're you and you're lovely. But I also want you with me to keep your brother away. If he'll listen to anyone it's you. And I don't want him anywhere near when this baby comes.'

'Are you sure, Em? He is the dad. He'll want to be here.'

'I'm the mother. I don't want him here.'

'Okay, I'll keep him out if you're sure it's what you want.'

'I'm sure.'

Chapter 24

'Is it time now, Mummy?' said Lottie for the third time that morning.

Emily smiled at her daughter, wearing wellington boots, and carrying her coat, face full of expectation.

'Yes, poppet, the chickens are hungry, I'll help you with your coat.'

Emily treasured the time she spent with Lottie feeding the chickens. They fed them every day, and Emily had fought with Ben to keep the ritual they had started when they first arrived at Cleeve House. It was one of the few occasions she had alone with her daughter.

'When can we eat another chicken, Mum?' said Lottie as the flock clucked in response to the shake of the bin.

Two of the older birds had stopped laying and gone to the table a week ago. And for a couple of days the family's hunger abated. The flock would be replenished by newly hatched chicks in the spring.

'Not for a long time now, poppet, we need the eggs from these, and without chickens you don't get eggs. So, we don't want to eat them all, do we?'

'But I'm hungry,' said Lottie.

'So am I. When we've finished here you know what we'll do, don't you?'

Lottie whispered, 'Sneak around the back and keep it secret.'

'That's right. No one must know, not even Daddy.'

'Not even Daddy,' repeated Lottie in her best conspirator's voice.

Crouched behind the chicken house, the egg basket containing seven eggs between them, Emily stroked her growing belly and said, 'Which one would you like, and which one shall your little brother have?'

'I want that speckled one, and little brother should have that little one because he's little.'

Emily took a small cup from her pocket, cracked the speckled egg into it, whisked it with a teaspoon, and handed it to her daughter. Lottie's initial reluctance to drink raw egg had long vanished and she gulped it down. Emily prepared her own egg in the same way and swallowed it at a gulp. Then she ate the shells, her body craving the calcium her growing baby needed.

'How many eggs are in the basket now, Lottie?'

Lottie counted them while pointing at each in turn, 'One, two, three, four, five. Five eggs.'

'Very good, so if anyone asks you how many eggs we collected today, what will you say?'

'We collected five eggs today.'

'That's right, good girl.'

'Only five?' said Lucy when Emily gave her the basket.

'We are two birds down and it is the middle of winter. I think we're lucky to have these,' said Emily.

'One for Lottie and one for you only leaves three for

everyone else.'

'Shouldn't I have one? Is that what you mean? Or Lottie?'

'No, Em, I don't mean that, of course you must have them. I'm desperate I suppose. The meals are getting thinner and thinner. I'm worried it won't be long until...' Lucy didn't continue but took the eggs and locked them away in the bare cupboard.'

'Until what?'

'Until someone keels over from hunger, I suppose. I know I don't have the energy I used to have. I don't know how I manage sometimes. It must be doubly tough for you, feeding two.'

Chapter 25

Faye looked at Marcus standing in the doorway to the hovel, a cold wind pushing past him and through the gaps in the boarded window, his face torn between question and concern.

'What choice do I have? It's not like I wanted this to happen,' said Faye stuffing the few things she had into a small bag.

'Just say no, don't go, stay here,' said Marcus. 'And you haven't been here long, we've hardly...'

'I know exactly how long I've been here. Seven freezing bloody weeks.'

'Is that all it is, it's too cold? I could make it warm, I could build a fire, I could...'

'It's the middle of December and it's like the Arctic. What do you think it's going to be like next month, and February?'

'I wouldn't mind it. And it wouldn't be so cold if there were two of us. We can...'

'We! It's not our place, Marcus, it's mine. And I'm leaving it and going to the house. It's too cold here.'

'I don't understand. Why do you have to? I could...'

'Oh, stop it, Marcus. I'm going to the house. I have to. Ben wants me there.'

'Why? What's it got to do with Ben?'

'Look Marcus, Ben's in charge, he's the boss, he wants me at the house, you think I should say no? Look what he did to Rob, and he was his brother. What do you think he'll do to me?'

'It's what he'll do if you go, I'm worried about. Can't you see that? I thought we...' Marcus turned away to hide his face, and his distress, from her.

Faye's voice softened. 'I'll always have a soft spot for you, Marcus. I'll never forget what it was like, being with you here on that day. If I don't go to the house Ben will come here and do what he wants with me anyway, and I'll be alone here, he could do anything, no one would know. He could kill me. No one would hear.'

'Do you think he would? I'll stay with you, watch out for you.'

'No, Marcus, I don't think he would, I don't think he'd kill me. I'm saying I'll feel safer in the house, there are people about who would hear me if I called out. Don't you understand? Imagine what it would be like for me out here, in the dark, in the middle of the night and him coming here. It would be more than scary.'

'What right has he to do this? It's horrible.'

'Yes, it's horrible, but who's going to stop him?'

'I'll stop him, I'll kill him.'

In the two weeks since Faye first brought him to the hovel Marcus had fallen completely for her. It had been easy. A shared look, a secret smile, a little flattery, and he fell. Now she feared for his safety. She could have gone to Rob, he might have had her back, but he'd left, chased away by Ben. She could have told Rob about Ben killing his father, he would have believed her, but what could he have done? Now Rob was gone. And Ben came most nights. She knew he would have her back at the house when he made Emily move into Rob's room. His own wife. What would he do to her if she told now? What would he do if she didn't go to him? She wished someone would kill him, but Marcus never could, he didn't have it in him.

'Marcus, no, you mustn't think that, let alone try it. I love you for wanting to, I really do, but you mustn't.' She watched the impact of her first use of the word insinuate itself on his psyche.

She busied herself packing her last items of clothing and said, 'If I go to the house Ben won't even know about you and me. If I stay here, he'll find out and he'll hurt you. I don't want you to get hurt. I don't want anything bad to happen to you.'

'Faye, what about us? I love you.'

The simple sincerity in his voice struck Faye like a slap. Now she hid her face and wiped a tear running down her cheek; not knowing if she shed it for herself, for Marcus, or for the secret she carried within.

'Oh Marcus, I don't know about us. Perhaps, when all this...' her arm swept an arc about her, 'is over. Maybe then we could be together.'

'It might never be over. I might only see you across the field and know what was happening in the house at night with him.' He spat the last word as if he'd discovered a wasp in his mouth.

'Why don't you stay here, in this shelter. You hate the barn, you told me. You could be private here, alone. You could make it comfortable, warmer. Maybe, if I can get away, I might find you here sometimes.' Faye threw straws at Marcus convinced he would grasp one.

'Stay here, do you think I could?'

'You'd have to persuade Ben.'

'He'd never agree, especially if you came out here,' said Marcus.

'He might if he believes there's nothing between us. If you acted like you didn't like me. If I'm going to the house, why would I care who stays here? You would have to be convincing, and not be hurt if I call you names. It would be part of the act. You might have a chance. Could you do it?'

'I could try.'

'Try wouldn't be good enough. If Ben thinks you and I... I dread to think what he would do.'

'Okay, I'll do it.'

'You'd better leave here now. Don't let him see us together. He's not stupid. Don't mention it now. Wait a day or two, maybe have a row with Stuart while Ben is there, or something. Tell him if you don't get away someone will get injured. He won't like that. Or maybe find the hovel by accident and go and see him and tell him you've found it. Be all excited and say you want to live there because you can't stand your brother. He'll believe it too, it's true, isn't it?'

Marcus nodded. 'Yes, I'll tell him that, I'll make it work. If it means I can see you again.'

Chapter 26

The ringing on the saucepan brought everyone running despite it not being time for a meal. One or two even began to salivate so accustomed had they become to the signal for food.

'Is everyone here?' said Ben, looking around the room, counting people off in his head. 'Where's Emily?'

'She's coming,' said Lucy, 'you need to cut her a little slack, it takes her a minute.'

'We'll wait, this is going to affect everyone.'

Ben had insisted they all gathered in the largest room in Cleeve House. They never met all together. Only Lottie didn't expect bad news, she played games behind a couch as if alone.

Emily arrived, holding her back and breathing heavily. Lucy gave up her seat.

'Okay, now we're all here, look at this.' Ben hoisted a large plastic bin onto the table.

'See this here, it's a rat hole. This bin did have twenty-five kilos of rice in it. Enough to feed us all for maybe a month.' After the enormity had sunk in, after the dismay had dwindled, when his glower quietened the room; Ben said, 'That's not all. Someone has been in the store. There are tins of ham and beans missing. Not a lot, maybe six or eight, enough to make a difference, especially after this.' He swung the bucket around so everyone could see the neat round hole left by the vermin. 'I want to know who's been in there. And I want to know now.'

The silence which followed was broken by a chorus of denials. Lucy shared a look with her mother and was about to speak when Connie shook her head. 'It was me,' she said into the cacophony. People quietened.

'It was me, Ben. I took them,' said Connie.

'Mum! Why?' said Ben.

'Don't be stupid, Ben. I took them for your brother. Do you think I would let my own son starve, after the way you treated him?'

'You couldn't have, not alone, they would have been too much for you to...'

'I could and I did. I didn't take them all at once, just one at a time, otherwise he would have gone with nothing, he wouldn't have stood a chance. Just like he never stood a chance against you, Ben.'

'You should have told me; I would have given him something.'

'A boot up the arse maybe.' She turned to the gathered people. 'If you want, I'll eat half rations to make up for what I've taken.'

'He was your son,' said Sue.

'Why should I go hungry so he could do a runner,' said Stuart.

'Stop!' shouted Ben as people began to debate. 'It was a small amount compared to the loss of rice. There will be reduced rations from now on. We're finished here, you can all go.' His head signalled the Reever family, who dutifully filed out.

When they had gone, he rounded on Connie.

'I don't think you understand what I'm trying to do here, Mum. If we're all to survive we must be disciplined. Lucy, Mum won't be helping in the kitchen anymore. Faye will help you prepare the meals in future.'

Chapter 27

Lucy now went to the cove alone, refusing all offers of help. Every week she tied a green ribbon around the post at the head of the path into Goff's Cove. Every week she returned with a gallon of seawater, now their only source of salt. Sometimes she brought back a fish or two.

Waves cresting on the shore drowned out small sounds whilst Lucy cast into the sea.

'Is this yours?' called a voice.

Lucy whipped round at the sound, heart jumping, then squealed in delight when she saw Rob. She dropped the rod and ran to him, leaping into his arms.

He grinned through his beard, the lost tooth gaping at her.

'It's good to see you, I've been worried, I thought…' she began.

'It's okay, I'm fine. Tired but fine.'

'Are you hungry? I've got a fish; it'll be enough for two.'

'Starving, of course.'

Lucy squatted by the fire, skewered the fish and set it to roast.

'Smells good,' said Rob.

'It is good,' said Lucy. 'Now tell me where you've been, what's happened, everything.'

Rob told of his journey, the four-hour hike to the deserted village of Histon. The afternoon trekking east and north, following the coast. How he'd spent the night in a deserted cottage. 'I couldn't have made it without the food you smuggled out for me.

'Towards the end of the second day I came to a fishing village. A few rough shacks thrown up by a river mouth. They had boats, a couple of small trawlers tied up, and some sail boats. They told me there had been a proper village, now under the water. You remember Selmouth.'

'Yes, course I do, we used to go crabbing from the harbour.'

'That's the place. It's totally under the water now, and most of the population drowned in the first flood. The harbour wall we used to crab from is about four metres down.'

'Poor people. It must have been like that all along the coast.'

'Yes, a few survived and made it to higher ground. And they've had some "walk-ins" like me. There's about thirty people there now. They fish every day. Go hungry when it's stormy.'

'They must catch loads of fish if they have boats.'

'They say the trawlers still have some diesel in them, but they can't use them because none of the electronics work, sonar and stuff. They're tied up so they won't crash into the smaller boats. They go out in the open boats, it's dangerous. They've lost people to the sea. There's no chance of rescue if you go in.'

'You don't go out, do you?'

'Lucy, they feed me, I have to do my share. Besides, I want

to learn how to handle boats. It's important now. We're trying to rebuild the village upstream, it's hard, all by hand with scavenged materials. The sea throws up a lot of stuff. We have to cart it up to where it's needed, well above high water.'

Lucy saw life had flooded back into Rob; life that had been squeezed out of him before he left Cleeve House. He looked ragged, filthy and tired, but he also looked happy, his eyes gleamed as he talked about the people at Selmouth. How they spent the evenings singing songs and how one of them had a guitar. Rob hit it off with him as soon as they played together. Lucy listened rapt while Rob talked. She wished Cleeve House held the same happiness of people in adversity.

'You see it, don't you,' said Rob.

'See what?'

'The difference. At Selmouth people say, "what can I do for you", at Cleeve it's "what can you do for Ben".'

Lucy bit her lip and blinked her single eye.

'I'm not saying it's all easy, all light and lovely,' said Rob. 'It isn't. It's hard and cold and dangerous. And we're always hungry. But there's this sense that the problems are ours together, we're striving for the same things. I don't know, it's just a lot easier to live with the hardship if you have friendly people about you.'

'You sound happy, though. If it's so good, I'm surprised you came back.'

'I haven't "come back". I've come to see you, Lucy, like I said I would. And to ask about Mum. But I haven't come back.'

'Mum's okay. She doesn't talk much. I don't think she's happy, it's not surprising, what with Dad dying and all this chaos. She doesn't blame you for going, she was surprised it took you so long.'

'She said that?'

'Yes. She must have known what Ben was doing to you without us telling her. She never talks about it. All she talks about is practical stuff, except to Lottie, she tries to be cheerful if Lottie is there, but can't always manage it.'

'It must be tough on her, seeing what's happening and being powerless. She'd enjoy Selmouth, but there are hardly any proper buildings yet. We're trying to build some. It's slow work.'

'Mum couldn't leave Cleeve House. Not after all this time. And Dad's buried there too.'

Rob paused for a beat, looked deep in Lucy's eye and said, 'You could, though.'

Lucy sat quietly, her gaze drifted away from her brother and travelled along the sea's horizon. She turned back to him, fierceness in her look. 'Could I? Just up and leave Mum, I could do that? And poor pregnant Emily whose time will be soon, leave her, could I? What about Lottie, swiftly turning savage, could I leave her too? You may have had good reason for going, and I'm glad you did, glad you've found a welcome elsewhere. What reason have I to leave? No one hurts me, no one pushes me around, starves me, bullies me. I love all my family, Rob, and don't want to lose any of them.'

Rob stirred the now empty skewer around in the sand at his feet and said, 'I'm only saying if things get bad for you there'll be a welcome at Selmouth. That's all.'

'What about Faye? Would she be welcome?'

Rob's eyes flashed at her. His hair, his beard, his dirty face, all camouflaged the expression. Lucy couldn't tell if it was anger or distress.

'Faye is nothing to do with me,' he said, his voice flat.

'She's pregnant.'

Rob went back to stirring the sand, then took the skewer,

broke it in half, and threw it towards the sea. He looked straight at Lucy. 'Is she saying it's mine?'

'She's said nothing, told no one.'

'How do you know she's pregnant?'

Lucy shook her head at him. 'Because I'm a woman? Because I hear her throwing up? Because she's automatically protecting her stomach with her hands? Could be any of those things, but I know.'

'Okay, she's pregnant. Why are you telling me?'

'I thought you might want to know. If she's having a baby, then…'

'Then what? It can't be mine. It's been months since we did anything together.'

'Come on, who else could it be?'

'I think it's obvious, isn't it? Look, Lucy, I didn't come here to argue with you, I came here because you're my sister, and to tell you there are people out there trying to do things in a different way. Good people working hard together.'

'I don't want to argue with you either. You're my brother. You could come back, you know.'

'I couldn't. If I did either I would kill Ben, or he would kill me. I've done a lot of thinking since I left. About all the years he's bullied me, how he used to make sure I got the blame so Dad wouldn't find fault with him. Yet I would come off worst. He was always Dad's favourite, you know, until you came along. But the pattern was set. He knew how to manipulate me, and I was always too young to understand how he did it. But I'm not now. I can see what he did, and he's continued doing it all my life, every time we meet. It's not going to happen again. If I see him, he'll carry on, and I won't respond to him, and he'll get more vicious. It wouldn't end until one of us couldn't ever answer back. I don't want to do that to Mum.'

Lucy watched her brother, his voice calm, his gaze gentle and unchallenging. She gave a single sob and hugged him.

'I've got to be heading back,' he said, breaking the hug. 'Tell Mum I'm okay, won't you?'

'Yes, she'll be relieved.'

'I almost forgot. I have something for you.' He rummaged in his bag for a book of piano music. 'I found it in the deserted cottage and thought of you. Merry Christmas.'

'Is it Christmas? I guess it almost is.' She turned the book over in her hands, ruffled the slightly damp pages, heard the tunes in her head.

'It will be in two days. That's another reason I must get back. We're having a feast.'

'A feast? Turkey and everything?'

'No, fish of course. It will be much the same as any other day, except there'll be singing and dancing too.'

'Will I see you again?'

'Yes, I don't know when. It's a tough journey in this weather. Perhaps four, six weeks, more if there are storms. Maybe not until spring. It's two days' walk.'

Lucy hugged him to her, soaked him up into her. 'I think of you all the time, Rob. I always will.'

Rob hugged her back. 'And I you, Lucy, but I must go, I need to get to shelter before it's dark.'

He gently peeled her arms from around him and kissed her cheek below her eye patch, before turning away from her to begin his return journey.

Chapter 28

The sun had set, and twilight dissolved into a clear winter night, the sky bright with stars and a half moon near the zenith.

Faye stood on the threshold of the empty hovel, looking here and there, not sure what to do. Though dim, enough moonlight spilled through the open door to see by. Marcus had made the hovel his own. A rough wooden frame with sides of thin woven branches formed a bed. He'd excavated a small fireplace in the opposite wall, what looked like the beaten bonnet of a car formed a cowl and old metal piping a chimney. She ran her hand over the ragged clothes hung on pegs hammered into the mortar of the stone wall near the bed, a mean and makeshift wardrobe.

Faye sat and waited. Marcus wasn't much of a back-up plan, but she could trust him to do what she asked. She couldn't trust Ben at all.

He was quiet, but she still heard him and stood before he came in the door.

Marcus dropped the armful of timber he carried and stepped back; then a flash of recognition crossed his face.

'Faye. I'd given up hope.' He stepped towards her; arms outstretched. She turned and looked away from him.

'I said I would if I could,' said Faye. 'It's been difficult to get away. I have so much to do, and I always feel tired, and it's been hard because…' Faye left the sentence hanging, hoping Marcus picked up the sadness she tried to convey.

'I know, it's hard for all of us, Faye. Don't give up.'

'It's not the ordinary hardness of it all, it's not just that, Marcus. Oh, I'm sorry, I shouldn't have come. I'll go away, leave you alone. You seem to be doing okay here on your own, you've made it comfortable. You'll be better off having nothing to do with me.' She walked towards the door, passing close by Marcus. He stepped in front of her.

'Don't go, Faye, not yet. I think about you all the time and…'

Faye put her finger on his lips. 'Don't say anything. I'm sorry, I must go.' She made to push past him, but he held her arms.

'Something's wrong, I can tell. You can't hide it from me, not since… Why don't you tell me what it is? Sit down, just for a minute. I'll be worried if I don't know why you came.'

Marcus brushed and smoothed a part of the bed and Faye sat, hands on her lap, head down.

He crouched, gazing up at her, trying to meet her eyes. 'Now what's wrong, are you ill?'

'I think I might be, sort of.' Her small voice forced Marcus to lean forward to catch what she said, he took her hands.

'Tell me all about it; you know how much you mean to me. I'll do everything I can to help.'

'I've been sick.'

'Sick?'

'Yes, throwing up.'

'Today?'

129

'Yes, today, and yesterday, and the day before.'

'How long has this been going on?'

'Ever since…'

'Ever since when?' said Marcus.

Faye lifted her head and looked at him, even in the moonlight the innocence of his gaze struck her, eroding her resolve, but she wasn't doing this just for herself. Holding his eyes, she said, 'Ever since the afternoon, when it rained, here in this shelter, when we…'

'When we what?' said Marcus.

Faye almost blurted it out, instead worried her lip with her teeth. She'd have to spell it out for him.

'When we… you remember, you told me you loved me.'

Realisation dawned on his face. Even in the moonlight Faye could see him blush. His confused look chased away first by worry, then by excitement.

'You mean you're…'

Faye drooped her eyelids, dropped her gaze to her hands, sat demurely on his bed, resolutely not speaking.

'… having a baby?'

'Yes, Marcus, I'm having a baby.'

'And you've been sick since… does that mean I'm the father?'

Faye didn't speak, only looked at him and gave a smile.

'I'm going to be a father. I don't know what to say. Faye, can I hug you? I won't if it will hurt, you know, but can I, just a bit, and can I feel it, I mean you, your tummy? This has never happened to me before.'

Faye suppressed the rolling of her eyes and shake of her head in response to Marcus. Instead, she said, 'Yes you can stroke my stomach, be gentle, it's been hard for me lately.' As she spoke, she thought, and when you've done that, we can talk about what I need and how you can get it for me.

Chapter 29

Emily gently placed the egg basket on the kitchen counter. Only three eggs sat in the centre of the large basket.

'It's getting worse. There's even less than before,' she said.

'There should be at least half a dozen.' Lucy's dismay rang around the empty kitchen. 'Even in the winter. I know the solar lights are still working.'

'Are you accusing me of stealing them, because if you are...'

'No, Emily, of course not. But something must be wrong.'

'Maybe something spooked them in the night. Put them off.'

'I'll have to let Ben know. If I give one to you and Lottie there'll be only one left.'

'What will he do? He can't magic eggs out of thin air.'

'No, he can't, Em, but he's bound to notice. He'll ask. If I don't tell him he'll think I'm covering something up.'

Emily recognised the picture of Ben Lucy drew. He would suspect even his sister. If she told Ben, he might want to take over the egg collecting or come with her.

'Why don't you keep these today. Will they be enough?

The hens may be back to normal tomorrow.'

'Lottie needs the protein, and so do you.'

'We'll manage for a day. If it's as bad tomorrow, you can tell him.'

The next day there were again five eggs in the nest boxes. When Emily tried to take them all back to the kitchen, Lottie tugged her sleeve.

'Mummy, don't forget the secret, not even Daddy. I'm hungry.'

Emily caved and hurried Lottie behind the coop. Each ate an egg; Emily again eating the shells.

'I'll have to tell Ben now,' said Lucy as she locked the three eggs away.

'Do you have to? Lottie and I could go without for another day if you need us to.'

'No, I can't let you do it again. You have an unborn child, Em. If anyone needs the protein, it's you. I can't decide what to do about this on my own. He has to know.'

'Where's Emily now?' said Ben after Lucy had told him.

'I think she's in her room, but it's not her fault, anything could have happened, the hens may be broody, it may be too cold, anything,' said Lucy.

'I still need to talk to her.' He stomped off as Lucy locked the cupboard.

Lucy followed him, stopping before she reached Emily's room. She didn't need to get any closer to hear Ben's voice.

'I can't believe this. You have one thing to do in the whole place and you mess up. We're on the edge of starvation, and you can't keep your eyes on a few chickens. You're just useless baggage here.'

'It's not my fault if the hens stop laying, is it? I can't help it if that's all there is. It's no good blaming me.'

'You're so fucking free with your own eggs though aren't you. The last thing we needed was another baby, and you had to go get pregnant.'

'How can you be so hurtful, Ben, it's not as if you had nothing to do with it.'

'It wasn't me who didn't like taking the pill.'

'It was you who didn't like using a condom.'

'And how do I know it's mine anyway. It could be anybody's, maybe it's creepy Simon you keep going on about.'

'He was only a friend.'

'Just a friend, yes, I bet. Just how friendly did you and he get I wonder.'

'I don't believe I'm hearing this. All you have and you're still insecure.'

Lucy heard a crack and a yelp from Emily and the door yanked open. She ducked out of sight as Ben stormed past.

Lucy found Emily sitting on her bed. Tears shined her eyes, a red mark on her cheek dwindled as Lucy watched. It disappeared before she could speak. 'Are you all right, Em?'

'He hit me,' said Emily. Outrage, shock, and sadness, battling to express themselves. 'He's never done it before, Lucy. He's been angry, he's stomped off in a strop, he's even broken things, but he's never hit me.'

Lucy went to hug her, but Emily held her hand up and stopped her. 'It's okay, I'm not going to cry. If anything, I'm likely to laugh. To think I loved this man for all those years, and I'm carrying his child. We've had rows in the past, now I see they would never have stopped, they would have only got angrier.'

'I didn't know,' said Lucy.

'Of course you didn't, it was nothing to do with you. It's not as if this was anything to do with me. It's not my fault if the bloody chickens don't lay. He needed someone to blame. And I'm easiest.'

'I'm sure he didn't mean…'

'Oh no, I'm sure he did mean. I'm sure he meant to hurt me. I think this is to make sure I never return to his bed. Faye must have talents I've never possessed. Well, he needn't be worried. I swear on this unborn child, he'll never touch me again.'

The vitriol in Emily's voice stopped the words in Lucy's mouth. She saw Emily as a friend but didn't recognise the face contorted with hatred in front of her. Lucy took a breath and calmly said, 'He's doing his best for us; he is under a lot of stress.'

'He's doing his best for Ben. I don't think he gives a toss about the rest of us. He hit me, Lucy. Before all this happened,' she waved her arm in a large circle, 'that would have been grounds for divorce. Now, there's no law except Ben's law. I'll be heaving a large piece of furniture across the door from now on.'

'Em, think about your baby. You can't do that now.'

'You're beginning to sound like your brother, telling me what I can and can't do when I'm pregnant. Don't you think I know what I'm capable of? What would you know about it, anyway?'

Lucy couldn't hold Emily's challenging glare and looked down at her hands, finding her fists clenched, nails digging into palms. She relaxed and rubbed the impressions of her nails away with her thumbs. She took a breath and released it slowly, focussing her attention anywhere but Emily's eyes. When she felt composed enough to meet the challenge, she looked straight at Emily.

'You're right, Emily, I know nothing about what you're going through. Only what you tell me.' Lucy turned to leave.

'Wait,' called Emily, 'wait, Lucy, don't go. I shouldn't be giving you my anger. It's not you I'm angry with.'

Lucy paused and turned back to face her.

'Look, there isn't anyone else I talk to. There'd be no one if you cut me off. I'm sorry,' said Emily.

'That's okay, Em. I know things are tough for you, perhaps more than anyone else. Everyone's having a tough time, and though I don't agree with everything my brother does, I do think he's doing the best he can for us all. Imagine where we would be without him. There would have been no stores in place, no chickens, and no eggs at all anyway. Yes, he's overreacted. It must be as if everything he's worked for is falling apart.'

'Can we stay friends anyway?' said Emily.

'Of course,' said Lucy.

This is almost too easy, thought Marcus, as he opened the nest box behind the coop and put his hand in. Faye had explained it to him. Emily had an egg because she was pregnant, everyone knew; and Lottie had one because she was a little kid. And kids need eggs if they are in their mother's womb or not. It was only fair Faye should have one. And she couldn't slip away in the night to help herself, could she? And Marcus was certain he remembered her saying he should have one too. He had to keep up his strength if he was going to be a good dad. And it was cold in the hovel on his own, it was only fair he should have an egg to himself. Why Faye wasn't staying in the shelter with him, he didn't fully understand. She'd said she would be, but it wasn't the right time to tell anyone about her baby yet. It was bad luck to mention a new baby too soon. No one else knew except him.

She'd go and get the egg herself, in broad daylight, but there'd be trouble if anyone saw her, and she didn't want trouble. It all seemed to make sense the way Faye explained it.

Marcus soon got into the habit of creeping out, long after dark, to the run. Light leaked from the roof making the chicken house an easy find in even the darkest nights.

He took a couple of eggs and pulled his hand out, fastened the box behind him, and turned to leave.

'What brings you out here in the dead of night?'

Marcus almost dropped the eggs. The quiet menace in Ben's voice sent shivers down his spine.

'What have you got? Hand them over.' Ben stepped out of the shadows. Marcus put the eggs into his outstretched hand. 'You thieving little gobshite.' Ben swapped the eggs to his left hand and made a fist of his right, then changed his mind. 'I'm not going to risk breaking these, I'll deal with you later. Now fuck off.'

Chapter 30

Ben climbed into bed in the dark of his room. Different ways of punishing the thieving Marcus ran through his head. He didn't want to injure him so badly he couldn't work, but he couldn't be allowed to get away with his stealing; he would be an example to the rest of them.

Next to him Faye turned and moaned, disturbed by Ben's return. 'What is it? Can't you sleep?' she said.

'No, not yet.'

'What's wrong? You sound angry, it's not something I've done, is it?'

'No, it's someone else.'

'What's someone been doing?'

'I caught a thieving bastard with their hand in the chicken run, stealing eggs. Now I've got to decide what to do with them.'

'Is it serious?'

'Not on the face of it. A couple of eggs missing. But if it's been going on for days or weeks, everyone else has had less than their share. They used to cut people's hands off for stealing. Then cut the other hand off if they did it again.'

Ben couldn't see Faye blanche in the darkness, but he felt her.

'I'm not going to hack his hands off, though I'll have to punish him somehow.'

'I bet it was stupid Marcus, he's only a kid really. I expect he thinks it's all a game,' said Faye.

'He won't be thinking that when I've finished with him. If I hadn't been holding those two eggs, I would've beaten him black and blue.'

'What are you going to do?'

'I don't know yet. I only know it's going to hurt.'

'Do you have to beat him? Isn't there some other way of punishing him, can you give him extra work to do?'

'There isn't anything else. And he's pretty useless, he couldn't do much. Why should you be worried anyway?'

'I'm not worried, he's just so pathetic. If you hit him, he might break something and need looking after. He won't be able to do the little he does. I feel quite sorry for him, stuck out on his own in the shelter. It's perishing out there.'

'It was his choice. He practically begged me for your place when you moved in here. I wonder if that's why. There'd be no one to see him sneak off to steal the eggs.'

'Do you think he's that devious? Or even bright enough to plan so far ahead?'

Ben rolled over, face to face with her in the dark of his bed. 'Why are you asking me? You should know shouldn't you. He's had the hots for you as long as he's been here. Hasn't he come on at you in all that time?'

Would she deny it? If she did, would he be bothered? She kept him warm for now, did he care if feeble Marcus had made a play for her? Not if she behaved herself now.

'He tried to. You know, he's such an innocent, I don't think he's ever been with a girl. And what chance has he got here?'

'Might as well be a kick in the knackers then. It'll put him off thieving and he's no use for them anyway.'

Faye snorted into the bedclothes at this. He expected she'd react, but wasn't sure if it was a false laugh, or tiredness. She yawned too, so he let it pass. 'It's okay, you can stop worrying about your poor little innocent, I'm not going to beat him. I've decided what his punishment will be. And he's going to wish I'd beaten him when I let him know.'

'What are you going to do?'

'You'll find out.'

Ben held off looking for Marcus, left him to stew. And Marcus did all he could to avoid Ben.

When Lucy banged on the old saucepan lid to call the daily meal, they all came scurrying, including Marcus.

Lucy and Faye served a meagre ladle of some sort of vegetable mush. No one asked about the ingredients anymore. The answers weren't pleasant, it was easier to eat without knowing. Marcus lurked at the back of the queue, until everyone else had a full bowl, then proffered his bowl. Ben's hand stayed Lucy's arm.

'Give me your bowl, Marcus,' said Ben. He handed it over. Ben released Lucy's arm and the ladle filled the bowl.

'Now sit down,' said Ben. They all sat with their meal. Except Marcus who sat with nothing. Ben raised Marcus's bowl. 'Marcus has kindly decided he would like Lottie and Emily to eat his meal today.' Ben divided the meal between the two and gave the empty bowl back to Marcus. 'Now, let's eat.'

'Why isn't Marcus having any?' said Sue, mouth full. Her hunger getting the edge on her mother's instinct.

'Do you want to tell her? Or shall I?' said Ben.

'It's all right, Mum,' said Marcus. 'I'm not really hungry.'

The words didn't match the bereft look on his face, the intensity with which he watched the others eat, and watched his meal disappear down Lottie's and Emily's throats.

'Something's not right here,' said Sue, her bowl now empty like everyone else's.

'Do you want to complain?' said Ben. 'If the service isn't satisfactory here, we wouldn't mind if you chose to eat elsewhere.'

'I'm not complaining,' said Sue. 'I'm worried about Marcus. Andy, tell him, I'm not complaining, am I?' She poked Andy with her elbow.

'She's not complaining, Ben,' said Andy. 'We've no complaints at all.'

'Good, maybe she should shut the fuck up.'

Connie waited until everyone except her eldest son had left before speaking. 'What was that for, Ben? The poor lad's starving. Whatever he's done, your father wouldn't have treated him like that.'

'He deserved to miss a meal; he might miss another.'

'Why?'

'He's been stealing eggs.'

'Perhaps it is right for him to miss a meal, but it isn't right for him to be humiliated in front of everyone. And to make him watch the others eat his food, it's plain cruel.'

'You call it cruel; I call it setting an example. If we don't put them off stealing, they'll have it all. I've told you this before, Mum, it's time you understood.'

'I understand well enough. You just like to throw your weight about. You made it plain when you spoke to the Reevers like that. Threatening them with starvation too. You want to be careful, son. You seem to be good at making enemies, even in your own family. The time may come when you need friends.'

'What I need is some discipline, and I'll have it. I'm not a toddler to be told off by you anymore, Mother. The game has changed, things are desperate, it's likely some of us will starve to death. It won't be me or Lottie. Or Emily.'

'You almost forgot to add Emily, Ben. You're not feeling guilty for stealing Rob's girlfriend, are you?'

'I've nothing to feel guilty about, I didn't steal anyone, and I don't have to listen to this nonsense.'

Chapter 31

Connie knew before she arrived at the coop. The usual chorus of clucks and scrapes were absent. An ominous silence spread from the chicken roost like a rolling fog, enveloping her, pushing the sense of disaster deep inside; throwing her back to another morning, years before, when she'd experienced this for the first time.

She saw the door of the coop was ajar, the latch hanging open, and knew what she would find. Slaughtered, every last one.

She found no sign of damage to the latch. Emily locked them in at night, and yesterday Ben had been arguing with her again. Emily had enough to contend with. Connie took a nearby rock and pounded the hasp until it fell off.

Back in the kitchen Connie found Emily and Lottie about to collect the corn bin.

'There's no need to go today,' said Connie.

'We like feeding the chickens, don't we, poppet?'

'We like the chickens, Gran,' said Lottie.

'Emily, a fox has been in during the night. There aren't any chickens left to feed.'

'You mean...'

'Yes, that's what I mean,' said Connie, eyes flicking towards Lottie and back to Emily.

'How...?' Emily's eyes locked with Connie's then darted about the room, her hands went to her coat, fumbling at the buttons.

'It looks like the latch is broken.'

'What?'

'Yes, broken. I've kept chickens a long time and it looks broken to me. That's what I'll be telling Ben.'

'Surely they're not all dead, a fox couldn't eat them all.'

'Once they're inside the house the chickens panic, the fox kills them by instinct.'

'What's Ben going to do?'

'There's nothing he can do, the latch was broken, a fox got in, it's nobody's fault.' Connie spoke gently to her daughter-in-law, watching her as the rising panic began to subside.

'I don't know what to say,' said Emily.

'Probably best if you don't say anything. It's done, there's no point in making it a bigger problem than it is already.'

'Oh, Connie.' Emily hugged her. 'How can I ever...'

'Shh, it was a fox, that's all.'

'You must have left the door unlocked. How else could a fox get in.'

'I...' began Emily.

'The latch is broken,' said Connie. 'Why don't you look instead of letting fly without knowing anything?'

'I will.' He stomped out towards the run.

Emily began to follow him.

'Don't go, Emily, you'll be a target. Let him see it's broken, because it is, and when he gets back, he'll have calmed down.'

Ben returned after a few minutes. 'Okay, this is what we'll

do. We'll cook and eat the carcasses. We have to do it immediately. There may be a risk, if we cook them hot and long, we should be okay.'

'The carcasses haven't been bled,' said Connie, 'and it's too late now.'

'You don't have to eat any if you don't want to,' said Ben. 'Come on, we need to get this done.'

They ate chicken for three days until it was gone. No one got ill, no one complained. The people were cheerful while they feasted, but beneath the cheer ran the knowledge that starvation would loom even quicker without the eggs the chickens had provided. By the middle of January all trace of game and livestock had disappeared, hunted beyond the limits of a day's hike, their only source of protein now the scant few tins remaining in store, dwindling rapidly.

Chapter 32

Lucy, wrapped in all the clothes she possessed, broke the ice on the water butt and lowered the bucket in. She filled it half full, but still struggled to heave the bucket from the butt. Hungry and weak, she had all morning to pass until she could prepare the only meal of the day. Ben found her struggling towards the kitchen, trying not to spill the water.

'You need to come with me,' he said.

'Where? Is it far?'

'Not far, just to the storeroom.'

'Why are you bringing me here?' said Lucy, her voice echoing around the now empty space.

'Do you know the date? It's mid-February. I said this would happen. Here,' said Ben, taking a tin of ham from an otherwise empty shelf and handing it to her. 'You'd better use it for today's meal.'

'What about tomorrow?' said Lucy.

'There won't be anything tomorrow.'

Lucy had seen weight fall from everyone. They weren't getting enough to eat now, despite spending countless hours scavenging the fields and hedgerows. Game and livestock had long disappeared. They'd found Manuka's remains in the forest months before; no one owned up to the dog's slaughter.

'Some people seem to suffer more than others,' said Lucy.

'What do you mean?'

'Everyone's lost weight, but you don't look too bad, and nor does Stuart.'

'What are you suggesting, Lucy? I'm stealing my own food? I said people would starve when the Reevers first arrived; you didn't want to listen. If they hadn't been here, these shelves would be full.' He waved his hand over a couple of empty shelves on the other side of the room.

'So why does it look like you've lost hardly any weight? Faye is stick thin.'

'It's the way it is. Some of us will die, others might survive.'

The tin began to weigh heavily in Lucy's hand, and she put it back on the shelf.

'Don't you want it?'

'Yes, I do. It's just heavy. I'm getting weaker, we all are.' Lucy scratched her head, her hand clawing out clumps of hair. 'How long do you think we can go on?'

'I'm not sure, not long, days, maybe weeks. I'm not going to let Lottie starve. I'll think of something.'

'What about the rest of us? What about Mum, Emily, Faye?'

'You're looking to me for a solution. I had one, I was ignored, why should I help anyone?'

'Ben! Because it's your family. I've helped you; I knew we had to defend ourselves, I've backed you up when you cut the rations, I've been as careful as I could be with the stores.'

'Are you talking about yourself here? Of course I'll help you.'

'No, I'm not only talking about me. You can't just choose who to help and leave others to starve. What does that make you? Some sort of evil tyrant playing God with other people's lives. I can't believe my brother would be so callous. It has to be everyone.'

'If the Reevers hadn't pitched up there would be plenty.'

'You've said it before, but they're here, and you have to accept it. We are where we are now. Come on, Ben, don't go all stubborn on me. We can't afford it. We must work together. There's nothing we can do about the past; all we can do is go forward.'

'That's what I'm doing. Going forwards. With fewer people.'

'You know I disagree with some of the things you've done, especially Emily and Faye, but it's really none of my business —'

'You're right, it's none of your business,' Ben bristled.

'That's why I haven't said anything about it, it's your personal life. But everyone needs to eat. Everyone deserves a chance at life. I don't believe my brother Ben, my childhood hero, would allow people close to him to starve to death while he looked after himself. I don't believe you could be so heartless. You're a better person than that.'

'Okay,' said Ben. 'I hear you, Lucy. I'll go out hunting one more time, see if there's anything to be had. I'm not hopeful.'

'Do you want me to come with you?'

'No, I don't think I do. I'd be able to go further without you. It will have to be soon.'

Chapter 33

Ben led Stuart into a small room at the back of the house.

'You're wondering why I've asked you here,' said Ben.

'Yes, you hate us. What do you want?'

'You're mistaken, Stuart. It's not you or the Reevers I hate; it's weakness. We need to be strong to survive. Weakness will kill us; don't you agree?'

'Yes, we must defend ourselves, keep what's ours. You do it pretty rigorously. Sue thinks you're deliberately starving us.'

'We're all starving, it's nothing personal to you lot. Since the chickens went nobody's getting enough to survive. Mainly because there's more to feed here than we planned for. I made provision for only the Marchand family, then you lot arrived.'

'We had no choice, the house was burnt down, you saw it yourself, your father welcomed us.'

'My father's poor judgement is not a reason for my family to starve.'

'And mine should?' Stuart spat the words through clenched teeth.

'It's okay to be angry,' said Ben, 'but it won't solve anything.'

'What will?'

'I have a solution. A way we can all survive, but I can't make it happen alone. That's why you're here.'

'You want me to help you?'

'I want more from you than help. I want to trust you. Trust you to back me up, trust you to do what I ask, no matter what.'

'What's in it for me?' said Stuart.

'Besides survival? You get to be number two here. You'll get extra rations, respect from the others. You won't have to take orders from anyone, except me. That's what's in it for you. If you're up to the job.'

'And in exchange all you're offering is a bit of extra food.'

'Think about it. The way things are, some of us will for sure starve, and some won't. Which side of the line do you want to be on?'

'I could do the job. Like you, I know how to deal with awkward younger brothers. But there's something else I'd like besides extra rations.'

Stuart's sideways glance and measured words caught Ben's attention. 'There is? What?'

'Your sister.'

Ben laughed. 'Lucy! I don't think you're her type.'

'I'm serious, I want her. I can't help it. She's all I think about.'

'Have you spoken to her, asked her? Not that I think it would do you any good, you're too—'

'Too young for her? What bollocks. You wouldn't be saying the same about you and Faye, would you?'

'I was going to say crude, unsophisticated if you like. Lucy's got brains and she's cultured. She dumped anyone who wasn't her intellectual equal damn quick.'

'That was then. Before the intellectuals, as you call them, got wiped out by having to work to eat. She doesn't have a lot of choice now, does she?'

'Have you asked her?'

'She turned me down.'

'What do you expect me to do. I can't make her change her mind, can I?'

'It was a bit vague. If I come on at her any stronger, she'll go running to her big brother, won't she.'

'You mean if you threaten her; is that what you're going to do?'

'No, come on, you know what it's like. You get the eye from someone and come on at them, then they start being all coy and playing games, making out they aren't "ready" or wanting to take things slow. You've been there.'

Ben remembered awkwardness and misunderstanding in his early approaches with women, girls they would have been, but never any doubt about whether things would develop or not.

'What is it you're really asking of me?' said Ben. 'You want me to ignore my sister if she asks me to protect her. Are you for real?'

'You asked me what I wanted, and I told you. You still haven't told me what it is you want me to do. I've no idea. Maybe you should be asking someone else.'

Ben ran through the others at Cleeve, mentally dismissing each in turn. Nobody else had the ruthless streak Stuart had. And he looked fit and strong despite the scarce rations.

'I can't promise Lucy to you, you know that. I can say I won't get in your way; I'll sing your praises to her if she comes to me. But I can't make it happen for you. You'll have to do it yourself.'

'What if she starts accusing me of stuff?'

'What stuff?'

'Come on, you know what I mean, what if she accuses me of forcing myself on her? Are you going to get in the way?'

'You mean rape? You want me to stand by while you rape my sister?'

'No, I don't mean rape, I mean overcoming a little reluctance, that's all. She only needs a bit of persuasion. There isn't anyone else here. What am I supposed to do?'

'If Lucy comes to me and tells me she's been raped, I'll kick the shit out of whoever's done it.'

'If she accuses me...'

'I haven't finished. If you have to resort to rape to get what you want, you're a sad bastard who deserves a kicking. Now hear me out. If you rape my sister, you'll wish you'd never been born. But if she tells me anything else. If you've been pestering her, or coming on at her, I'll let it go. I'll even big you up to her. Tell her how helpful you've been, what an all-round good bloke you are. It's the best I can do. If it's not good enough, maybe you should piss off.'

Stuart sat still a moment, then said, 'It'll do. I think we'll be able to work together.'

'I thought I was clear; we won't be working together. You'll be working for me as my second in command. Understand?'

'Yes, I understand.'

'There's something else,' said Ben. 'This offer isn't a shoo-in, I need you to prove you can do the job first.'

'Is this where I finally find out what you want me to do?' said Stuart.

'You remember those men who attacked us when my father died?'

'Yeah, that was ages ago. We've been keeping watch and

they haven't been back, have they?'

'Not that we know of, but they might.'

'The poor bastards are probably starving, like us,' said Stuart.

'Yeah, they probably are. When was the last time you weren't hungry?'

'I'm always hungry.'

'This is the deal. Go out there, find their camp, hunt one of them down, and kill him. The younger the better. Bring the body back. Then I'll know I can trust you and I'll do what I can to help you with my sister.'

'You want me to kill someone?'

'You've done it before, haven't you?'

'That was different, we were defending ourselves.'

'This time you'll be the attacker. Say so now if you haven't the stomach for it.'

Stuart paused for a couple of beats. 'Alright, I'll do it, but the whole body! Can't I just bring back the head or something. It'd be a lot easier to carry.'

'No, it won't be enough. We need the whole body; it's going to solve the other problem we have.'

'The other problem?'

'The protein problem.' Ben watched as he laid these words before Stuart. He saw confusion give way to understanding, revulsion give way to acceptance, hunger give way to determination.

Stuart weighed Ben's words. 'If I do this, you won't get in my way when it comes to Lucy?'

'If you do this, I won't come between you and Lucy,' said Ben.

'Can I trust you to keep your word?'

'You have a choice. You don't have to do this. But if you don't and you go anywhere near my sister, I'll tear your balls off with my bare hands and stuff them down your throat.'

'Okay, I'll do it, but I'm going to need a hand. Carrying a body back from God knows where will be tough.'

'I'll be with you. We'll go during the night,' said Ben.

Chapter 34

At the edge of the woodland the two men crouched.

'Down between the ash trees. Here, take a look.' Ben handed the binoculars to Stuart. 'Can you see it?'

'Yeah, it's defo a light of some sort. I think it's flickering, it's too far away to tell.'

'We only need to know it's there. Come on.'

They trekked down the night shrouded hillside. The wet ground sucked at their boots, and occasional old fences snagged at their clothes, but they maintained a straight line towards the light source, until they came to the wall.

'This is where the road is,' said Stuart.

Stuart put his hands together and formed a step for Ben, boosting him to the top of the wall. Ben heaved Stuart up in turn. They jumped down and stood in the lee of the wall, catching their breath.

'How far?' hissed Stuart.

'Not far I reckon.' Ben sniffed the air. 'Can you smell it?'

'Woodsmoke?'

'A fire.'

'It doesn't mean there'll be anyone there.'

'Someone lit it. For a reason.'

A tawny owl added its haunting hoot to the night as they crossed the road. They worked their way along the hedge until they came to a farm gateway. Ben signalled Stuart to stop and pulled him close to whisper in his ear.

'It's got to be in here. We can't hesitate. If whoever's there sees us, we kill them.'

'Suppose there's loads of them?'

'Then, my friend, we're fucked.'

They crept into the farmyard and saw the glint of light shimmer in the farmhouse window. Ben pointed to the chimney from where a steady plume of smoke rose into the starlit sky.

Against the farmhouse wall, Ben leaned over, snuck a glance into the window. In the firelight he saw the back of a sofa, the top of a man's head visible on the arm, along with the barrel of a shotgun. He lay still.

Pulling Stuart's head to him he whispered, 'One of us distracts him at the window, the other goes inside and kills him.'

'If there's anyone else, whoever's inside will cop it.'

Ben picked up a small pebble, put his hands behind his back. 'Choose,' he said holding his fists out. 'Whoever gets the stone goes inside.'

Stuart chose, Ben's hand uncurled to reveal a pebble.

'I'll count to twenty slowly then put a rock through the window,' said Ben.

Stuart drew his knife and made his way to the door.

In the darkness Ben discarded the pebble from his other hand as he picked up a rock. He threw the rock. Glass smashed. The blast of the shotgun hid Stuart's boot crashing the front door open.

Ben heard the gun being broken open and cartridges

dropped to the floor. The gun clicked closed again. Ben froze hard against the wall of the house as footsteps crunched on broken glass.

Stuart burst into the room. From his throat came a cry of blood lust. As he leapt the man began to turn the gun, but Stuart was on him. Plunging his knife deep, twisting it, yanking it out. The man stumbled. The gun went off again. Ceiling plaster fell. Stuart yelled again, stabbed his arm, his shoulder, two quick hard stabs. The gun fell. The man clutched his stomach. Stuart screamed, stabbed him again and again and again. The man fell, and Stuart fell with him in a frenzy of stabbing.

'I think he's dead now,' said Ben coming into the room.

Stuart paused, knife held aloft, and looked at him, eyes glazed. His face, arms, his whole body, splattered with blood. He nodded, a gruesome smile forming. 'Yes, I reckon he is.' The smile became a grin.

'I looked. There's no one else. We'll use the fire.'

Stuart wiped his knife on the dead man and sheathed it. 'What for?'

'Dinner, my friend, dinner. Sit down and have a slug of this, you've earned it.' He handed Stuart a bottle of whisky.

Stuart popped the cork, upended the bottle, took a gulp, and coughed at the sharpness of the alcohol.

'Where'd you get it?'

'In the kitchen, there's nothing else,' said Ben. He knelt by the corpse, drew his own knife, and cut into the stomach.

Stuart watched, taking sips from the bottle. Ben exposed and excised the liver, stuck a fork into it and propped it in front of the fire to toast.

'Is that dinner?' said Stuart.

'It is, we should eat the heart, out of respect, but I can't be arsed to saw it out.'

Blood dripped and sizzled from the liver as it roasted in the heat of the fire. The smell filled the room.

The two men sat side by side on the sofa, drinking whisky from the bottle and eating the liver.

'Fuck, this tastes good,' said Stuart.

Ben laughed, almost spilling his drink. 'Food always tastes better when you've caught it yourself.'

'We're not seriously going to cart him all the way to Cleeve.'

'Nah, we'll hack off the best bits. They'll make a good stew.'

They both burst out laughing.

'It's a shame though,' said Stuart.

'What do you mean, a shame, what is?'

'It might have been a woman.' They both roared with laughter again.

'If it's a woman you want, there's one upstairs, waiting for you,' said Ben.

'You're pulling my plonker.'

'No, really. Behind the only closed door, go take a look.' He handed Stuart a torch.

Ben waited as Stuart climbed the stairs, then laughed again when he heard the shout from Stuart.

'You bastard, you might have said.'

'Pretty gruesome, isn't it. I guess we know how this bastard survived.' He nodded his head over the couch at the body on the floor. 'We'd better get busy. I want to be back before anyone's up. And this is finished.' He upended the now empty whisky bottle.

The work of butchering the corpse, stripping the meat from legs, arms, body, was hard and filthy. Stuart's frenzy had punctured many intestines, contaminating much of the meat on the torso. They stripped all they could from the bones to lighten the load they would carry.

'It's not as much as I thought it would be,' said Stuart; hefting his backpack before they left.

'Next time we'll be more careful about how we slaughter the prey,' said Ben. 'Think about how you'd deal with a deer. You'd keep the meat as clean as you could and bleed the body.'

'There'll be a next time?'

'Oh yes, there'll definitely be a next time.'

Chapter 35

They snatched a couple of hours sleep before beginning work in the kitchen.

'D'you think everyone will be up for this?' said Stuart, barricading the door.

'They will be when they smell it,' said Ben, hacking the meat into pieces. 'We'll cook it all now, have a feast, let everyone know what can be done if you're determined enough.'

The large pot with meat in began to sizzle as they fed more wood into the stove, keeping it hot and the room warm. They had little to add to the meat, some salt water from Lucy's last fruitless trip to the cove, a little pepper, a few dried herbs, nothing of substance; no onions, no garlic, no celery, no carrots, no cabbage, no potatoes. Still the smell of cooking invaded their senses, filled the room; their mouths watering long before the meal was ready. At every opportunity they indulged the "chef's prerogative" and tried the meal as it cooked. There were no adjustments to be made, no additions of this or that to alter the flavour, but their stomachs spoke loudly, and they tasted and tasted, until they were almost sated; nodding smiled encouragements to each other as they fed.

Someone tried the kitchen door, then banged on it.

'What's going on in there, who is it?' They recognised Lucy's voice.

'It's okay, sis,' said Ben, 'everything's under control. I'll let you know when we're ready to eat.'

'What is it, Ben? My mouth's watering.'

'You'll have to wait and see. Come back in an hour.'

They were all there when Ben opened the kitchen door and stepped out to speak to them; a waft of cooking meat swirling about them, driving their bodies to find the resources to drool.

'There's enough for everyone. You'll all eat well today. Come in.' He led them in and stood behind the large pot, a ladle in his hand.

The families pushed in. Ben watched them. They all bore marks of hunger and starvation. His sister, once beautiful, now greasy haired and sallow skinned. Andy's beer belly now an inconvenient flap of skin. Connie had lost a tooth from her receding gums. Sue also had teeth missing. Marcus showed less physical change than most, but he had always been a skinny lanky teenager.

Ben looked over them all, crowding the counter, holding their bowls out, keening for food.

'Quiet,' bellowed Ben, 'children first.'

Lottie, squeezed to the back by the throng, was pushed forward. Stuart took her bowl and Ben ladled it full of the meaty stew. Every eye followed the bowl's journey to the table and watched as Lottie began to eat.

'Emily next,' said Ben.

She too struggled from the back of the crowd, protecting her pregnancy as best she could. Her hollow cheeks and thin arms contrasting her enormous belly.

'I know you need enough for two, there will be plenty. This is just to begin with,' said Ben, filling her bowl.

As each of them presented a bowl Ben spoke kindly to them, promising more where this came from. All accepted their bowl of meat with thanks and smiles and sat to eat. Lottie finished before the last person arrived at the counter. It was Connie.

'Give me your bowl, I'll fill it up,' said Ben, smiling at his mother.

Connie could not control her drooling lips, salivation triggered by the smell of the meat, but she could control her arms and she held tightly to her bowl.

'What kind of animal is this meat from?' she said.

The room was quiet bar the sound of chewing.

'Does it matter as long as it feeds us?' said Ben.

'It may not matter to you, or anyone else,' she swept her arm around the room, 'it matters to me.'

'Come on, Mum, you're starving, look at you.' Ben reached over to try and take Connie's bowl. She held it tight against her and stepped back. The room fell silent.

'There's been no animals seen for months now. There's only one source this meat could have come from, and I'll not taint my soul by the tasting of it.'

The sound of chewing ceased; spoons were laid to rest within the bowls. The silence as pregnant as Emily's womb.

Lucy looked up from her partially eaten meal. She hadn't given a thought to the source of the meat, but was eating with gusto, driven by starvation. Now she scanned the room, her face burning, her shame wrestling her hunger. She stole glances at the hesitant diners, saw her own shame mirrored in Sue's face, confusion in Andy's. Watched as Faye shrugged, picked up her spoon and began to eat again. One by one she saw the same hunger win the struggle in all the people around the table, all bar her mother.

'But Grandma, it's so good,' said Lottie, breaking the silence in the room.

Ben laughed, 'And you shall have some more, Lottie. Fetch your bowl.'

'Come on, Mum, you must eat, you're starving,' said Lucy.

Connie's eyes flashed at her. 'I must, must I. I don't think so. What's happened to your humanity? You know what you're eating don't you.'

Lucy dropped her eye from her mother's glare. 'If we don't eat...'

'We'll die,' finished Ben. 'I'm not going to allow my daughter to die of starvation when there's a simple solution.'

'It might seem a simple solution to you, to me it is savagery, pure evil. I'll have nothing to do with it.'

Connie mustered what dignity she could and would have swept from the room imperiously, had it not been for her stick like frame and unsteady gait.

'There's plenty left, who wants some more?' said Ben. The silence continued for a beat, none seemed willing to break it.

'I do,' said Sue. She strode up to the counter and looked Ben in the eye, holding her bowl out.

Ben matched her look while filling her bowl. 'I might have known you'd be first,' he said.

Soon the rest followed.

When all bowls were replenished Ben and Stuart sat amongst the satiated crowd.

Ben called for quiet. 'It's through Stuart's strength and skill we all eat today. I want you all to know he is now my second in command here. I expect you all to give him the respect he's entitled to.'

Murmurs of gratitude spilled from some.

Ben paused, looked at them all and said, 'This is how defeat of our enemies gives us strength.'

As the room echoed in agreement Lucy whispered to her brother, 'I'm going to check on Mum, see if there's anything I can do.'

'It's her choice, her funeral if you like,' said Ben. 'I understand you want to go to her, but I don't think you'll get anywhere.'

'I have to try,' said Lucy.

Chapter 36

Lucy paused halfway up the stairs on her way to see her mother. Something wasn't right. She passed her hand over her eye patch, it hadn't changed, ran her hand over her body, feeling her ribs, and came to her stomach. Her hand stopped as she realised what it was. For the first time in what felt years but was only a few months, she didn't feel hungry. She smiled at the absence of the gnawing gap in her belly. Her mother deserved this. She would persuade her.

'Mum, it's me, can I come in?' Lucy tapped on her mum's door.

Connie's lined face displayed a deep sadness when she opened the door. Since Lucy's arrival at Cleeve House her mother's shining well cared for grey hair had become wild and filthy, overgrown and cropped by hand. Patches where Connie's scalp showed through told of hair loss. Her eyes, still fierce, now protruded from their sockets. Her skin sagged beneath her chin, her cheeks hollow, gaunt.

'I shouldn't have barked at you, Lucy, I know you were only trying to help,' she said, waving Lucy in.

'I'm worried about you, Mum. You must eat something,

anything.'

'I understand what you're saying, Lucy. Please think about it.'

'What is there to think about? It's obvious, isn't it? Either you eat or you die.'

'I had such hopes for you, as did your father. You were his favourite you know. We never planned to have you, that's why there's such a gap. And suddenly, there you were, our late sprung chick, and I'm so glad you're here.'

'Mum, why are you telling me this?'

'Because it will help you understand. There's something I want you to do. We were proud when you went to Oxford. And not surprised when you got head hunted to the States, you're so bright. It was pride with a bitter kernel. We knew we would hardly ever see you. Your dad was like a child when he heard you were coming back. Despite all the doom and gloom in the news, about the flood and everything, when you came home everything brightened for us. It's selfish, I know, but there we are.'

'I was glad to come home too. I wouldn't want to be anywhere else during this horror.'

'Let me finish. Before you were born, Ben let us know how he felt about Rob. He had that pushed out of the way feeling when new babies arrive. It didn't matter what we did, extra presents, special time alone with him, whenever Rob had anything, Ben would take it away. Whenever Rob cried, we always knew why, but Ben always lied about it.'

'It must have been hard on you, and Dad.'

'When you came along, Rob was seven and Ben ten. We feared for you, what he might do to you, he was much bigger than when Rob was born. He surprised us. You seemed to calm him down just by being there. The two of them could be fighting, but when I put you in the room with them it stopped. As if they both knew you were precious, special.'

'Oh, Mum,' said Lucy, tears now blurring her eye.

'I used to hear them talking to you before you could even say their names. Telling you they'd look after you. It made my heart swell.'

'And they did look after me, Mum, both of them.'

'I know, and you looked after them in return. You might not know it, but the arguments and the fighting practically ceased because of you. Then they started to leave, go to college, become adults. There was less violence, their disagreements meant nothing, arguments about music, politics. Like ordinary families. By the time you went to university and the States they had their own lives away from here and seemed happy enough.'

'I still don't know why you're telling me this?'

'Because I want you to do something for me, on my behalf if you like, after I'm dead.'

'Mum...'

'Don't, Lucy. I understand how important life is for you. You might have a future. I don't. Think about the poor person whose remains lay in the kitchen, would they have been as old as me? Probably not. I can't take a young life so I can live an old one. And it's not a life I want to live. A life of brutality and pain. A life watching my children and grandchildren turn into savages. I've been lucky to be blessed with beautiful children and a loving partner. I've thought about this a lot since James died. While I could be useful, it was okay, I could be sort of happy, knowing I was helping my children. But now? Do you understand, Lucy? It would mean a lot to me if you did.'

Lucy mumbled her assent. 'What is it you want me to do?'

'Ben is beyond help and he's taking his daughter with him. I want you to be there for Lottie, and Emily. When this is over, remind them of the gentle things in life, remind them of art, stories, music.'

'I can do that, but Rob —'

'Hush, there's more I want from you. I want you to keep contact with Rob but keep him away from his brother. I saw what Ben did to him. He'll kill Rob if he returns. Please, for me, keep him away, promise me.'

Connie took Lucy's hands in hers and looked in her eye and said again, 'Promise me.'

'Yes, of course, I'll do all I can to keep him away. But he might insist.'

'All you can do will be enough.'

For a moment the two women sat, gripping each other's hands, staring into each other's souls, as if in some form of higher communication, without words, without gestures.

'There's just one more thing,' said Connie, breaking the grip on her hands. 'It's time for you to have this.' She slipped her wedding ring off her finger and handed it to Lucy.

'Aw, Mum, I can't, I...'

'There isn't anyone else. It carries everything I hold dear in the world. Love, family, trust, loyalty. I want you to have it to carry these things with you. I don't know if there ever will be weddings again. I don't know if you'll ever find someone like I found your father. Still, I want you to have these things. Please take it.'

Chapter 37

Lucy and Emily were alone in the lounge. They found a quiet time to sit together every day.

'It's not going to be long now,' said Emily, 'and I don't mind admitting I'm petrified.'

'Is there anything you want me to do?' said Lucy.

'You'll be there when it's time?'

'Of course, I've already promised. But I've never been pregnant, let alone seen a birth. I'm not sure what use I'll be.'

'I was going to ask Connie...'

The two women sat silently for a few moments.

'She would love to see the new baby,' said Lucy.

'She might if she hangs on, or at least eats something.'

'I know, Em. I try to persuade her every day.'

'I'm sorry. I didn't mean it to sound like that. I'm scared shitless, that's all. With Lottie there was the NCT, the ante-natal clinic, yoga with a couple of other mums. There was the midwife, the hospital and scans, everything. Now there's nothing, there's only me. Suppose it's complicated, suppose the cord's around its neck, what am I supposed to do?'

'I don't know, Em. I might be able to help with the cord

thing. Have you talked to Sue?'

'I haven't. I never even thought about her. Ben won't like it. You know how he feels about the Reevers.'

'We don't have to tell him, once it's done there'll be nothing he can do about it.'

'Have you never been afraid of your brother?' said Emily.

Lucy laughed. 'Ben! He can be opinionated at times, but he's always been there for me. No, I've never been afraid of him. The opposite really, he's always made me feel safe and secure. A real big brother.'

'That's how I used to feel about him. Since Lottie's birth he's changed. Now we're here it seems to have brought the worst out in him for me. Sometimes he seems to be cruel just because he can be.'

'He's not still hitting you, is he?'

'No, he's not physically hurting me. But look at Faye, poncing around as if she owns the place. He'll get tired of her, she's too young for him. She'll soon find out what he's really like.'

'It must really hurt, Em.'

'It does and it doesn't. In a way it means I can tell him to sod off if he comes near me. Which he won't do for a few weeks after the baby if last time is anything to go by. The more I think about him... maybe I shouldn't be telling you this. You're his sister after all.'

'I'm also Lottie's aunt, and your friend.'

'If I'm honest, I don't give a toss what Ben thinks right now. I'm more concerned about my baby. I reckon I've less than a week to go.'

'I'll do whatever I can, Em, to make sure you're okay. But I'm a bit out of my depth here.'

'Thanks, Lucy. I am worried though, this baby doesn't seem as settled as Lottie was. It feels more uncomfortable. I could do with talking to someone about it. Sod what Ben thinks, will you ask Sue to come and see me?'

'You're coming down in the world visiting us in our hovel,' said Sue, opening the barn door to Lucy's knock.

'I haven't come for me, Sue, but for Emily. She's scared witless about her baby, and I know next to nothing about having babies. She would have spoken to Connie...'

Lucy paused and watched as Sue's initial confrontation slowly subsided, her face softening at the mention of Emily and her baby.

'I understand, of course she's scared. Anyone would be in these times. If you think it will help, I'll come and see her.'

'Thanks, I'm sure it will. I haven't a clue about what's normal and what isn't.'

The two of them strode across the yard to the house.

'How far on are you now?' said Sue after Emily had welcomed her into her room.

'About thirty-eight weeks I think.'

'When do you feel it will be?'

'To be honest, I'm not sure. Some days I feel it could be anytime, others as if there's weeks to go. This one doesn't feel the same as Lottie.'

'How does it feel different?'

'I seem to be getting kicked in all sorts of strange places, and I feel a lot more pressure on my lungs somehow. I get much shorter of breath than I did last time.'

'Can I see the bump? I'm not an expert, I don't know lots about this. But I've had a couple.'

'I would love you to have a look, I'm worried.' Emily lay on her bed and rolled her clothes over her pregnant belly.

Sue rubbed her hands together before placing them on

Emily's stomach. 'Hope they're not too cold,' she said, running her palm over Emily. 'Ooh, I felt a kick there.'

'So did I,' said Emily.

'I remember mine at this stage, it feels like you're carrying a sack of spuds strapped to your front, doesn't it? It didn't get any easier with the second either,' said Sue as she prodded and pushed at Emily's bump like she thought she remembered her midwife doing. She paused. 'You say you're about thirty-eight weeks? Have you felt the head engage at all?'

'No, I didn't feel it with Lottie either.'

Lucy saw a frown pass over Sue's face. 'Have you found something?' she said.

'Is something wrong?' said Emily, her voice a semi-tone higher.

'I'm not an expert,' said Sue. 'I don't really know anything.'

'You think there's something wrong, don't you?' Emily's voice was now sharp and snapped the words from her.

'I don't know,' said Sue, continuing to feel Emily's stomach, 'it's just...'

'What?! Tell me, what is it.'

'I don't know, calm down a minute, let me think. Lucy, can you feel here?' Sue indicated a part of Emily's belly to the side and above her navel. Lucy felt. 'Now here,' said Sue, pointing towards the low part of the stomach. 'Which feels hardest to you?'

Lucy pressed on each part with her hands. 'Are you okay with this, Em?' she said.

'Yes, I just want to know what's going on.'

'I think this bit up here is a bit harder than down there, it's hard to tell,' said Lucy.

'That's what I think,' said Sue. 'Emily, if you're thirty-eight weeks, and you look it, the baby's head should be down now.

It feels like it's up here.' Sue stroked the region where she thought the head was.

'You mean it's a breech,' said Emily. She started to sob. 'Which means…' She couldn't say anymore as tears engulfed her.

'Is it a problem if it's breech?' said Lucy.

'What it means is if there was a hospital, she'd be having a delivery by C-section. But there isn't.'

'What will happen?'

Sue glared at Lucy and hissed, 'If she's lucky only the baby will die. And Emily knows this, now stop your stupid questions.'

Lucy's eye flicked from Sue, frowning with concern and worry, to her friend, shedding tears of desperation. A sense of helplessness gripped her and forced its way to her voice. 'There must be something you can do. Can't you turn it round or something?'

Sue's anger flashed in her eyes. Her eyebrows rose, and her mouth opened to spit fire. Then she stopped, calmed. 'I had a friend once, years ago, who had this. I didn't see it, but she told me the midwife had moved the baby round, turned it, and she had a normal birth. Emily, did you hear me. I had a friend…'

'Yes, I heard you. Can you do it?'

'I don't know.'

'Try anyway.'

'I'm not really sure how, I might hurt him.'

'Not as much as a breech birth will. Please try.'

'Okay, I'll try,' said Sue, unsure of herself. 'You need to relax, and it might be uncomfortable.'

'It's bloody uncomfortable anyway.'

'What do you do? Push the head down?' said Lucy.

'No, that wouldn't be right. You put your hand here,

above the head, so it doesn't turn away or go any higher. I'll try and move the baby's bum upwards, maybe he'll turn by himself.'

Sue pushed her hand and thumb into the lower part of Emily's bump.

'How does it feel, are you okay?'

'Yes, I'm fine, nothing's happening,' said Emily.

'He's kicking, I think it's a good sign,' said Sue as she brought her other hand next to the first and slowly increased pressure on the baby. 'Just relax, don't think about it.'

'Don't think about it? You're joking,' said Emily.

'Sorry, my love, I'm doing my best here. Did he move? Did you feel anything, Lucy?'

'Maybe a little, I'm not sure.'

'I don't want to hurt you, Emily,' said Sue.

'You're not, it's just feeling a bit weird, like there's another pair of legs kicking me, from the outside.'

'Oh,' said Lucy, 'I think the head's moving.'

'It is,' said Emily, 'I think he's going.'

Sue's hand followed the legs of the unborn child up Emily's stomach while Lucy traced the path of the head downwards.

'God, he's moving, he's doing it,' said Emily.

'I reckon he's going to be an acrobat when he grows up, cartwheeling like that,' said Sue.

Emily laughed as tears of relief streamed down her face. The other two women couldn't contain huge smiles.

'Best make sure he gets settled in the right position hadn't we,' said Sue as she helped Emily stand.

Emily pulled Sue to her, hugged her as tight as her pregnancy would allow. 'I don't know how to thank you. I don't know what to say.'

They all three laughed together.

'It wasn't just me. If Lucy hadn't have said about turning, I wouldn't have remembered Clara. And she had a right bonny boy.'

'How are you feeling now, Em?' said Lucy.

'Better,' said Emily, 'better. But still bloody uncomfortable.'

All three laughed again.

'Sue, will you be there when my baby's born? I'd love it if you could be.'

'It would be an honour, but remember, I'm not an expert.'

Chapter 38

The rain lashed Cleeve House, a howling westerly tore at the trees and the buildings, rivulets of muddy water streamed through the yard on their way to the river. The water butts were all overflowing. The fields holding the few precious late plantings of kale, cabbages, broad beans, were quagmires.

Certain Rob would not be at the cove, Lucy stayed at Cleeve House, preserving her energy, keeping the weakening Connie company. Ben and Stuart had brought home a whole carcass. Connie still refused to eat. Now she hadn't the energy to sit let alone stand and walk. She refused to see Ben but was glad of company from Lucy or Emily.

'It's not that I don't want Lottie to see her,' Emily told Lucy. 'But she may try and persuade her not to eat.'

'She's dying, Em, it could be any time now. It would mean a lot to her if she could see Lottie once more.'

'She doesn't have to be dying, it's her own fault. She could eat, then she'd be okay.'

'You were there that first time, you heard what she said. She won't give in. And I doubt she'll last another day,' said Lucy.

'Ben wouldn't like it either, not that I care about what he thinks.'

'Do it for me, Em, a few minutes can't hurt. Lottie won't see her again otherwise.'

Even at midday the curtains were closed, the room dim. Lucy spoke in hushed tones to her mother, recalling her childhood adventures and explaining her life choices. Connie lay in bed, occasionally shifting position, murmuring an acknowledgment.

The gentle knock on the door signalled Emily's arrival. She stood in the doorway, gripping Lottie's hand. 'Remember, Grandma is very poorly; she won't be able to play with you like she used to.'

Lottie clutched her favourite, and only, teddy bear as she came into the dim room. Lucy left her seat next to her mother, indicating Lottie to take it.

'Hello, Grandma,' she said.

Connie's eyes opened, her mouth smiled, she took a breath. 'Hello, Lottie,' she rasped, lips parched.

'Poor Grandma, you sound very poorly.'

Another breath, 'Don't you worry about that, let me look at you.'

'I bet Daddy could mend you.'

Emily and Lucy shared a panicked glance.

'He is very clever, your daddy, but even he couldn't mend me.' Another rasping breath.

'He said he could, but you don't want him to.'

'I don't think he…' began Emily, but a glance from Connie quietened her.

'I see you have Ted with you. How is he?'

'He was really really hungry, but now he's just ordinary hungry,' said Lottie.

'That's good,' another breath, 'maybe he won't be hungry at all one day.'

'I'll ask him.' Lottie whispered secret words into her teddy's ear. 'He says he'll be hungry forever and ever now, so he might as well get used to it.'

Emily recognised the words from a conversation with Ben the previous evening. 'I'm sure there'll come a day when he isn't hungry,' she said.

'But you don't know anything,' said Lottie, 'Daddy told me.'

Lucy watched Emily's face crumple. 'Why don't you tell Grandma about all the water in the yard. She hasn't seen it,' said Lucy.

'I don't want to. I don't like the big water.'

'Good,' said Connie, 'I've had enough of water too.'

'Grandma, Daddy says you're going to die, like the chickens did.'

'That's right, sweetheart, but don't worry. I don't mind.'

'Where will you be when you're dead?'

'I don't know, I won't be anywhere I guess.'

'You won't be in a hole like Grandad?'

'I might be. Wherever it is I won't mind.'

'Will I be able to come and see you, like you go and see Grandad?'

Lucy watched a single tear run from the corner of Connie's eye and soak into her pillow.

'Only if you want to. But there isn't a lot to see.' Connie took a breath. 'I never saw your grandad; I just went to remember him.'

'Would you have forgotten him if you didn't go?'

Connie smiled; she might have laughed if she had the energy. 'I have something for you.' From under her pillow Connie took a heart shaped locket on a golden chain.

'Grandad gave this to me before your daddy was even born.' Her fingers fiddled with the clasp holding the locket closed. She gave up trying to control her unwilling hands. 'Lucy, open this will you?'

Lucy clicked the locket open and gave it back to her mother.

'Lottie,' said Connie, showing the locket, 'this is me when I was younger than Aunty Lucy, and this is Grandad when he was younger than Uncle Rob.' The two small photos on either side of the locket smiled out of a time long past.

'I want you to have this, Lottie, and if you ever want to remember me, or Grandad, you only have to look inside.' She closed the locket with a click and gave it to Lottie. 'You can wear it if you want to.'

Emily strung the golden chain around her daughter's neck and tucked the locket in her clothes.

'It feels funny,' said Lottie.

Connie didn't reply. Her eyes were closed.

'Is she dead?' whispered Lottie to Lucy.

'No Lottie, she's only sleeping. She's very tired.'

'Oh,' said Lottie, a hint of disappointment in her voice.

'Come on, poppet, we'll let her sleep,' said Emily, taking her hand.

'But I want to see her dead,' said Lottie as they got to the door.

After the door had closed Connie's eyes opened. 'Thank you, Lucy.'

'I didn't do anything, it was Emily.'

'I know you did. Emily wouldn't have brought her, I'm glad I've seen her once more.'

'You might see her again.'

'No, Lucy, I won't be seeing her again.'

'What about Ben? Will you see him?'

'No. I don't want to sully what memories I have. I fear for him, and the rest of you while he's in charge, but there's nothing I can do now.'

'He's doing what he thinks is best. Anyway, can I get you anything else, some more water, anything.'

Connie didn't answer. Then she looked directly at Lucy. Fear in her eyes.

'Lucy...'

Lucy took her hand and Connie gripped it. 'What is it, Mum?'

Connie's other hand went to her chest, the fear in her face changed to pain, her grip on Lucy tightened. She took a sudden, gasping breath, holding Lucy's gaze. Then her eyes lost focus, her grip slackened, her breath left her.

Tears welled in Lucy's eye as she watched her mother's lids droop and felt her hand limp in her palm. There was no point in calling for help, there was no help to be had, nothing to be done. The life ebbed away from her mother as Lucy sat beside her holding her hand, watching her jaw slacken, her body slump.

Lucy tucked her mother's hand beneath the blanket, then gave vent to the wail of grief she had been holding for days. Now she was an orphan. In four months both her father and now her mother had died. Rob would have understood, held her, given her a shoulder to cry on, if he had been there.

Chapter 39

After covering her mother with a blanket, Lucy took her grief to her brother. He was an orphan now, too. He'd understand, help her with a funeral as she'd helped with their father's.

'She's gone, Lucy, she's dead. It doesn't matter what we do with the body, she won't care anymore.'

'What's the matter with you, Ben? We have to bury her next to Dad.'

'Remember the Himalayan tribe who used to leave their dead for the sacred vultures to eat? It wouldn't be any different to that,' said Ben.

'I don't believe I'm hearing this. You're being incredibly callous. She was our mother. We can't dump her body in the woods. Remember Dad's funeral? You were happy to dig a grave for him. What's changed?'

'A lot's changed. It's pointless, a waste of energy and resources.' Ben watched the distress growing in his sister, her single eye beginning to fill, her hands pulling their fingers, her voice high and fast.

'You're not planning to eat her, are you? Our own mother?' The horror in Lucy's voice matched the look on her face.

'Of course not. How could you think that of me? No, we can't eat her. Look around, everyone is worn out, exhausted and starving. I'll be using my energy to go hunting to feed everyone. I won't be digging any graves. And I won't be telling anyone else to either.'

'Then I'll dig it myself,' said Lucy, and stormed out of the room.

Rain fell in squalls as the recent storm lost its power. Ben watched Lucy pull her coat collar up and her hat down and stride to the tool shed. She disappeared inside for a couple of minutes before coming out carrying a spade and marching off towards the cairn where her father's grave lay.

When she was out of sight Ben donned his own coat, crossed the yard, and let himself into the Reevers' barn.

'What do you want?' asked Sue.

'You're so friendly, I'm surprised anyone ever speaks to you,' said Ben.

'You might have knocked at least. We could have been doing anything.'

'Yeah, course you could. Where's Stuart?'

'Are you stealing him away from us again?' said Sue.

Stuart appeared from the back of the barn. 'You want to see me?'

'Yeah, step outside with me, this is private,' said Ben, giving Sue a steely look.

They stood in the shelter of the house eaves where they couldn't be overheard.

'I've got something for you. If I tell you what it is you're going to owe me big time.'

'Owe you what?'

'You want to get on Lucy's good side, don't you? Now's your chance. She's at the cairn digging a grave for our mother, single handed. You should go and give her a hand.'

'Why aren't you helping?'

'Because I thought you would want to. If you don't…'

'No, no, I do. I'll go up there now, I'll take a shovel.'

'You've got to make it seem like an accident. As if you're on your way somewhere. And think, if in doubt don't speak at all, she's my sister, she'll know if you're lying. And take the stupid grin off your face, she's just lost her Mum, get serious. If you blow it, I figure there's no hope for you.'

Lucy marked a rectangle in the mud next to her father's grave. Her anger at her heartless brother gave strength to her blows, and the hard work soon had her sweating despite the chill of late February.

She hadn't finished removing the first layer of mud when she felt someone approaching. Her arms ached and she hoped it was Ben coming to help, but when she looked, she saw Stuart.

'What are you doing in the mud?' he called.

'Keep away, or you'll feel the edge of this spade.'

Stuart stopped and spread his arms out showing open palms. 'Okay, I'm not coming closer.'

'Why are you here anyway?'

'I was coming to check the gates, have a look down The Lane. I know it's raining but you never know when they may decide to attack again.'

'I don't think they ever will, even if they are still alive. Go on and have a look if you must, then leave me alone.'

Stuart walked to the gate and peered down The Lane, then came back to where Lucy was excavating around a large stone. 'Why are you digging, Lucy? It looks like hard work.'

'If you must know I'm digging my mother's grave, now sod off and leave me alone.' Anger at her brother, at Stuart, drove her to dig, and now she had the spade wedged against the stone, trying to lever it out. It wouldn't budge. She began digging again.

'It's not going to be easy, hefting that out of the hole,' said Stuart. 'Can I give you a hand?'

'No, you can't, I'll manage. Why don't you just leave?'

'Okay. I understand why you want me to go, and I'm sorry about that. I know I've been stupid. Just let me help you get the rock out of there. You could injure yourself.'

The lack of arrogance in his voice surprised Lucy. She'd hardly spoken to him since Goff's Cove, avoiding him as much as possible. She didn't trust him, but the struggle with the rock frustrated her, and he was right about it. It would be easy to slip and drop the rock on herself.

'Okay,' she said, 'you can help with the rock. Then you can go.'

Despite the rain Stuart took off his coat and lay it on the cairn before stepping down into the shallow beginnings of the grave. He bent and gripped the rock in both his arms. He strained to lift it, but it stuck fast despite his best efforts.

'I'm going to need the spade,' he said.

'I can dig,' said Lucy.

'It'll be quicker if you let me.'

Lucy stuck the spade in the mud and climbed out of the grave. She watched as Stuart took it in his hands and set to. Despite the paucity of diet, Lucy saw well defined muscles in Stuart's shoulders and arms. He circled the stone, taking a full spade depth of mud from around it as he went. When he'd completed the circuit he handed the spade to Lucy, bent, and wrapped his arms around the rock again, and heaved it from the sucking mud and onto the edge of the grave.

'I don't think you could lift that, Lucy. It probably weighs more than you do. I'm going to roll it over to the cairn. Then if you still want me to go I will. If you'd like me to help finish the digging, I'm happy to do it. It's knackering, we could take turns, give each other a breather. You next.' He waved his hand at the grave as he stepped out.

Lucy didn't say anything as she began digging again. With each spade full she watched Stuart. He was taking an age rolling the rock the few metres to the cairn.

Stuart took his coat from the cairn and put it on. Laboured breathing the only sound from Lucy. Stuart adjusted the position of the rock, glanced at Lucy again. The rain stopped.

'Do you want me to take a quick turn before I go?' he said.

Lucy looked at him. Her aching arms were beginning to tremble with exertion. She was on the point of taking a rest. Did he know? Had he been watching her for just this sign? The grave wasn't half dug. She left the spade in the grave and climbed out, sitting on the rock.

Stuart took that as a yes and began to dig, throwing earth out of the grave. The hole grew under Stuart's onslaught. Soon it was deep enough, and he stopped. He had left a step at one end to make climbing out easier. He handed the spade to Lucy.

'It needs finishing at the bottom. You should do that.'

Lucy couldn't let Stuart's hand be the last to dig, her mother's grave would be sullied if she didn't finish it. She used the step into the bottom and began to smooth the lumpy floor of the grave, removing small stones and spades of soil when she needed to.

When she tried to climb out her muscles began to give up in protest. She struggled, despite the step, to pull herself out. Lucy used the spade as a prop to push down on. When she lifted her knee onto the graveside the spade sank into the mud, tipping her off balance. With one knee on the edge and a foot in mid-air she would have fallen into the grave. Stuart was there in an instant. As if he knew this would happen, he grabbed her hand. Relief and horror struggled for control of Lucy's emotions as Stuart hoisted her from the grave.

As soon as she was safely out, he let go of her. 'I'm sorry,' he said, 'I didn't want you to hurt yourself. I think we're done here; I'll leave now.' He turned to walk down the hill to Cleeve House.

Lucy watched him go. After he had gone fifteen paces she called to him, 'Stuart.' He turned to look at her. 'Thanks,' she said, looking at him for a moment before turning away.

Chapter 40

Emily's nights consisted of occasional slumber interspersed with restlessness and a struggle for comfort. Her baby didn't understand diurnal rhythms and the need for sleep. Not for the first time that night she hoisted herself from her bed and onto the bucket serving as a commode. Nine months of pregnancy sitting atop her bladder brought the absence of running water and electricity into sharp relief. She lumbered back onto her bed, trying to slow the breathing in her restricted lungs. As her heartbeat slowed and sleep approached, again a kick woke her.

'Come on, baby, give me a break, Mummy needs some sleep, she's knackered,' Emily cooed at her belly. The response was a contraction. She'd been having them on and off all day. Emily held her bump and felt the wave sweep downward through her bulging abdomen, gasping at the sudden onset of pain, and breathing again at its release a minute later.

'Oh God, I guess this is it, you're on your way. Couldn't you wait until the morning?'

A couple of minutes later another wave overtook her and she knew it wouldn't be long. With Lottie she'd been in labour a scant two hours, to the envy of her friends. Now the prospect of a quick labour scared her. She waited for the wave to pass and yelled as loud as she could, 'Lucyyyyyyy,' then a breath and another yell, 'Lucyyyyyy.'

It took five piercing screams of her name before a bedraggled Lucy arrived. A candle sitting on the dresser beneath the window, the only lighting in the room, guttered as Lucy came in wiping sleep from her eyes.

'Lucy, it's happening. They're only a few minutes apart. Get Sue, quick.'

'Is there anything...'

'Just go and...' Emily paused, a contraction stealing her ability to speak. 'Go, now, Sue,' Emily hissed.

Lucy turned and ran.

'Not yet, baby, not yet. Hang on a little while,' said Emily into the uncomprehending ear of her unborn child.

It seemed ages. Emily lost count of the number of contractions she'd had since Lucy left; she knew the time between them was shrinking. She prepared as best she could in the minutes between, trying to clear space on her bed, pulling off the pants she wore. Then they were there, just as the panic of aloneness threatened to overwhelm her.

'Thank God, you're here, Sue, I... ugh,' and again Emily couldn't speak.

'They never do choose a convenient time,' said Sue.

Emily could only grunt as her belly clamped tight.

'Let's have a look at you.' Sue made to take the candle up from the dresser, Lucy's arm held her back.

'Here,' said Lucy handing Sue a head torch.

'Lord, where d'you get this from,' said Sue, pulling the strap around her head and switching the light on.

'I thought it might come in handy. You okay, Em?'

'I think so. I don't think it will be lo... ugh. Long. Lottie was quick she only took... ugh.'

'Take it easy,' said Sue, 'you'll need your energy.'

Despite the cold of the night, beads of sweat stood out on Emily's face as she panted through another contraction.

'It's not... ugh, giving me much... ugh, choice. I really want to push.'

'I know you should be fully dilated before you start pushing,' said Sue. 'You can't be by now, surely.'

'Are you all right, Em?' said Lucy.

Emily attempted a nod as she moved on the bed. 'I need to be... ugh...I need to be on all fours. It's better.'

Lucy and Sue helped Emily turn and crouch, her body hot to the touch and slick with sweat.

'I'm holding off. But baby won't be much longer. It was like this... ugh, with Lottie. She was quick, two hours. Ugh... This one is even keener than Lottie... ugh...'

'The waters haven't broken, have we towels, or something?' said Sue.

'It's an "or something",' said Lucy, pulling the curtains she'd pinched from the lounge from under Emily's bed. 'I'm hoping to save one for the baby.'

Sue took one of the curtains and tucked it beneath Emily.

Emily let out a scream as she surrendered to the next contraction and the waters broke.

'I think you'd best start pushing, my love,' said Sue, 'I can see the head now.'

'He's amazing, Em,' said Lucy. 'So are you, utterly amazing.'

'I don't know about me, I think I'm just relieved, but yes, he is amazing isn't he.' Her eyes fixed on the tiny child, cradled in her arm, and wrapped in an old curtain.

'Lucy's right,' said Sue. 'It's just wonderful, that's what it is, wonderful.'

'We should be drinking champagne, the best there is, Krug, or Cristal,' said Lucy.

'Never mind champagne, I could murder a decent cup of coffee,' said Emily.

Laughter rang around the room and baby moved his head.

'Can he hear us?' said Lucy.

'Of course he can, and he's probably wondering if he'll ever get fed. Come on, baby, on you go,' said Emily, nuzzling the child to her breast.

'There's still the placenta to come,' said Sue. 'What do you want to do with it?'

A question formed on Emily's brow.

Sue explained. 'I've known people who freeze it and keep it until the child's a year old then bury it somewhere secret. There was one who ate it. She said animals eat the placenta to replace the nutrition they've lost. I saw a cow do it once, after she'd calved in the field over the road.'

Emily grunted as her womb began to contract, and Sue caught the placenta in a porcelain dish.

'A couple of months ago I don't think I could even have thought about it. Right now, I'm starving.'

'Do you want it cooked or as it is?' said Sue.

'There's nothing to cook it with,' said Lucy. 'There's no fuel for the stove, no fat to fry it in. Looks a bit like liver, onions would be great if we had some.'

'Stop it,' said Sue, 'you're making my mouth water.'

Emily eyed the placenta lying in the dish then looked at her baby. 'He's going to need every calorie I can give him,' she said, and held out her hand. 'Give it here.'

Chapter 41

Ben withdrew his hand from Faye and rolled away to his side of the bed.

'You're fucking pregnant, aren't you?' he said.

Faye flinched at the undertone of disgust in Ben's voice.

'I think I must be,' she said, her heart pounding as she injected a note of innocence into her words, hoping his reaction would change.

She had been careful not to show her growing belly. The winter helped. It gave Faye plenty of reasons to wear whatever she could find. It was fine during the day, and during the night darkness hid her. But she couldn't hide from his hands.

'It's enough hearing her screaming away downstairs without you shoving your bulging stomach at me.'

'She's having a baby, Ben. You can expect her to scream.'

'I don't have to like it. And now you're having one.'

'Is it a problem?'

'It's not a problem for me. How far gone are you?'

Faye knew exactly. Her memory of conception in the hovel was vivid and the date burned in her head. She'd even kept a secret calendar ever since, counting off the days with a growing fear of discovery.

'I'm not sure. Four or five months maybe.'

'It's nothing to do with me. Probably my brother's. You're going to have to piss off, you know.'

His anger dissipated to a distant calmness which threw Faye and she burst into tears.

'It might be your baby, aren't you pleased?' she said between sobs.

'Why should I be? I've already got one to look after, and she's having another. Why would I want any more? And you can turn off those tears. They don't work with me. Take what you need for tonight and go and sleep in the lounge. You can collect the rest of your crap tomorrow.'

'How can you be so heartless. I can't live in the lounge, everyone uses it.'

'You're right, you can't. It's only for tonight. Then you'll have to find somewhere else.'

'But I'm pregnant,' Faye wailed.

'Yes, I know,' said Ben, getting out of bed and pulling on his clothes. 'Look, we had a good time together for a few months, now it's over. This must have happened to you before.'

Faye didn't speak until after he'd finished dressing.

'Suppose I won't go?'

Ben laughed. 'You'll go all right. I don't care if you end up at the bottom of the stairs with a broken leg, but you're going. You only get to decide if you go after you've dressed or before.'

'Can't I go in the morning?'

'Nah, you can go now. To be honest you have the stink of pregnant woman hanging about you. I've been wondering what it was for a week or two. It all fell into place when I felt your stomach. You should have owned up. Then it wouldn't be the middle of the night. You see, it's all your own fault.'

'You bastard, you should treat me better than this, I know...' she stopped. She couldn't say she knew he was a murderer. What would that do except get her killed. He'd already threatened to throw her down the stairs.

'What do you know? That the brat's mine. I don't think so.' He leaned over and pushed her out of the bed.

'Ow, that hurt,' she said, falling on the floor. 'Be careful of my baby.'

'I don't give a toss about your baby. Now get your stuff and get lost.'

Faye crept into the lounge wrapped in all her clothes and carrying a small bag containing everything precious to her. She heard voices coming from Emily's room, women's voices. They sounded cheerful; someone was laughing. Faye recognised Lucy's voice amongst them. As she pulled the door closed behind her, Faye was certain she heard a baby cry. Her hand went instinctively to her stomach.

'I've never seen that before,' said Sue as Lucy let her out of the house, 'she positively wolfed it down.'

'She did,' said Lucy, 'and I understand why. Little Adam is going to need all the help he can get in this world.'

'He is. And what a great name for the little tyke. I wonder if it was Ben's choice.'

'I don't think Ben had any say in it.'

'It is inspiring though isn't it, seeing a baby born.'

'You're not thinking of having anymore are you, Sue?'

'Me! No fear. I'm past all that. I was thinking you might.'

'That's not going to happen, I can assure you. Anyway, it's freezing here, and I'm worn out.'

'Sorry, my love, I'll let you get off to sleep.'

Lucy closed the door behind Sue and tiptoed past Emily's room to the stairs. She had one foot on the bottom step when she heard a voice. She thought it might be Emily and turned to go back to her. She heard it again, it sounded angry, and it was coming from the lounge.

Clouds scudding across the sky allowed a shaft of moonlight through the curtainless windows as Lucy pushed the lounge door open.

'Faye? Is it you?'

'Lucy! I'm sorry, I know I shouldn't be here.'

'It's okay. Who are you talking to?'

'No one, just myself. I'm sleeping here tonight.'

'What's going on? We used to be friends before...' Lucy couldn't bring herself to say, "before you slept with Ben and destroyed Emily".

'You don't want to talk to me. You don't even like me.'

'I can't make you talk, that's for sure. Only you can do that. If you don't want to talk to me, I'm going back to bed.' Lucy turned to leave.

'Wait, please,' said Faye.

A plaintive, almost pleading tone in Faye's voice stopped Lucy from leaving. She turned again and went to the couch where Faye lay. 'Budge up and I'll sit with you,' she said.

'Lucy, I don't know how to say this... I'm pregnant.'

Lucy almost burst into laughter. 'Yes,' she said.

'You don't sound surprised,' said Faye.

'I'm not. I figured you were weeks ago. What are you crying about? And why are you here at this time of night? Shouldn't you be with Ben?'

'He's thrown me out, Lucy. Kicked me out in the middle of the night. As soon as he found out I was pregnant. I don't know what I'm going to do.'

'You knew he'd do this. He did it to his own wife.'

'I know, but I thought it would be different with me. I thought he'd, I don't know what I thought, I'm an idiot.'

Lucy put her arm around Faye's shoulders and gave her a sideways hug. 'How pregnant are you?'

'Twenty-two weeks. I'm so stupid. I can't stay here, I have to leave, he told me,' said Faye.

'Leave Cleeve House?' said Lucy.

'No, I meant this room. I hadn't thought about leaving Cleeve, I don't know where I'd go. I don't know where to go anyway.'

'You won't like it in here; I stole the curtains for Emily's baby. There's only Mum's old room. Next door to mine. It's only a few days since she died; it still feels like her room.'

'I am sorry about your mum; she was always kind to me.'

'I don't know if you can stay there. I guess you'd have to ask Ben.'

'Do you think he'd say yes? I hope so. I'll ask him tomorrow. Lucy, can I ask you to do something for me?'

'I don't know, what is it?'

'I know I've been a fool, but we used to get on okay. I like you; I trust you. When I have my baby will you be with me?'

Lucy could only respond positively to the desperate note in Faye's voice. 'Yes, of course I will. But right now, I need some sleep.'

Chapter 42

Lucy woke late the next morning with memories jostling in her head; Sue strapping on the head torch; Adam's first cry; Emily suckling him. After the miracle of a new baby the memory that grabbed her attention was Emily's post-delivery meal. Lucy again saw Emily's mouth chewing, the small slick of placental blood escaping from the corner of her mouth, and Emily's tongue stretching down to lick it.

She shook herself, climbed out of bed, dressed, and went to see the mother and child.

'Isn't he marvellous,' said Emily, barely glancing at Lucy as she came in. 'I've hardly slept a wink and I'm utterly knackered, but I just want to watch him.'

'He is gorgeous,' said Lucy.

'I was scared I would never see him, but he's here and he's lovely.'

The two women admired the squashed, flat face of the half-day-old Adam poking from the grubby old curtain serving as swaddle.

'He's got the lip,' said Lucy.

Emily laughed. Adam already displayed the prominent

upper lip, a feature of both Lucy's and Ben's faces. Lucy spoke about finding Faye in the lounge the night before.

'The little bitch has copped it has she. I guess she thought it would be different for her. Serves her right.'

'She's frightened,' said Lucy.

'She's right to be. She won't get any support from Ben.'

'It might not be Ben's baby.'

'Then she's even more stupid than I thought.'

'Does Ben know about Adam yet?' she said.

'He came this morning. I told him I'd decided to call my son Adam. I thought we'd have a fight about it, but he agreed. "It's fitting" he said. I was surprised. It was a bit like the old Ben. Still, I don't trust him.'

'Will he want you to go back?'

'Probably, now he's kicked Faye out. Not right away, he'll wait until I've recovered before trying it on. But I'm not going back. I've finally realised what type of man he is. As far as I'm concerned, I'm on my own now. And I don't want to get pregnant again.'

'Ever?'

'Absolutely ever. Frankly, it gives me the heebie-jeebies thinking about what I went through. Imagine if Sue hadn't been able to turn him. It would have been a breech birth and... Enough of what-ifs. He's awake, pass him to me, will you?'

Lucy took the tiny child from the old dresser drawer that served as a crib and passed him into the waiting arms of his mother.

'I don't even know how much he weighs,' said Emily.

Leaving Emily, Lucy looked for Faye in her mother's old room but found no sign of her. On the landing she met her brother.

'Have you seen Faye? I saw her last night and she told me what had happened.'

'And?' said Ben.

'I wondered where she was that's all. I told her she might be able to use Mum's old room, and to check with you first. Now I can't find her.'

'She can't use Mum's room. I've told her she'll have to move out of the house.'

'But it's empty. And Faye's pregnant and...'

'It's not going to be empty for long. Someone will be moving in soon.'

'Who?'

'I've told Stuart he can have it. It makes sense for him to be closer to me. And he is second in command now.'

'But...' Lucy began, then stopped, her eye darting to the room and her brother, her hands clutching each other, her heart pounding. She'd never told Ben about the cove, and now it seemed too long ago, Ben would dismiss it.

'But what, Lucy?'

'I think it's a bit unfair. Faye will need somewhere warm and dry while she carries, and Stuart's already got somewhere to stay.'

'I've told you; I want him close by in case I need him. We may have to go out together to feed you all. You don't want to stop eating, do you?'

'No, but—'

'All these "buts" Lucy. Have you something against Stuart? Is that why you're keen on Faye having the room?'

'Yes, no, I don't know.' Lucy looked at her brother, searching for her protector of old, but he wasn't there. 'There's something about him. I'm not sure I can trust him.'

'I trust him, Lucy. He's a damn good hunter, a great shot. Most of the meat we eat comes from his crossbow. Maybe you need to look at him in a different way. This is not a time for weaklings and contemplation, this is a time for strength and action. I'm going to tell him he can move in. We need to prepare for tonight's hunt.'

'Where's Faye?'

'I don't know why you're bothered about Faye. She'll have found somewhere, well out of my way, I hope. Now I have to go.'

Chapter 43

Rain beat on Faye's head, soaking her and her doubts as she approached the hovel. Over two months had passed since she'd told Marcus about her baby. Her confidence drained away like the rain draining from her clothes and her hair.

At the sight of smoke puffing from the makeshift chimney, a small smile spread across her face. Before she would have marched straight in, confident of a generous welcome from Marcus. Now she hesitated, a sense of fragility and insecurity enveloping her. She took a breath, firmed her resolve, and knocked on the makeshift door.

Faye stood shivering hearing noises from inside. The door opened a crack and Marcus peered out into the rain, saw who it was and swung the door wide.

'Faye! I wasn't expecting you. Come in quick before the heat all goes.'

Faye stepped in, leaving wet footprints behind her. When Marcus swung the door shut, smoke from a small fire in the hearth billowed into the room, stinging her eyes.

'You're soaked, do you want to take your coat off?'

Faye nodded and began to shuck her coat from her

shoulders.

'Here, sit by the fire.' Marcus showed her a crude stool he'd arranged from a stump of tree trunk.

Though small, the heat from the fire made steam rise from Faye's sodden clothes. She hadn't yet spoken, and as she sat, an unusual reticence gripped her. How was she going to ask Marcus for what she wanted? The machinations of her earlier contact with Marcus now seemed cruel to her. She knew who her baby's father was, and Marcus had nothing to do with it, yet she'd allowed him to believe it was his, and he was thrilled by it. Marcus's innocent welcome touched her and for the first time in her life she recognised what guilt felt like. She almost confessed, then Marcus spoke again.

'I hoped I'd see you soon. How is my baby? How's he growing? It must be tough on you. I'm sorry I got caught with the eggs. You had a few, didn't you? I'm not Ben's favourite person though. Nor anyone else's.' He paused. 'I'm sorry, I'm talking like an idiot. I don't get to speak to many people these days. Mum talks to me sometimes, Stuart cuts me dead. Unless I'm getting orders.'

'Marcus, I'm sorry, it's all my fault.'

Marcus crouched on the floor beside her and took her hand. 'No, it's not, you're the best thing that's ever happened to me.'

'If it weren't for me, you wouldn't have stolen the eggs, you'd be fine. Everyone would be okay with you.'

'But I wouldn't be having a baby, would I? And I wouldn't have met the most beautiful woman on the planet.'

'You're sweet,' said Faye working hard at holding back tears, trying a wan smile.

'Are you crying? What's the matter?'

'No, it's just the smoke in my eyes. I'm fine. I just wondered if…' she left a pause.

'Wondered what?'

'I wondered if you'd like us to spend a bit more time together?'

'I'd love it, it would be fantastic, but wouldn't Ben...'

'I've left him.' It was a blunt statement. Faye justified it to herself as the truth.

'Won't he—'

'No, he won't, he wanted me to go, so I did. I've been thinking about you more and more lately and it must have shown.'

'Where are you sleeping? Have you moved into the old woman's room?'

'I could have done. It's comfortable there. I wondered if...'

'If what?'

'If, maybe, you'd like it if I stayed with you?'

Faye watched the answer blossom on his face, a broad smile threatened to crack from ear to ear and he shook his head in amazement, mouth agape. Before he could speak there was a knock at the door. Marcus, startled out of his reverie, leapt to his feet, and again pulled the door open, this time to find Lucy standing in the rain.

'I'm sorry to intrude, Marcus, I was looking for Faye and—'

'I'm here, Lucy,' called Faye from inside the hovel. 'Don't keep her in the rain, Marcus.'

Again, smoke billowed into the tiny shelter as Marcus closed the door.

'I'll hang your coat up... somewhere if you like,' said Marcus.

'I won't be here long. I came to see Faye; I said I would yesterday.' Lucy turned to Faye. 'I heard you're not staying in Mum's old room because—'

'That's right, I wanted to stay with Marcus, and I'm

pleased to say he said yes.' Faye's interruption was immediate and her look at once piercing and fearful.

Lucy swung around to find Marcus grinning. 'You do know Faye's—'

'Expecting a baby,' interrupted Faye again, 'of course he does. Don't you, Marcus?'

'I'm really pleased about it. I never thought this would ever happen to me,' said Marcus.

Lucy turned again to look at Faye. Her eyes pleaded with Lucy as her head gave a tiny shake.

Lucy turned back to Marcus. 'Faye has asked if I would be with her when her baby is born. I expect you'll be seeing a bit more of me.'

'I'm glad,' said Marcus. 'I haven't any idea what I'm supposed to do.'

'Maybe we'll talk about it later. I just wanted to make sure Faye got here all right. I'll be off now.' She turned to go. 'Can we meet up for a chat soon, Faye?' said Lucy.

Faye nodded. 'I'll come down to the house tomorrow.'

Heading back towards Cleeve House, distracted by her thoughts about Faye and Marcus, Lucy forgot what Ben had told her about Stuart. It wasn't until she was halfway up the stairs and saw him on the landing she remembered. Her heart tumbled in her chest as she paused on the middle step, she couldn't turn around, he'd seen her.

'Hi Lucy. It looks like we're going to be neighbours.' His grin fell on her like an axe.

'Yes, it does,' she said. She tried to keep the quaver of distress out of her voice, but her chest was tight, her lips drawn, her mouth dry, and the sound she made was simultaneously husky and high pitched.

Stuart had a couple of boxes and a bag on the landing and

the door to her mum's room was open. She would have to stop thinking of it as Mum's room. There was nothing of her mum there, especially now.

Lucy climbed to the top of the stairs to go to her room. Stuart stood there, not exactly blocking her way, not moving aside either. She would have to pass so close she could smell him. Smell the sweat of his labour, smell the maleness of him. She suppressed a shudder as he put an arm out against the banister, blocking her way.

'I want to get past,' she said, her eye looking towards her room, avoiding his stare.

'I know,' he said, 'before you go can I say something to you?' He kept his hand gripping the banister, preventing her passing.

If Stuart had been a couple of years younger, she might have tried to knock him aside. Now, at nineteen, he carried bravado and strength. Lucy knew she couldn't break his grip by force. 'I'm listening,' she said.

'You remember when I helped you with Connie's grave, what I said, about being stupid, I meant it. What I did at the cove was stupid, cruel, I'm sorry, I really am.'

'You've told me, I want to go now,' said Lucy.

'I haven't finished.' There was anger in his voice as if a flare had been let off and immediately extinguished. 'There aren't a lot of people here, Lucy, and you are one who I really respect. I can't change what's happened but is there some way we could at least be friendly. I mean, we're next door to each other.'

'It's not so simple for me, Stuart. If I hadn't been able to stop you, how far would you have gone?' She turned her head and looked him straight in the eye. He couldn't hold the accusation in her gaze and looked away. 'You see, it's a matter of trust, Stuart. Why should I trust you?'

Lucy saw his fingers begin to relax their grip and she went to push past him. But he redoubled his hold.

'Twice a week I go out hunting, risking my life. I've been injured, not seriously, not so you'd notice, but it could have been. It's only a matter of an inch or so for a blade or an arrow to kill instead of a harmless flesh wound. I do this again and again. And every time I do it, I think to myself, Lucy will be eating this. Lucy will be stay alive because I'm risking my life. I'm not asking for anything from you, only a little politeness, see me as another human being and stop looking at me as if I'm an animal. That's all I'm asking. Think about it.'

Stuart let go of the banister picked his boxes and bag up, stepped into his room and kicked the door shut behind him.

In her room Lucy leaned against the door, heart pounding. She took the only chair in the room and propped it beneath the handle of the door, testing the door to make sure it wouldn't open.

She rummaged into the back of the wardrobe, found the old hockey stick she'd used at school, and hefted it in her hands. It might have been heavier, but it would have to do. The tape on the handle showed the stick's age, fraying and grubby. The hook had a couple of splinters. She leaned it against her bedside table, lay on the bed and practised grabbing the stick and whacking it at the air above her body.

Chapter 44

The hedgerows greened, and the families turned their hands to earthing up potatoes and preparing canes for beans. In the two months since Ben and Stuart had brought home the first meat, Lucy had become adept at its preparation. Initial reluctance at dealing with human flesh had given way to acceptance and finally economy. She and Faye eked as many meals as possible from a single contributor.

In April the spring onions, sown in January, had grown into a small forest of thin green needles. Lucy thinned them, placing each tiny stalk she pulled into an old plastic tub.

She hummed a tune while making her way to the kitchen to meet Faye.

'We're not reduced to eating grass now, are we?' said Faye.

'Close your eyes,' said Lucy. She rubbed a stalk under Faye's nose.

'Onions! God, I'd forgotten about onions. They're a bit small though.'

'It's early yet, these are thinnings. We'll add them to the meal today, see if anyone notices.'

The meat, chopped small, cooked fast using little fuel.

Cracked bones allowed the marrow out, and supplements of foraged leaves and mushrooms completed the meal. They cut the onion stalks in half to release flavour into the broth. They were at the end of a carcass and the pot contained small bones, parts of rib and upper vertebrae.

'I can smell the onions,' said Faye leaning over the pot, breathing in the steam as if it could feed her by smell alone. She took a taste from the wooden spoon. 'It's delicious, I can hardly wait.'

'Let me taste,' said Lucy. Faye relinquished the spoon. 'It is, isn't it? It's ages since I've tasted onion. And there'll be more, they'll grow bigger and bigger, until we have whole onions floating in the broth, along with beans and peas and carrots and—'

'Stop, stop,' said Faye. 'I can't stand it, I'm starving, and I have to feed two and you're making my mouth water.'

'So's mine.'

The two women laughed together; the hope they shared made manifest in a handful of thin green stalks.

When the call to eat went out everyone wolfed their bowl of broth as if it might disappear before them. Lucy tried to watch them, to see if anyone noticed the new ingredient, but she lost her concentration when the first spoonful entered her mouth. She focussed solely on eating. Like many others she found a bone in her bowl. It was a vertebra. Her teeth made light work of the few strands of meat clinging to the processes, and her tongue investigated the foramen. When all else was finished she sucked it dry.

Lucy looked up from her bowl, still holding the bone between her hands, and caught Faye smiling at her.

'That was so good,' said Faye.

'It was,' said Lucy, looking about the room at the ragged people, at the black fingernails, the scrawny beards of the men, the straggling, rat-tailed hair on the women. The noise and concentration of eating fell away as each inspected other's bowls, in case of forgotten fragments. Many looked in envy at Emily, with her extra portion, trying to hold Adam with one arm and protect her meal with the other.

Lucy looked at the bone in her hands. Yesterday, and all the previous days she could remember, at this point she would feel regret and longing for the next meal, but holding the bone her mind splintered, her thoughts cast adrift. What have we become? What am I holding? This was a person, now they are only food. I don't know their name, if it was a man or a woman, or even a child. What is happening to me? Her mother's words came back to her. Yes, she had to eat, she had to survive to be any use to Lottie or Emily, and now Adam. Today she hadn't eaten only to survive, she'd eaten with pleasure, with gusto, enjoying the consequences of someone's murder. She held the bone in the palm of her hand and watched as people began to leave the kitchen. She closed her hand and slipped the bone into a pocket, vowing to remember the sacrifice this person had made so she could survive.

'Lucy, are you all right?'

She felt a hand on her shoulder and looked up to see Faye's concern.

'Yes, why?'

'You seemed to have drifted away, gone off somewhere, completely blank,' said Faye.

'No, I'm fine,' said Lucy. 'I've just woken up, that's all.'

The kitchen, the people, the meal, created a growing sense of entrapment in Lucy. She slipped out to the yard and headed for the cairn and the graves of her mother and father. She paused by the two rough graves, marked by small piles of stones, before climbing the gate and walking down The Lane.

Before the river, she turned off into the woods, along a narrow path, the carpet of last autumn's leaves sweeping her feet. She arrived at the clearing overlooking the river.

Sitting on the log, Lucy took the vertebra from her pocket, held it in her hands to examine it, turning it back and forth, intent, focused.

'I have no idea who you are. Have you left loved ones behind? Children? Are you missed? Are they looking for you, worried and concerned? What were you like? Were you kind, generous, loving? Were you nasty, brutal, selfish? Whatever you were, you died so I could live.'

Lucy cried for all the people she didn't know who had died so she could eat. She cried for their families, for their friends. She cried for the grief their deaths had caused. But mostly she cried for herself, for what she had become.

'I am a monster. I don't deserve you,' she wailed.

Exposing her thin forearm, Lucy used the bone to saw at her arm until it cut, and blood oozed. Kneeling on the ground, she excavated a hole in the forest floor with her bare hands, and in it placed the bone, letting her arm drip blood over it.

'Here, what remains of your mortality, I mark with my blood. I shall repay the sacrifice you have made. You have served me. When the time comes, I shall remember.'

A sense of reconciliation settled on her as she filled in the hole. Yes, she may need to eat this meat again, but she will never forget where it came from, and what it means to eat it.

In the weeks and months following, Lucy watched Faye's belly grow rounder, just as Emily's had. She encouraged Faye to take extra food from the pot in the kitchen before they called everyone to the meal; helping Faye's unborn child receive the nourishment it needed. As crops from the garden came into the kitchen the meals grew; there were onions, broccoli, sprouts, in the stews served. Around Lucy the people became cheerful, almost happy, as the weather warmed, and the diet improved. Still Ben and Stuart chased down prey and returned with the source of protein and fat.

From each carcass Lucy secreted a bone and carried it to the clearing to bury with the others. At every visit she would remove all the bones, count them, then recite the names she had invented for them. Finally, she would repeat her vow and sacrifice a few drops of her own blood.

After midsummer, when Faye looked like she might deliver at any time, the garden produced lettuces, radishes, early courgettes. Runner beans climbed poles and flowered, broad beans were harvested, thick bulbs of onions were pulled to give others room to grow larger. The first potatoes were dug and the space freed planted with leeks. Strawberries were in flower and the first fruits picked, blackcurrants and raspberries would follow. Apples and pears began growing fruit for the autumn, so were pumpkins.

Lucy saw this fruitfulness and wanted her heart to swell, wanted to believe in redemptive new growth, but saw it for what little it represented. They could survive on the garden alone only for a scant few months before starvation would loom again. They needed a source of protein and Ben seemed content to continue as before. There were no fish in the river, never had been, and Lucy's trips to the cove were often fruitless, returning only occasional bounty. Nor had she seen Rob since before Christmas. She feared for him, worried he had drowned whilst fishing. Despite diminishing hopes she kept faith with him, and the promise she gave her mother, and each week visited the cove.

Chapter 45

In late June, Emily took four-month-old Adam to see Sue.

'There's something not right about him,' said Emily. She held her son in the crook of her arm. 'He's got a big enough appetite, but he isn't active like Lottie was.'

'He's a boy, slower to mature aren't they,' said Sue, sitting next to Emily on one of the hay bales in the barn.

'I'm not sure. He doesn't look at me the same way Lottie did.'

'Here, let me hold him for a minute, see if I can see anything. He's only little yet, you can't expect much from him. Give him another month or two and he'll be chortling away and laughing at you,' said Sue. 'He's a lovely little baby, sweet as I've ever seen, aren't you, my love? But right now, I bet you could do with a change couldn't you.'

'Not again,' said Emily, 'give him here and I'll go clean him up.'

Sue looked at Emily's face, seeing the tiredness of sleepless nights. 'Is he keeping you awake at night?'

'And all day,' sighed Emily. 'Lottie was great, slept five hours from about four weeks old. I don't think I've had two hours together with this one.'

'Why don't I clean the little chap up and you can go and have a nap.'

'Oh, Sue, I'd love that. Do you mind, really?'

'No, it's fine, my love. I'll come by just before dinner with him. It'll give you chance for a good four hours.'

Emily dragged herself from her dream of life in London to hear the knocking on her door.

'Here, Emily, I've brought him back like I said I would. I've cleaned him and everything.' Sue held Adam in her arms while Emily pulled herself awake.

'Thanks, Sue. I was knackered.'

'Anytime you want me to look after him, I'll be happy to oblige. He's been no bother.'

Emily took the sleeping Adam in her arms. 'He certainly looks peaceful now. I wonder if it will last past dinner. It would be good to eat a meal without him wriggling away.'

Adam surprised Emily by sleeping right through the meal. He didn't wake until she returned to her room. Then he cried, a loud wail. She tried to feed him, but he wouldn't suckle.

She changed him, rocked him, cooed in his ear. Still he cried. She wrapped him in her arms and went outside to distract him. In the warm and dry early summer evening Emily walked up to the cairn with him and back towards Cleeve House. Adam cried all the way.

'What's wrong with him?' said Lucy, seeing Emily in the yard. 'He's not usually like this is he?'

'No, he's not. I don't know what's upsetting him.'

'Give him to me, I'll carry him for a bit.' It made no difference, still the baby cried. 'Is he hungry?'

'He's always hungry, aren't we all? And he's such a

guzzler, much more than Lottie was. I feel drained, literally, after he's had a go at me.'

In her room Emily settled in a chair, exposed a breast, and held her arms out for her son.

'Is there anything you want?' said Lucy.

'You wouldn't get me some water, would you? I always get thirsty once he's clamped on.'

'Sure, I'll bring it now.'

Lucy poured a glass of water from the daily jug and took it to Emily.

Emily was encouraging Adam, but he wasn't cooperating.

'He doesn't want to feed, it's not like him. Look, he's fallen asleep now.' Emily lay him in his crib. 'Maybe it's something to do with when he was with Sue.'

The two women watched the sleeping child for a few moments, the sun, low in the sky, beaming orange shafts through the window. Emily pulled a curtain across to keep the light from her son's eyes. At least now he was asleep she could have an adult conversation.

'I never understood what you did in the States,' said Emily.

Lucy laughed. 'It seems an age ago now. The most utter useless thing you could think of in today's world. I used to be a consultant in cyber security.'

Emily joined her laughter. 'I bet it paid well.'

'It did, I earned a lot of money, and it did have a use for me at the end.'

'How?'

'When the rumours started about the flood it panicked everyone. Palo Alto is low lying and was bound to be hit. There were no seats on any flights. I hacked the BA system and booked myself a business class flight to Heathrow.'

'That's pretty damn cool.'

'It didn't feel like it. I was waiting for a hand on my collar all the way through customs and over the Atlantic. At least I'm here now, but sometimes I feel useless.'

'You're not. You're so organised. I would never have thought about sowing and planting stuff early. Think where we'd be without the vitamins in those greens of yours. Even worse off than we are.'

'Look, I think he's waking up.'

Adam grizzled and his eyes flickered open, he cried again. Emily picked him up and tried to feed him.

'There's something not right. Does he feel hot?'

Lucy felt his forehead. 'I'm not sure, maybe a little warm.'

'He's still not feeding, it's too long now. I'm worried. Fetch Sue for me, will you? She better not have given him something while she's had him.'

'He was fine when he was with me, right as ninepence,' said Sue. 'But you're right, he doesn't look too well now. Maybe he's just tired out.'

'You didn't give him anything when he was with you, did you?' said Emily.

'No, course I didn't. What could I have given him? I couldn't even give him a crust. Has he got any teeth yet?'

'Maybe that's it, maybe he's teething,' said Emily. She licked a finger as clean as she could before slipping it into Adam's mouth, running it over his gums.

'I can feel the teeth there, they may be breaking through. Would teething cause a temperature? I don't remember it with Lottie.'

'Mine had red cheeks when they were coming through, chewed on me something rotten they did,' said Sue.

'Adam doesn't have red cheeks. If anything, he looks pale.

213

Are you sure you didn't give him something?'

'Look, I already told you. I haven't given him anything. The little chap just lay on the straw slumbering the whole time. I don't know why you have such a problem with him.'

'Something's not right,' said Emily.

'That's what you said when you brought him to me. Maybe it's new mum worries, all those disturbed nights and what have you,' said Sue.

'You think I should ignore it?'

'What else can you do?'

'I don't know, that's why I asked you here. I'm worried about him, and I don't know what to do.' Emily's rising voice and flashing eyes spat accusation at Sue.

'It's not Sue's fault,' said Lucy, 'she's only trying to help.'

'How old is he now, four months?' said Sue.

'Don't you remember, you were there. It's seventeen weeks and three days ago he was born,' said Emily.

'I don't see that I can do anything more to help him. I'm sorry if it's not good enough for you. I've had sick babies myself. I think it's probably best if I go.' Sue turned to Lucy. 'You know you can call on me if I can help.'

'Fat lot of use she was,' said Emily after Sue had left. 'Look at him, what am I going to do?'

Adam gave a short wail and clamped his mouth closed. His eyes tight shut.

'Feel him,' said Emily, 'he's really hot.'

'Does he need a drink?' said Lucy.

'I've tried to feed him. He won't. There's something seriously wrong.' Emily stood up, cradling her son in her arms. 'Come on, baby, what's the matter, drink something.' She offered her breast to the child again, but he turned his head away as if finding it difficult to breathe.

'He's too hot, he's burning.' Emily began to take the clothes off the child. Pulling his arms from the tiny jacket he wore, taking off his leggings.

Lucy caught his hand as Adam's arm fell. 'His hand feels cold to me,' she said.

'That can't be, feel his head, his neck.'

Lucy ran her hand over the infant's head. 'It does feel hot.'

'I don't know what's wrong, I don't know what to do.'

'Maybe if you lay him down, he'll cool down a bit,' said Lucy.

'You're right, maybe he will.' Emily lay him down in the middle of her bed and sat and watched him. His breathing laboured, she could hear him wheezing, struggling to take a breath.

'What's wrong, baby, what do you need, give me a clue.'

Adam gave another wail and shuddered and shivered before his arms and legs spasmed as a convulsion overtook him.

'What's happening to him?' said Lucy.

'I don't know, I don't know.'

'What are those spots on his legs?'

'He didn't have those before; I don't know what they are. Lucy, I'm frightened. What's happening to my baby?'

The two women stared helplessly at the suffering infant laying on the bed. The convulsion ceased and Adam vomited bile and began to choke.

Emily turned him over, wiping the vomit away and clearing his mouth so he could breathe. The child didn't respond to her, didn't open his eyes to her voice. Didn't react as Emily's tears splashed onto his head.

The rash extended behind his legs. Emily stroked his head and felt a protrusion of the fontanelle at the crown. She wailed. 'Feel here, Lucy.'

Lucy's hand swept over the infant's head. 'What does it

mean?'

'I don't know.' Emily's distraught face spoke as loud as the cry that escaped her.

Emily sat on her bed cradling her son. Sue, summoned again by a distraught Lucy, said, 'I haven't never seen nothing like it before.'

'Then you may as well fuck off, you useless cow,' said Emily.

Sue shook her head and left without a word.

'Why did I leave him with her?' wailed Emily.

For the next four hours she cradled him, his breath weakening, convulsions wracking his tiny body, withering him away, taking his life force with them.

Chapter 46

They buried Adam next to the grandparents he never knew, on a day which dared to dress a clear blue sky with a bright sun. Only Lucy, Ben and Lottie accompanied Emily, the Reevers forbidden from attending. Nothing Sue said could stop Emily from blaming her.

Ben carried the body, tightly wrapped in a fragment of waterproof blue tarpaulin, to the shallow grave and lay him in the bottom. Emily cried throughout as Ben wordlessly shovelled earth onto the tiny corpse.

'Why are you crying, Mummy,' said Lottie.

'Because your little brother is dead.'

'But he was only very small and didn't do much.'

'But he was a lovely baby.'

'He couldn't even talk or walk. Like I can. Am I lovely?'

'Ben, can you take Lottie please,' said Emily through her tears.

'Come with me, my lovely Lottie, Mummy doesn't understand it's the living who are important.'

'Mummy's being silly again,' said Lottie as she took her father's outstretched hand.

'He's stealing her,' wailed Emily to Lucy after they'd gone.

'You're still her mother, he can't ever break that bond,' said Lucy.

'He's doing his damndest, the bastard.'

Connie's words rang in Lucy's ears alongside Emily's. Lucy took hold of Emily's arm and said, 'I'll do everything I can to help you, Em, everything.'

'He's your brother,' said Emily, throwing Lucy's hand off. 'I wish I'd never met him, never had anything to do with the bloody Marchand family.'

They stood in silence, at the graveside, for half an hour.

'You may as well go back to the house,' said Emily.

'Aren't you coming too?'

'No, I need to stay here. Alone.'

Emily remained at the graveside of her little boy until the sound of the day's meal was rung. She turned away from the grave and walked down The Lane to the kitchen.

'No extra for you,' said Ben handing her bowl back to Emily. 'You're only feeding yourself now.'

'Does it mean we all get a bit more?' said Sue.

Ben's look demolished her. 'No, Faye's pregnant; she'll be getting the extra.'

'Feeding another of his bastards,' whispered Sue to Andy.

'If you have something to say, spit it out,' said Ben, 'or you can piss off, whichever you like.'

'I'm not complaining,' said Sue. 'The lass is pregnant; she needs the extra.'

'You have to shut it, Sue. If you carry on it might be you in the pot,' Andy murmured.

'This is the last of the meat,' said Lucy handing Ben his bowl.

'Stuart, it looks like we'll be going out tonight.'

'Again? It's getting harder to find prey,' said Stuart.

'Hear this, everyone, "It's getting harder to find prey" he said. Remember who it is who's keeping you all alive.'

For the first time Ben and Stuart came back empty handed from a night's hunting. The day's meal was what could be ravaged from the garden, doubtful greens plucked from the hedgerows, and dubious mushrooms found in the woods and fields.

Only Emily, wracked with grief, didn't notice. In the two days since Adam had died, Emily spent the first part of each morning crying at his graveside.

The third morning after Adam's death Emily again stood alone by the side of his small grave and cried. After shedding tears, she turned to leave. Hunger had weakened her. She stumbled and fell. Her arm, stretched to cushion her fall, landed on her child's grave, and plunged elbow deep into the soil. Emily let out a cry of distress, but her arm did not meet the body of her child, nor the tarpaulin it had been wrapped in.

She pulled her arm out and looked closely at the grave. The small pile of rocks she had built at the head were disturbed, fallen over, scattered. Had she done it when she fell? She couldn't recall feeling the stones. And the soil, it was loose everywhere. Had it always been so?

Emily found an old piece of wood to help her hands dig the soil from the grave. Ben's voice came back to her. "It only needs to be shallow, that's why he's wrapped in the tarp." But the tarpaulin wasn't there, and neither was her son.

She screamed as she ran to the house. Screamed as she tore up the stairs. Screamed as she battered on his locked door with her fists. 'You bastard, you complete bastard. How could you do this, your own son.'

The door swung open, and Ben stood there, filling the frame. 'What do you want?'

Behind him Emily could see Lottie sitting on his bed, watching her. 'You know,' she screamed, 'you know what you've done. You're evil, a monster. You're not fit to have Lottie here. Will you eat her next?'

Ben reached out and grabbed both her wrists, shaking her. 'Calm down, stop being hysterical. What are you talking about?'

'The grave, you've stolen him, Adam, your own son.' Emily's voice shrieked but weakened as she spent her strength struggling against Ben's grip.

'I don't know what you're talking about, show me. Lottie, you stay here, you'll be fine… I'll be back soon.' Ben pulled the door behind him and pushed Emily towards the stairs. 'Take me there, let me see.'

'Wait, wait, what about Lottie? Who's taking care of her?'

'Lottie is fine. I don't want her witnessing your hysterics. Go on.' And Ben pushed her to the top of the stairs.

Emily turned to the steps, fearing Ben might push her down. She didn't see Lucy and Stuart appear on the landing; she didn't see the shake of the head Ben gave Stuart as she preceded Ben down the stairs.

'Come on, Emily, show me what you're screaming about,' said Ben, following her out of the door.

On the landing Lucy moved to follow them. Stuart stepped in front of her, blocking her path to the stairs. 'I don't think you'll be needed, Lucy,' he said.

Lucy paused for a moment, her palms suddenly sweaty, her face hot. She felt herself shrinking under Stuart's glare. No, she would not let this happen, not in her family's house. Heart beating hard, fast, her single eye wide open, she forced herself to speak. 'Get out of my way. This is a family affair and nothing to do with you, Stuart Reever.' She pushed past him, waiting for him to grab her, not knowing what she would do if he did.

'I'm only trying to help; it won't do any good following them.'

By the time he'd finished Lucy was down the stairs and out of the door chasing her brother and Emily up to the cairn.

Lucy could see the two of them talking. She could hear Ben shouting, 'And you think I did it? You think I stole the body of my own son? You really are a sick woman if you think I could have done this.'

Ben caught Lucy's eye. 'Hi, Lucy. I'm sorry, Emily's not very well.'

'It's not me who's sick, it's you.'

'You're mad if you think I did this. I want to know who it was as much as you. I'll kill the bastard when I find out.'

'You already know, you did it, you—'

Emily's scream of accusation stopped dead as Ben's palm connected with her cheek, sending her spinning to the ground beside the grave. Ben stood over her. 'I'm only going to say this once more. It wasn't me. And whoever it was will pay for this. But you? I can't stand the sight of you anymore.' And to Lucy he said, 'See, she thinks I've dug the body of my own son out of his grave and eaten him. I'm not putting up with this anymore. Only a few days ago I dug his grave, I wrapped his body and carried it myself, and now she thinks this of me. Can you believe it?'

'No, Ben, I don't think you're capable of that. You can do many things, but I don't think that would be one of them.'

Ben's shoulders slumped. 'I can't bear to speak to Emily again. I'm going to find out who's done this, and when I do, they'll pay.'

Chapter 47

On her regular visits to Goff's Cove Lucy always tied the ribbon around the wooden post, now bleached grey by the weather. Her heart held as little hope of seeing Rob as the ribbon had colour. Half a year had passed since she last saw him. She worried something horrible had happened to him.

Once at the cove she recovered the hidden rods, baited, and cast them, then gathered driftwood.

It took an hour of patience before she had a bite on either of the lines. The fish, too tiny to eat, she used as bait. She had cast and reset the rods when she saw a flash of sail out to sea. It disappeared in the swell; reappearing attached to a small boat. The wind would drive it along the coast, but the sail turned and pushed the little open boat towards the cove.

Lucy couldn't make out a figure but felt the eyes of the unseen pilot upon her and shivered. Should she hide? She wouldn't have time to stow away the rods and she couldn't allow them to be stolen. She checked her boot, making sure her knife was handy, and retreated from the coastline preparing to run. The boat bobbed in the water, struggling to breach the waves beating against it.

Then she heard her name. 'Lucy! Lucy!'

Her heart leapt when she heard Rob's voice from over the sea. There he was, standing, wobbling, in the little boat as he lowered the sail, then hauling hard on oars.

Lucy ran to the water's edge, smiling, waving, excited. Finally, he made landfall, and she embraced him on the edge of the ocean. Together they pulled the little boat away from the water's drag.

'It's good to see you. I wasn't sure you'd be here, I haven't been up to the post.' Rob's words tumbled from him.

'I'm here nearly every week. I've been worried about you, thought something had happened. You look... thin, but great.'

'You're not exactly plump yourself,' laughed Rob, 'and something has happened to me. I've got a boat, isn't she grand.'

Rob's grand boat might have spent its previous life on a park lake. A clinker-built rowing boat with thwarts for four and a short mast holding the small sail, now reefed. A pile of netting lay between the thwarts.

'Let's eat, look,' said Rob and from under the netting he pulled a large fish.

'I never know what to do with dogfish. They're a tough one to skin,' said Lucy.

'There's a knack, watch.' Rob cut a couple of small nicks in the skin near the head and with his knife freed a small flap of skin. He rummaged in his coat and pulled out a pair of pliers. He clamped the jaws around the flap of skin and holding the fish's head in his other hand, pulled backwards.

'You've got to have a strong grip,' he said as the pliers slipped their hold. After three pulls the skin was off.

While the fish toasted, Rob said, 'How's Mum?'

Lucy looked away a moment, then turned back to face her

brother. 'Oh Rob,' she said, 'I don't know where to begin.'

'What's wrong, has something happened to Mum?'

While Lucy told Rob about Connie's death and burial, she watched him. Saw his brows knit together, his mouth turn down, his eyes fail to blink away a tear. Until finally she had told it all. Rob's grim face told of more than grief.

'Is that what you're eating now? People?'

'There isn't anything, Rob, what are we supposed to do? Starve? What do you eat?'

'Fish,' said Rob, 'lots of it, and the occasional game that's hard to find. And we're growing stuff.'

'I hardly catch any fish here, two or three maybe all day, and that's with two rods. Many times, I haven't caught anything.'

'You wouldn't, you need a boat if you're to catch enough. It's why we're on the coast. What about Emily? I expect she's had her baby by now.'

Lucy told Ben about Emily's baby, but she baulked at telling him about the grave being disturbed. She felt guilty and didn't know why; she hadn't robbed the grave, but someone had, and nobody seemed interested now, except poor Emily. 'She visits the grave every day. Spends hours there. It's so sad,' she said.

'I never really got on with Emily, but I wouldn't wish that on anyone,' said Rob. 'Poor woman. She should have been at Selmouth. We have a proper doctor with us now. She turned up about two months ago and has already saved one life; and fixed a broken arm.'

'You haven't asked about Faye,' said Lucy.

Rob looked out to sea. 'I do think about her sometimes,' said Rob, 'she's Ben's now, he can keep her.'

'She doesn't belong to anyone,' flashed Lucy. 'You men, sometimes you're such arrogant shites.'

'Okay, okay. I didn't mean it to come out like that. Has she had her baby yet? She can't have, it's too soon.'

'She hasn't, but it won't be long. You might be the father.'

'Lucy, we've talked about this. I'm sure I'm not. She isn't saying I am, is she?'

'She isn't saying Ben is either. Poor Marcus thinks it's his.'

'Marcus Reever? He's only a kid. Why does he think he's involved?'

'Why do you think? After Ben threw her out, she went to stay with Marcus. There must be something between them for him to think it's his baby. And he's totally besotted by her.'

'Ben threw her out? After what he put me through. He's a bastard.'

'He likes to have things his own way, but it's mainly him keeping us all alive. I think we'd have starved long ago if he hadn't…' Lucy couldn't bring herself to finish the sentence.

Rob did it for her, 'Murdered people so you could eat them. Is that what you mean?'

'Do you think I enjoy it? Do you think for a minute I'd do this if I had a choice? Look.' Lucy rolled up her sleeve and showed Rob the row of scars running up her arm, some old, some newer. 'See, one for every person who's kept me alive and who I owe penance to.'

Rob stared grim faced at the mutilated arm of his sister. 'Lucy, you don't have to do this to yourself, you could…'

'I could what?'

'You could come with me. Both Mum and Dad are gone now. What's to stop you from leaving?'

'I'd love to come, I really would, I want to come, but Rob, I promised Mum.'

'Promised Mum what? You'd stay and eat people?'

'That's not what I mean, and you know it. Don't make it

225

any harder for me than it is. I don't want to… '

'You still do it. At least eating fish we can be cheerful about it. You don't have to go back; you could just get in the boat with me.'

Three paces and she could be in the boat and leaving the horror her life had become. She could be starting a new life in a community that valued its members. And Rob was there, the brother who sang her songs, played games with her, made her laugh. Ben may have been her protector when she was young, but Rob had been her entertainer, her comforter. Her mother's voice echoed in her head, "I want you to be there for Lottie and Emily". And her promise to Faye to be at the birth of her child.

'I can't, Rob. I want to and I can't. I promised Mum.' Lucy's head swung from side to side, her eye pleading with Rob.

'She'd understand if you had to break a promise. She wouldn't mind. She won't even know.'

'I would. I'd know. And I couldn't live with myself. Maybe later, when things are settled, when Faye's had her baby, when Lottie is older.'

'I can't risk her in the boat if she's nearly due. After Faye's had the baby, if she wants to leave Cleeve House, let me know. She can come and stay at Selmouth, she'd be welcome.'

'That's kind of you, I'll let her know. I like Faye. I think she'll really want to. Who wouldn't want to get out of there?'

'She can't stay with me though, I'm… There'll be somewhere else for her. She's young and healthy, it's what we need.'

'Did I hear a bit of hesitation there, Rob? Is there another person in your life?'

Rob smiled at Lucy's teasing. 'Maybe, I'll tell you more next time.'

'You can't leave it like that. Come on, who is she? What's she like? What's her name?'

'It's all a bit new, Lucy. I really don't want to say anymore right now, it might not work out.'

'I'll tell Faye about your offer if you promise to tell me more about your mysterious woman friend.'

Rob laughed. 'Okay, I'll tell you more next time, I'll know by then. And tell Faye I'll take her in the boat. Instead of a two-day hike it's about four hours if you get the tides right.'

'Does this mean I'll see you more often?'

'Maybe, I'm getting better at reading the sea, learning a lot from an old salt. Talking of tides though, this one has turned. I'll need to be going soon. I have to ride it up the coast and get home before it turns again.'

'Do you have to go already?'

The tide was flowing now. Rob watched it with a keen eye.

'Yes, I do. Come with me.'

'I can't. Not yet. There are people who need me.'

'The offer will still be there next time I see you. Now I must go, or I'll be stuck here until tomorrow.'

Lucy felt his arms embrace her and he almost lifted her off her feet. She wondered if he would throw her in the boat and sail off with her. And she wondered if she would do anything to stop him. She hugged him back and helped him launch the little boat. He jumped in to wrestle the tide until he'd manoeuvred into the open sea. Lucy watched him unfurl the little sail and the wind and the current sped him away.

Chapter 48

'I have something to tell you, but you can't tell anyone else, not even Marcus,' said Lucy when she next saw Faye.

'I can keep a secret from Marcus.'

Lucy told Faye about seeing Rob and what she knew about Selmouth. 'And Rob said you'd be welcome there if you wanted to go. After you've had the baby.'

'That's fantastic, I'd love it. It would be good for my baby not to... you know. I didn't think Rob would have anything to do with me again. I was horrible to him. You're lovely for thinking of us.'

'I didn't ask him to do this, it all came from Rob.'

'And they have food there?'

'Rob says it's mainly fish, and they have a doctor.'

'You're thinking about my baby, aren't you?'

'Yes, after what happened to Adam.'

'What about Marcus, can he go too?'

'I don't know. Would you want Marcus to go with you?'

'Why wouldn't I? Don't you think he'd make a good dad?'

'He would, but...'

'But what, Lucy? Don't you think he's the father of my

baby? He does. Why do you think he's convinced? He may be a bit of a pushover, but he's not totally stupid. And does it really matter who the father is so long as they look after and love the baby?'

'You're right,' said Lucy. 'Next time I see Rob I'll make sure it's okay for Marcus if it's what you want. Please don't tell him yet. It will get me into all sorts of trouble.'

'I guess Ben doesn't know you're seeing him.'

'No, and he mustn't. You saw what he did to Rob.'

'It's okay, your secret's safe with me. And I really appreciate the invite from Rob. I'd love to get away from here. Why can't I go now?'

'It's over thirty miles away. You'd have to walk and there's nothing to eat on the way. Rob says he'll take you in his boat, but it's only tiny. If you end up in the water, you could lose your baby and your life.'

'It'll be fantastic to start a new life with my baby.'

'You seem pretty relaxed about this baby, despite what happened to poor little Adam.'

'I know. I don't know why, but I feel sure my baby will be fine. There'll be nothing wrong with him at all and he'll grow up to be really lovely.'

'Suppose it's a girl?'

'The same. To be honest I don't really care so long as they grow up happy. I think it's why I'm glad about Rob's invite. Selmouth sounds great.'

'Yes, it does.'

'Are you going?'

Lucy looked at Faye, saw the enthusiasm for life bursting from her, saw the excitement of a new beginning both in her pregnant belly and in Selmouth. And she was jealous. Jealous of the freedom to decide Faye had, jealous of her lack of concern, part of her was even jealous of her being pregnant.

She watched as Faye frowned, wrapped her arms around her stomach and gave a grunt.

'A little contraction,' she said. 'It won't be long now, maybe tonight or tomorrow.'

'Are you scared?' said Lucy.

'No, I'm excited.'

Chapter 49

In the hovel, Marcus feigned busyness while Faye stood, sat, lay down on her side then her back, stood again. She held her pregnant belly in her arms while standing, stroked it while laying down. Occasionally she'd give a grunt at the Braxton Hicks contractions.

'You okay, Faye?' said Marcus. 'Comfortable enough?'

'Of course I'm not fucking comfortable. Who would be with a great lump like this stuck on their belly?'

'I was only asking. I don't suppose it'll be long now.'

'You don't fucking suppose? And what, exactly, do you know about it? It could be today, it could be tomorrow, it could be in ten minutes. I've no idea.'

'Look, I'm sorry. Do you want to be alone? Do you want me to leave you for a bit?'

'Yes, go, give me some fucking peace.'

Marcus stepped out of the shack into the bright June sun. The green of the hedgerows cheered him, another month and there might be blackberries. He didn't talk about it to Faye, or about his feelings. She had become grumpier and grumpier as the baby had grown inside her.

Her moods swung back and forth like a kid's swing, and he always seemed to get the blame for them. She went to bed grumpy and woke worse. She seemed to resent that Marcus would just fall asleep and not even notice when she was up in the night, except when she deliberately woke him to fetch her something. That happened most nights now, though he soon fell asleep again. Faye told him she didn't sleep all night. Marcus couldn't say he didn't believe her, even though he didn't. He'd tried it once and she'd been incandescent, accusing him of not understanding women, of being selfish, of being useless. That had hurt, so he kept a tight rein on his tongue, kept his thoughts to himself; what did he know about women, especially pregnant women?

He found he'd crossed the field, away from Cleeve House to the gate they had climbed the first time Faye had shown him the hovel. A day etched deep into his soul; the rain, the sodden clothes, the tiny shelter with its hay bale bed, and Faye, naked and warm, beside then beneath him.

It was too soon to go back, so he climbed the gate and made his way through the woods, heading for the clearing where they'd first met, running the movie of his memories while he walked.

Through long habit his footsteps in the forest were gentle and smooth. Since he first discovered the animals living in the woods, he tried not to disturb them, instead watching, marvelling at their hidden lives. He'd seen deer in the years before the flood. They'd vanished, eaten he supposed, along with any mammal which would fit the pot. Still there were shrews, mice about and if he stayed still and silent, they would show themselves. It wasn't forest animals he heard near the clearing, but a woman's voice.

As Marcus approached, he saw Lucy, kneeling on the ground, her voice somewhere between singing and reciting.

He couldn't make out the words but saw no one else. Remembering his embarrassment when he first saw Faye in this same spot, he deliberately trod on a stick, broke it with a crack, coughed, and brushed a branch as he made his way into the clearing.

Lucy's head went up and her voice stilled at the first sound, scanning the woods. Marcus called out to her.

'Hello, Lucy. I don't usually find anyone here.'

Lucy scrabbled to her feet, pulling her sleeve over her arm. Marcus saw blood dripping from her fingers.

'Are you all right? Is that blood?' he said.

'I'm fine, it's only a scratch. You surprised me. I thought I was alone.'

'I often come here, it's where I first met Faye.'

'I didn't know. How is she?'

'To be honest, she's really grumpy. I can't seem to do anything right. I do my best, but it's never good enough.'

'Were you looking for me because the baby's coming?'

'Not yet. She told me I had no idea what was happening, and it could be tomorrow or next week or in ten minutes.'

'Ten minutes? Was she serious?'

'No, I don't think so. Although sometimes it's difficult to tell with Faye.'

'Maybe we should go and make sure she's okay.'

'She told me to leave her in peace, but it may be all right to go back now.'

'Come on,' said Lucy heading out of the clearing.

'You'll have to climb the gate,' said Marcus.

'I can manage a gate. You go first.'

Following Marcus meant she didn't have to speak to him, answer any questions. She would have to find another place for the bones, more secret. Lost in her thoughts, she didn't notice when they had left the forest. Marcus had stopped by the gate.

He pointed. 'Look, there's the shelter.'

'Yeah, I know, I did live here most of my life.'

'Course, sorry. Do you want a hand over?'

'I'm not an old woman,' she said, climbing the gate. Maybe she was to Marcus's eyes. Much older than Faye.

'Where the hell have you been, I think it's starting, can you get...'

'I'm here,' said Lucy, stepping into the hovel behind Marcus.

Faye stood leaning against the bed Marcus had built, holding her stomach, groaning.

'Lucy, thank God you're here. I think it's started. I've been up all night with contractions, now they're getting stronger.'

Lucy had no idea what to do. 'How often do they come?' She remembered Sue asking Emily.

'I don't know, there's one coming now.' Faye groaned and held her stomach as the contraction overtook her body.

'When they come close together, we'll send Marcus to fetch Sue,' said Lucy.

'I don't like Sue. That's why I asked you to be here.'

'She knows a lot more than I do, she's had babies herself and she was great with Emily...' her voice trailed off. Memories of Adam flooded her head, please don't let it be like that, she begged to whatever deity might be listening.

'Yeah, I'm sure she was, and look what happened to her baby,' said Faye.

'Okay, I'll do the best I can, but if I feel out of my depth, I might want to ask her to help.'

'She's my mum, Faye. She'd love to help with her grandson,' said Marcus.

'I don't want her here. I have...' Faye was overtaken by a contraction as Marcus and Lucy shared looks.

'That was a doozy,' said Faye. 'Anyway, who's having this baby, me right! And I don't want her here. She can come and see the baby after it's born. I don't want her faffing around me.'

Marcus paced about the tiny shelter long faced, until Faye could stand it no longer.

'Will you stop wandering about. Do something useful. Get some wood for the fire, or something.'

'Okay, okay, I've already got loads, I'll get some more.' Marcus went to leave.

'Don't go too far, Marcus,' said Lucy.

Chapter 50

Throughout the afternoon Faye's contractions became more frequent until only a few minutes separated them.

'How long does this take?' asked Faye. 'I'm knackered.'

'I don't know. It was quick for... some people, yet I've heard it can be twenty-four hours or more for others.'

'Twenty-four hours! I'll be dead on my feet. Can I speed it up some way? Do I need to push him out?'

'No, no,' a trace of panic in Lucy's voice. 'You're not supposed to push until you're fully dilated. You can injure yourself, or your baby.'

'When will that be? How can I tell?'

'I don't know. Like I say, I've never had a baby, that's why...' She waited while Faye had another contraction. 'Why I think it would be a good idea if Sue was here.'

'Alright, send for Sue, but before she gets here, I have to tell you something.'

'What?'

'I can't tell you while Marcus is here, send him for his mum, try and get him to take his time.'

Lucy opened the door and beckoned Marcus inside.

'It's not quite time yet. Faye's decided she would like your mum to come and help. Can you go and fetch her?'

'I'll be back in a couple of minutes.'

'There's no need to hurry, let Sue get anything she thinks she might need. And go to the house and get some more water on your way.'

After Marcus had left Lucy shut the door and said, 'Okay, what do you want to tell me?'

Faye's contractions were coming quickly now. Barely a minute between them.

'There's something you need to know,' she gasped out before losing herself to her body's insistence.

Lucy remained still, watching waiting, not knowing what else to do. Faye began talking again.

'It's about your brother.'

'Ben?'

'Yes. He, I saw him...' Faye was again racked by her body. 'God, I never knew it would be like this,' she said as the pain subsided.

'You can tell me later, it doesn't matter. You're having a baby, that's what's important.'

'I must tell you. I've been going to tell you for ages. I saw him, at the bridge...'

Was Faye delirious with the pain? Then she screamed, and Lucy watched, trancelike, helpless, as Faye began to heave and try to push her baby from her body.

Faye screamed again, surely Sue must hear, come running, but there was no sign of her yet. Lucy watched, saw the head crown and found words of encouragement for Faye.

'I can see the baby's head, not long, Faye, a big push now.'

Faye heard and Lucy caught the baby as he was born. With her hands on the slippery child Lucy felt a connection, a link that could never be broken. Something about this child, not much bigger than her two splayed hands holding him, touched her soul. Despite all she had been through, despite all that had happened, here was hope.

She smiled and laughed at Faye. 'It's a boy, he's gorgeous,' she said, and handed the child into Faye's outstretched arms, the cord still attached.

Faye looked at the child, marvelled at the mewling coming from him, snuggled him into her, offered her breast to him.

'Does he have a name yet?' said Lucy.

'He does, don't you,' smiled Faye. 'Lucy, meet Quinn.'

'Quinn, a lovely name.'

'It means "Wise". I hope he'll grow up wiser than his mother, or father.'

'I think you're pretty wise,' said Lucy.

'No, I'm not. I'm just a scared little girl, that's why I've never told you about your brother.'

'You mean he's the father? I'd sort of guessed.'

'No, I mean what he did to your dad.'

'To my dad?' Lucy's face wrinkled in confusion. 'What are you talking about?'

'On the bridge, the day of the fighting. I saw him.'

'He was there, he said he was.'

'Yes, I know, and I saw what he did, Lucy, he pushed your dad, pushed him into the river.' Faye's face creased in pain. 'I have to push again, don't I? Get rid of the placenta.'

'Oh God, yes, I'd forgotten.'

Lucy remembered Sue tugging the cord to help deliver the placenta and she began to pull. Her head was spinning, Ben pushed her father. Faye must be confused, he wouldn't, would he? Lucy answered her own unasked question. Ben's cruelty to Rob, his betrayal of Emily, his callousness to their mother and now his desertion of Faye.

'It was deliberate, I'm sure. I've been frightened of him

ever since,' said Faye, 'always done whatever he asked. If he could kill his own father, what could he do to me, so I... oh, it hurts.'

Lucy let go of the cord. 'We may have to wait for Sue. I don't really know what I'm doing here. And Ben, he really...'

'Okay if you want, but I think it's coming now. I can feel it slipping out. I feel dizzy.'

Lucy looked, and yes, there was the placenta, and so was a lot of blood.

'Faye, are you all right? Jesus, you're bleeding, there's loads of it.'

Blood from Faye soaked, spread, and began to pool on the bed covers.

Faye turned glazed eyes on Lucy. 'What? I... I'm...' her head slumped and her body went limp. Her grip on Quinn slackened and he began to fall. Lucy reached up and grabbed him before he fell to the floor. She tried to staunch the flow of Faye's lifeblood with any rag she could get hold of. A shirt lying nearby, grabbed and pressed between Faye's legs, soaked through in seconds and blood still oozed around Lucy's panicked fingers. Holding the baby in one hand and trying to close the faucet of Faye's blood with the other, Lucy froze as the horror before her became real.

The flow of blood began to slow.

'I think it's stopping, Faye; it's slowing down. Faye... Faye!' This last a yell torn from Lucy's throat as she realised she held a motherless child in her arms.

Chapter 51

Lucy cradled baby Quinn and let herself cry as questions and guilt flooded her panicking head. Whatever the answers it was all her fault. She was to blame for Faye's death. Ben murdered her father; she was sure of it now. But she had neglected the life of this young woman. Had she torn the placenta from her, caused the haemorrhage? And in her arms she held an infant with no mother, an infant who was crying, an infant who was hungry.

The door to the hovel opened to Sue and Marcus.

'Oh God, what's happened?' said Sue taking in the scene, nostrils flaring at the iron in the air.

'Faye!' yelled Marcus who dashed the few steps across the hovel to her side. 'He turned to Lucy. 'What's happened? What have you done?' his voice loud, stretched, hoarse, unbelieving.

His mother put an arm around him, but he shrugged it off, went to hold Faye's limp body in his arms, the shock and grief overtaking him, his voice keening 'No, no, no,' over and over.

Lucy sat holding baby Quinn crying, 'It's all my fault, I'm

a fool.'

'She's haemorrhaged, love, she's bled to death.'

'I pulled the cord, I tried to help. I tried to pull the placenta. It wouldn't come, I've killed her,' she wailed.

Marcus wailed, Lucy wailed, Quinn wailed. Sue stood and looked at Faye then Marcus, then Lucy and finally at the baby. She went to try and take it, but Lucy wouldn't let go. Sue knew not to get into a tug of war, so pulled her arm back and slapped Lucy.

Lucy, stunned to silence, raised a hand to touch her reddening cheek, and looked at Sue, standing over her, watchful.

'I don't know what happened, I don't know how it happened, but I do know you,' said Sue, 'and you wouldn't have done anything to have hurt the poor girl. You have a crying new-born in your arms and if something isn't done about him soon, you'll be holding another lifeless body. Now pull yourself together.'

Lucy looked about at the bloody chaos surrounding her, at the infant in her arms.

Sue went to Marcus. She gently pushed her arms around him and pulled him away from the dead Faye. She wrapped him in a mother's embrace while he sobbed onto her shoulder. She'd never known him as happy as he'd been these last few weeks with Faye; and now it had been taken from him. She held him tight for a minute then said, 'Come here, my love, look, there's nothing you can do for Faye now. She's in a better place than this for sure. Now you have a son to think about. And if something isn't done about him soon, you'll lose the baby too. Calm down a little. There'll be all the time in the world for grief later.'

Marcus's sobs subsided under the gentle persuasion of his mother until he turned his head to look at the baby. His eyes slid away from Lucy, wouldn't meet her single sorrowful eye.

'Faye said to call him Quinn. Do you want to hold him?' said Lucy.

'Quinn,' said Marcus, cradling the baby in his arms. 'He's lovely, he's beautiful, he's gorgeous, he's…' wracking sobs of despair and delight interspersed Marcus's words as he gazed first on the new life in his arms, then on the lost life lying beside them. 'Oh God, Mum, this is all too much.'

Sue looked at his son holding the baby and tears were in her eyes too, but she held back her sobs. 'We need to do something about the mite, or he'll starve. He needs milk.'

'Milk! We don't have any, we haven't had milk for months. For milk we need a cow or a goat. Where are we going to get milk?' Lucy's despair joined Marcus's. She had killed Faye and now her beautiful baby would die, and it was all her fault.

'There's one place the baby might get milk,' said Sue.

Chapter 52

'Emily,' said Sue, answering the unasked question. 'It's barely a week since she lost Adam. If she's willing, she could feed Quinn. Marcus, give Quinn to Lucy, she has to take him to her.'

'Why me?' said Lucy.

'You're the only one here she'll listen to, my love. She won't listen to me; she thinks I made Adam to sicken. Marcus hasn't got the gift of the gab like you have. You know how Emily felt about Faye. She'll need persuading. And the sooner the better.'

'But he's my baby, my son,' said Marcus, and saying the words he stood straighter, pulled his shoulders back.

'Yes, and you want to keep him alive, don't you? Lucy will explain everything to Emily. You go too, if you want, but stay out of the room unless you're invited.'

'What about Faye?'

'More than anything she'd have wanted her baby to be all right. I'll do what I can here while you're gone. Now come on, it's been too long already.'

They wrapped the baby in the spare clothes Faye would

no longer need. Lucy snuggled him tight under her shirt before she and Marcus stepped out of the hovel.

'You go and wait in the lounge,' said Lucy.

'Quinn's my baby, remember,' said Marcus, still avoiding Lucy's face.

He blames me, she thought, and he's right to. I've killed the woman he loved.

'I remember, I'll do everything I can. I'll let you know what's happening soon.'

She knocked on Emily's door.

'What's happened to you?' said Emily, 'you look worse than you did when you'd been shot, come in.'

Lucy's clothes were soaked with Faye's blood. It hadn't seemed important. Now she looked down at herself.

'It's not my blood, Emily, it's awful, it's Faye, she's...' before she could speak Quinn made himself heard with a squawk from inside Lucy's shirt. She drew him out, still wrapped in Faye's ragged clothes.

'Emily, this is Quinn.'

'Faye's baby, she's had it?' Emily's mouth tightened; her eyebrows creased. 'Where's Faye?'

'She can't feed him, Emily, she's dead.' Lucy's look pleaded with Emily, pierced her humanity with spears of desperation. Emily's face began to soften.

Quinn began to cry, a weaker cry than Lucy recalled in the hovel. 'He's...' began Lucy.

'Hungry, yes I know, I can feel it.'

Lucy wasn't sure what she meant until she saw Emily's shirt displaying damp stains. 'Any crying baby always used to set me off when I had Lottie. Give him here,' she said, unbuttoning her shirt. 'I had reasons not to like Faye, but I didn't wish her dead.'

As Quinn nuzzled into Emily's breast Lucy began to shake. Guilt, relief, sadness, joy, anger, all swirled around her, overwhelming her senses. Lucy shook and cried while Emily murmured encouragements as she fed the new-born child.

'It must have been horrible for you,' said Emily. 'But before healthcare haemorrhages weren't uncommon, you shouldn't blame yourself.'

'It's not just Faye, Em. If anything, it's worse. It's Ben.'

'Has he finally got round to bullying you? There must be no one else left.'

Emily paused in feeding Quinn and switched him to her other breast. 'Have a go on this one too, got to keep balanced.'

'No, he's not bullying me.' Lucy looked at Emily. The baby occupied almost all her attention, her words to Lucy mere asides. She couldn't tell her about Ben now, couldn't break the bond forming between them by telling Emily the father of her daughter was a murderer. She couldn't tell anyone. Faye must have felt like this for nine months. Carrying the dreadful secret almost as long as she carried her child. Carried it in fear and solitude, not able to tell anyone until today. Now Lucy carried the burden. 'It's nothing,' she said.

'It might not work, you know,' said Emily when the baby was sated and sleepy, and Lucy had calmed. 'It's not the same as the first milk a mother produces. But it's better than nothing. I'll do what I can.'

'I'm grateful, I don't know what to say,' said Lucy, 'Marcus is outside waiting, can I bring him in?'

'Marcus? Why is he here?'

The atmosphere held a beat before Lucy responded. 'He says he's the father,' she said, into the growing silence between the two women.

Emily looked down at the child. Looked at the features of his face, recalled her own son, remembered Lottie as a babe.

'Who do you think is the father?'

'Does what I think matter? What I do know is Marcus would love him, look after him, sacrifice himself for his child. It's hard for me to say this, but I don't think I know of any other man here who would do that.'

Emily sat for a moment, rocking the baby, and gently nodding her head. 'You're right,' she said, 'I think Marcus would be a great father for Quinn. Bring him in.'

Chapter 53

The smell of Faye's blood leeched from Lucy's clothes, but it was futile to change while the body still needed her attention.

She let herself out of the house to go back to the hovel, her tread slowed by the dread waiting there.

While she walked, she searched within herself for some kind of explanation, some understanding of Ben's actions. Such a big part in her life she strove for mitigation and found none. All she found were small remembrances of Ben's lack of respect for their father, the barely hidden insults, the contempt. Had Ben seen his father's injury as an opportunity? Had it been cold blooded, premeditated? Maybe, maybe not; it didn't matter now. Now she knew, but what could she do?

Before she could answer her questions, she arrived at the hovel and heard sobbing inside.

Sue, sitting on the stool with her head in her hands, quickly stood, wiping her eyes on her sleeve as she did. Faye's body lay where Lucy had left it.

'I'm sorry, I haven't done a thing since you left, I don't

know what came over me. I just couldn't do anything.'

'It's okay, Sue. It's too much to deal with on your own anyway.'

'How's the baby? Did she take to him all right?'

'She did, he looked full and satisfied when I left.'

'And Marcus, where's he?'

'He's with them now, looking after his son.' They were the words Sue needed to hear.

'It's good of her. I always thought she was a bit stuck up.'

'She's not like that at all when you get to know her,' said Lucy.

'Do you think she'll mind if I go and see the baby sometimes, only...'

'I'm sure she won't, she'll need all the help she can get. It's going to be hard for her after her own baby... died.'

'That's what I mean. She thinks it was my fault.'

'Leave it a few days and see how things go. I'm sure Marcus will bring him to see you anyway.'

'I feel I've given him away, you know, given away my own grandson.'

Lucy looked around the mean accommodation the hovel provided; its rough stone walls held together with crumbling mortar, its crude hand-hewn wooden furniture, no water, no light save from the doorway. Finally, her eyes returned to this woman grieving for a grandson who wasn't her grandson, with the carcass of its mother a few feet away, and the air redolent of death and decay. She felt swamped, overwhelmed by the enormity of the day.

'We need to see to Faye. Why don't you go and find someone to help us with her, and get a wheelbarrow so we can get her down the path?'

Sue gazed vacantly at Lucy for a moment then came to her senses. 'Yes, I can do that. Andy will help and I'll get him to ask Stuart to bring a wheelbarrow. I'll let Ben know, he might come himself.'

Lucy's heart somersaulted. 'No, don't tell Ben, I… It will be too crowded in here. Maybe just Andy will be enough for now. Ben and Stuart will be tired from hunting. After we get the body out perhaps you could help me clear up?'

'Course I will.'

The hovel somehow seemed smaller after Sue had left, as if the walls were drawing in upon Lucy. The smell, the heat, the sight of the lifeless body, and the bed saturated with Faye's blood, all pushed into her fragile state. She resisted and resolved to act.

She opened the door and propped it with a stone, letting in fresh air. Her solitary eye, constantly drawn to the tragic figure of the young woman, could take no more; and a hastily thrown blanket served as a temporary shroud. Only minutes ago, it had been Faye, full of life and vivacity, now it was just a husk of who she had been. Lucy looked around the hovel for personal possessions of Faye, mementos for Quinn to link him to his mother.

A rough plank on a tall log made do as a bedside table and held some of the detritus of the life just gone. An empty scent bottle with a hint of eucalyptus and patchouli still in evidence, a tobacco tin, decorated with a painted mandala held nothing. Lucy took these, a legacy to give to Emily for safe keeping. They might be all the child had from its mother. A comb with strands of Faye's hair sat on the table.

This is what your life is reduced to, thought Lucy as she picked up the comb. It slipped from her fingers to the floor. She knelt to retrieve it and saw a shred of plastic tucked behind the head of the bed, wedged in. She tugged at it and pulled out a plastic bag.

The old carrier bag held a purple covered sketchbook. Gothic handwriting on the cover identified its owner as Faye. This would have to be saved for Quinn. Lucy sat on the wooden stool and began to leaf through the drawings. Some were fantastical gothic buildings inhabited by black-clad people. Others were pastoral scenes often centred around trees with gnarled, face-like bark, and branches like arms and hands. Lucy imagined Faye at college, making these drawings, showing them to friends. Turning the page, she came upon a simple pencil portrait of Rob and gasped. Faye had captured him in his best mood, his playful childishness sparkling from his eyes and mouth.

Faye's copperplate handwriting adorned every drawing with a date, and each carried her initials in florid letters. There was one of Cleeve House, changed to a gothic mansion with pointed turrets at the corners, and a tiny Rob waving from a window. Lucy couldn't help but smile at it. She turned the page again. The last entry in the sketchbook was a page of Faye's handwriting dated the 10th of December, illustrated with small line drawings.

The page began with a drawing of Faye herself in the centre of a circle of all the other people at Cleeve House, but distant from them, and while everyone else had a smile Faye's face showed a grim expression, her eyes blindfolded, her head throbbing.

I can't tell anyone. I feel alone; yet I'm surrounded by people. My secrets cannot be shared with any of them. I can't be myself amongst them. I have seen a crime of the worst kind and there is no one I can tell.

There followed a drawing of the bridge, two people stood on it, one with an arrow stuck in them.

Here's Ben and his father. There's been a horrible battle.

Attackers tried to invade. We were all scared. Ben led us to fight. We have won, and there are bodies of the enemy beyond the bridge. Ben's father is injured. They are arguing.

The next drawing showed a toppling James falling from the bridge and Ben peering over, watching him fall. Blood spurts from James' shoulder.

Ben hurt James. He pushed the arrow in him deeper; blood spurted out. Then he pushed him over the bridge. I heard James call out, but I did nothing. I was scared Ben would kill me if he knew I'd seen him.

A crowd of people were gathered in the next sketch. They were all kneeling or leaning over a prone body.

Ben climbed down to the river. I didn't hear him call for help. I think he was making sure his father was dead. When people came, then he called out. They lifted James onto the track. He was dead.

Lucy recognised the hovel in the next image.

It was only a week before the battle Ben brought me here, where I live. And it was here, on that first night we fucked. I knew he wanted to before we got here, but I wanted it too. I'm sure I got pregnant with him. Then he killed his dad, and I was too afraid to say no to him.

Then there were two drawings in the sketch book. Tiny portraits of the two brothers. Ben's rugged handsomeness tinged with cruelty, Rob's face easy going, relaxed.

I got bored with Rob, who was a bit dull, but I was never afraid of him. After he left, Ben treated me like a possession. He just took from me after the first night. Came here whenever he wanted me. I wouldn't tell him I was pregnant, not after what he'd done to Emily.

A brief sketch of Emily's face, streaked with tears, sat in the margin.

The next picture was another drawing of Cleeve House.

251

Again sketched as a gothic mansion, this time dark and ominous. The windows utterly black, deep shadows adding to the sense of gloom. Instead of a smiling Rob, from one of the windows hung a fearful Faye, her mouth open in a forever silent scream.

Now Ben says I must go back to the house and stay in his room. He can't be bothered coming up here to see me. He's bound to find out I'm pregnant. God, I'm frightened and feel so lonely. I don't know what's going to happen to me. I'm scared, pregnant and alone.

The last drawing depicted a heavily pregnant Faye kneeling in the middle of a desert, tears running down her face, hands clutching her belly, fear in her eyes. Beneath it she had written her full name in gothic script.

Faye Angelica Santory

Chapter 54

Lucy's vision blurred, a tear splashed on the sketchbook, smudged the ink. Reading Faye's text, looking at her sketches, she couldn't deny Faye's pain, or her accurate assessment of the family. If Faye had come to her, telling of her father's murder, Lucy knew she wouldn't have believed her, would have taken Ben's side. Rob might have, but how could she have told him? And then he left, forced out by his brother. She carried the secret alone, as she carried her child.

How could Lucy tell anyone? If Ben knew the child was his he might take him as he had taken Lottie. It would destroy Marcus if he knew. And what would the revelation do for Quinn? Faye had seen Ben for what he was before anyone else and carried that insight to her death.

If Ben saw this, he would deny it all, and Lucy wouldn't believe him and he would know, see it in her. And if he could kill his father... She stopped the train of thought.

A shiver ran down Lucy's spine. Her brother was a murderer, but what could she do? The question still unanswered.

Halfway through her third reading of Faye's note Lucy

stopped. Distant voices drifted in through the open doorway. She had forgotten about Sue. Dipping her head outside she saw Sue and Andy wheeling a barrow.

'Hope we weren't too long,' Sue called.

'No,' said Lucy turning away from them. Before they arrived on the threshold Lucy tore the page from the sketchbook, folded the thick paper in quarters and slipped it into a pocket. She added the sketchbook to the small legacy accumulated for Quinn and met the Reevers at the doorway.

'We need to get her buried as soon as we can,' said Sue. 'The heat won't help, and the flies are gathering.'

Andy backed the wheelbarrow into the space next to the bed. He slipped his hands under Faye's shoulders while Lucy and Sue each took a leg. They manoeuvred the body to the edge of the bed and heaved Faye into the wheelbarrow.

'It won't be easy, digging a grave,' said Andy.

'Maybe Ben and Stuart will dig one when they notice the stink,' said Sue.

After reading Faye's notes Lucy couldn't speak to Ben about a grave, wouldn't be able to meet his eye. Ben wouldn't dig a grave for his own mother, why would he dig one for a woman he'd discarded?

The silence in the hovel penetrated Lucy's consciousness. Sue looked at her expectantly, Andy, his hands on the handles of the wheelbarrow, waited. They were looking to Lucy for instructions.

Andy broke the silence. 'Where shall we put her?'

Why are they asking me? Why am I supposed to know? Why do I have to decide? Lucy's mind whirled with unanswerable questions. 'I don't know, I don't know where to put her. Can't you just go and bury her. I can't deal with this anymore.' Her eyes flashed anger at Sue, at Andy.

'Let me past,' she barked, pushing her way by an open-mouthed Sue, to run outside.

When she reached the clearing, Lucy knelt beside where the bones lay. She rolled up her sleeve and counted the scars that laddered her forearm. One for each of the victims she had acknowledged, some old and healed to scar tissue, some new and still scabbed, one fresh and oozing a little blood. She counted them slowly, reciting the names she'd given the victims as she did so.

Blood, it all seemed to be about blood. Blood of the victims she had eaten, blood of the baby, blood of the mother, blood of her father. She couldn't live like this any longer. The answer came to her in Rob's face conjured by Faye's drawing. She would go to Selmouth, live with the fisherfolk, leave this hellhole. But she had promised her mother. Promised to protect Lottie and help Emily. Ben kept Lottie by his side, except when he went hunting with Stuart, then he locked her away. Lottie drifted further from Lucy's influence as each day passed.

She was failing her mother, failing her niece, failing herself. She had to do something. Lucy stroked her hand over the scars and again recited the names of the victims and at the end, in a faltering voice, added her father. They were growing lots now; beans were being harvested along with greens and potatoes, courgettes and tomatoes. They didn't need to kill any more.

Dusk settled over the clearing, Lucy oblivious to the passing of time, until the evening calling of forest birds roused her, and she made her slow way back towards Cleeve House, her head bowed, her shoulders slumped.

Sue sat in the courtyard taking in the last of the sun when

Lucy arrived.

'I'm sorry I ran out on you,' said Lucy.

'That's okay, my love. I guess it was all too much.'

'Poor Faye, I feel bad about her. I should have called for you earlier.'

'There wouldn't have been anything I could have done. You've got to remember, in times before proper hospitals, thousands of women died in childbirth. It wasn't your fault, my love.'

'I tugged on the cord, I'm sure it made her bleed.'

'I would have done too, it would have made no difference, honestly, except it would be me feeling as if I'd failed the lass instead of you.'

'You're a good woman, Sue.'

'And so are you, my love.'

'What have you done with Faye?'

'When we got her down here, near the house, we saw Ben. He said to put her in the shed until tomorrow because it was late. To be honest, I was right pleased, we were all knackered. We wheeled her in and left her there.'

'I'll go and see her,' said Lucy.

'Why? It's not Faye anymore. I've got those things you put aside kept safe. I guessed you gathered them up for little Quinn. Do you want them now?'

Lucy had forgotten the legacy she had carefully gleaned from the detritus of Faye's life.

'They're all Quinn will have to remember his mother by.'

'He won't remember her, my love, he'll grow up thinking Emily's his mother, if she keeps him, and will it be a terrible thing? She needs to be a mother and he needs a mum.'

'I'll keep these things for him in case he ever needs to know what happened to him.'

Sue collected Faye's things from the barn and gave them to

Lucy.

'She was a proper artist,' said Sue, handing over the sketchbook. 'Not really my sort of thing, but I can see she was good. There's a page been torn out; I don't know why it happened.'

'There was a page missing when I found it,' said Lucy, the lie falling easily from her lips.

Lucy stowed the things away in an old cardboard box, tucked under her bed. Tomorrow she would go to the cove. She needed to see Rob.

Chapter 55

In the growing darkness of the short night, Ben followed Stuart making his way through the forest.

'There's no need to hurry, we've got all night,' said Ben from thirty metres behind.

Stuart didn't respond and pushed on.

Ben raised his voice. 'I said slow down, we've plenty of time.'

Stuart slowed and turned his head. 'You struggling to keep up, old man?'

He'd been getting cocky as the weeks passed, ignoring instructions with veiled apologies, joking at Ben's expense. In the woods, alone, at night, on the way to hunt seemed the perfect time and place to deal with the insubordinate twat.

'Yeah, hang on a minute, Stu,' he said, smiling, waving a hand.

'Hah!' A contemptuous expletive from Stuart who turned to lean against a tree, smirking.

'It's the hunger, we haven't had a decent meal for days, we need to catch ourselves a big one tonight.'

'You hungry? You should have said, I've got some meat.

Not far away,' said Stuart.

'Good where is it, where did you get it?'

'Ask no questions, you'll get told no lies. What's a good meal worth to you right now?'

Reaching the tree Stuart leaned against, Ben feigned a slight stumble, then brought his fist up hard into Stuart's stomach. 'It's worth me not killing you tonight, you gobshite.'

Stuart's solar plexus, unprepared for the blow, spasmed. His breath left him, he struggled to wheeze any air into his lungs. In the moonlight Ben saw a flash of panic in his eyes.

'Now, you bastard, just listen to me. I've had enough of your crap. You seemed to have forgotten our arrangement. You do as you're fucking told, understand?' Only Ben's hand pushing Stuart's shoulder against the tree prevented Stuart from sinking to his knees. But he didn't respond to Ben's question.

An instant later Ben's knife blade glinted against Stuart's throat. 'Understand?' he hissed.

Stuart nodded as vigorously as the close quarters would allow. Ben barked a laugh, stepped back, and released his grip on Stuart. The younger man collapsed onto his knees, gasping and wheezing, desperate to fill his lungs with air.

'It'll pass in about ten minutes, then you can have the pleasure of feeding me with this meat you have hidden away, okay?'

Stuart could only nod again.

Half an hour later Stuart led Ben into a small clearing. He rooted around on the forest floor and hauled a plastic bag holding a few small joints of meat. Ben cleared a small circle and laid a fire. Soon the joints were roasting on makeshift skewers.

'Okay, Stuart, tell me, why should I ever trust you again?'

'Come on, I was only having a bit of fun.'

'I don't think so. There's nowhere else to go for you except where I am. And I know you're a ruthless bastard, it's why I chose you. What are you going to do? You going to fight me to be leader? Is that it?'

'Nah, I wouldn't stand a chance, would I? I might beat you at running, but not in a fight; unless I had the jump on you.'

'That's why I'm asking the question. If I have to be wary of my second in command, I may as well top him and find myself another.'

'Who would it be? Marcus? My dad? There isn't anyone else.'

'It might be Lucy. How's that going for you? Is she willing to play yet?'

Ben leaned against a log and watched as Stuart fumed, keeping his gaze steady, appearing relaxed, inside he was wary, waiting for an attack. Unlike Ben's brother, Stuart didn't rise to the bait.

'She'll come round eventually.'

'Don't worry, you're only young. You'll get to pop your cherry sometime.' Ben saw Stuart's eyes narrow and maybe a tremor of rage in his hand as he turned the meat on the skewers, his lips tight sealed.

Ben slipped a hand, unnoticed, around the hilt of his knife as Stuart's head turned, anger in his eyes. Still he didn't rise to the jibes.

Ben spat a laugh at him. 'Come on, let's eat, we've got some hunting to do and I'm starving.'

'Okay,' Stuart nodded, pulled a skewer from the ground, handed it to Ben, and pulled one for himself.

The two men ate in a silence stamped with the hallmark of hunger. Hot grease dripped off the meat and into Ben's beard as he tore mouthfuls from the joint he held, eating with the gusto of arm's length starvation. Soon he'd picked the bone clean and tossed it into the fire.

'That was good, Stu, why have you been hiding this?'

Stuart finished eating and tossed his bone into the fire where it crackled and fizzed briefly before blackening in the heat. He stretched his arms and rose from the squat he'd maintained while eating. 'To be honest,' he said, 'I didn't think you'd want any.'

Ben watched him turn his head, a slow gaze meeting his own, inviting the question he asked without thought. 'Why wouldn't I?'

'I thought he might be a bit young and tender for your taste,' said Stuart, a slow, languid delivery, savouring each word as if they were to be eaten themselves.

It took Ben a few moments for the implications of his words to strike; moments that stretched into a leaden silence between the two men.

With blood roaring in his ears Ben leapt to his feet, drawing his knife, and lunging at Stuart. 'You evil cunt,' he yelled, his knife thrusting at Stuart's belly.

The younger man had learned well from the older and stepped away from the attack, tripping Ben as he passed, sending him sprawling on the ground. Stuart jumped for Ben's back, his own knife drawn, but Ben rolled away, Stuart landing in the spot Ben vacated. Ben threw a roundhouse punch at Stuart, catching him a glancing blow to his head as Stuart himself rolled away. The two men scrabbled to their feet, knives in their hands. Stuart had put the fire between them.

'What's the problem?' asked Stuart. 'You wouldn't want him to go to waste, would you?'

Ben took half a step and saw Stuart ready himself. He held

261

his back foot, forced himself to breathe, pushed his rage down. He recognised the tactics, the same he'd used on his brother. Anger, fear, rage, they were the companions of defeat. He quelled his racing thoughts, took another breath, watched Stuart through the flames and smoke.

Stuart tried again. 'Come on, old man. If you think you can take me, have a go.'

Ben paced as if looking for an opening, instead he cast his eyes around. Propped against a tree, were their crossbows. He needed time to draw the string, load a bolt, and aim. His head did the calculations, about fifteen seconds, a life-threatening time in a knife fight. He circled the fire, narrowed the space to the bow, Stuart mirrored his movements.

'If we fight and kill each other, everyone's done for,' he said. 'We need to sort this out.'

'Yeah, we do. We'll start by you putting your knife down,' said Stuart.

'That's not going to work, is it? You too, at the same time.'

'Okay, slowly now.'

Ben held Stuart's eyes as they began to crouch. When Ben dropped into a squat, and Stuart couldn't see through the smoke and flames, he reached out to a branch sticking from the fire. With the branch in one hand and his knife in the other he swept the embers of the fire upwards and towards Stuart, tossing them as hard as he could, ignoring the few embers landing, sizzling, on the skin of his hands and wrists.

Stuart raised an arm to shield himself from the deluge of ash, ember, and flaming wood, and prepared for an onslaught from Ben which never came.

After tossing the fire, Ben turned to the crossbows, strung one, slipped a bolt into the flight groove, and swung it to his shoulder.

Smoke and ash obscured his view. Ben waited for the

movement which would precede Stuart's attack, the crossbow aimed at his chest.

'Okay, Ben, okay. Look, I'm sorry, all right? I was teasing you. Come on, it was a joke.'

'You think it was a joke, do you? I'm not laughing.'

'I said I'm sorry, what more do you want?'

'I came out hunting tonight. There are people back there who need feeding. They won't care who they're eating, just like you don't. I'm sure your dad will enjoy the extra ration I give him. Before I tell him who it came from.'

'Come on, Ben. I'm your number two, your enforcer.'

'You're only talking to give you some more time, for another breath of sweet life before you get it. I know, I've seen enough of them, and so have you. But you don't have any time.' Ben's eye, and the crossbow followed the small movements of Stuart's body.

Stuart looked over Ben's shoulder, beyond him, his eyes elsewhere. 'God, no, don't…' he shouted into the distance.

Ben's head hardly moved, he knew a feint when he saw one, but his eyes swivelled a fraction, a reflex, and Stuart took his chance.

Ben saw him move, pulled the trigger. The bolt missed by less than an inch and thudded into a tree. Stuart was now running, zigzagging between the trees.

Ben put his foot in the stirrup of the bow, re-cocked the string, slid another bolt into the groove and raised it to his shoulder. Stuart, a dark form amidst dark trees twenty metres away, crashed through branches and undergrowth. Ben fired at the retreating figure. A yell from Stuart and a momentary silence told him he'd hit his target this time, then the noise of his retreat resumed.

'You might as well give up, Stuart. I know you're there; I'm coming for you.' Ben set off running to where he thought he'd hit Stuart.

He paused to reload the crossbow. In the moonlight, he could make out the route Stuart had taken, the broken trail through early bramble and bracken obvious. He paused to examine the spot where the bolt had struck home. A small dark patch on the forest floor might indicate a wound, but not how severe, and where was the prey? He heard him in the distance.

'I'm going to come for you, Ben, you bastard. I'll come for you. Remember that before you sleep.'

The noise of Stuart's retreat grew fainter. Ben wouldn't catch him if he gave chase. Stuart had been right about being the faster runner, and wherever the bolt had struck hadn't slowed him down.

He turned to begin his homeward journey. There would be no meat to take back tonight. But why should he care. He'd already eaten. As the thought entered his head the enormity of his last meal struck him, and his gorge rose. He cast the bow aside, fell to his knees and emptied his stomach in a heaving retch that shook his whole body. Though empty he retched again and again, sweat beading on his forehead, trickling into his eyes, the forest floor reeking of bile and vomit.

Chapter 56

Lucy turned a corner of the path to Goff's Cove and saw Rob sitting on a rock, staring out to sea. She called to him and waved. He'd never arrived first before. Descending the path, her brother slipped from view, hidden by a dip in the land. When he reappeared, he wasn't alone.

'Lucy,' Rob called and waved, stood and ran towards his sister. 'There's someone I want you to meet,' he said after they'd shared a hug.

'Not the certain someone you told me about?'

Rob laughed and took his sister's hand, pulling her along. 'Lucy, this is Ayisha.'

'I'm glad to finally meet you,' said Ayisha. 'Rob has told me so much about you, I said he had to bring me, and Stefan, to meet you.'

Stefan, a little older than Lottie, stood behind Ayisha, one hand holding her skirt, the other half covering his face.

Rob put an arm around Ayisha, smiling, reached behind her and ruffled Stefan's hair. 'This is my sister, Stefan, you can call her Aunt Lucy if you like.'

'Just Lucy will be fine,' said Lucy, showering the boy with

an effervescent smile. 'Does this mean you two...' her eye flicked between Rob and Ayisha, both wearing grins.

'Are together?' finished Rob. 'I guess you could say so,' he laughed.

'Don't tease her,' said Ayisha. 'Rob and I have been together for a couple of months now. I know how much he thinks about you and hope we can be friends.'

Ayisha's warm open smile shone into the fog of bad news Lucy carried. Something about this woman touched Lucy. Here was an honest, trustworthy person. Someone who met her gaze without the shade of secrecy she'd come to expect.

'Has Rob told you everything about me?' said Lucy.

'What man could ever know everything about a woman, even their sister,' said Ayisha. 'And being a man, he's probably only told me the unimportant things anyway.'

Lucy laughed.

'He told me about you,' piped Stefan, 'he says you can play the piano, and you'll teach me.'

'I didn't exactly say she would,' said Rob. 'I think there were a lot of "mights".'

Lucy reached out and touched Rob's arm, drawing his attention, her smile leaving her face. 'Rob, I'm sorry, I have bad news for you,' she said.

'I don't have any secrets from Ayisha.'

'It's not Ayisha I'm thinking of,' said Lucy, a frown furrowing her forehead and her eye piercing Rob's.

He thought for a moment before saying, 'Lucy and I need to have a walk, can you watch the boat?'

'Sure,' said Ayisha. 'Stefan will gather some driftwood and we'll have a fire and cook some fish.'

'Fantastic,' yelled Stefan, and sped off along the shoreline, clambering the drystone wall marking the boundary of the fields which were once there.

'Be careful,' called Ayisha after him. To Lucy she said, 'He's adjusted to the new landscape far quicker than I have. I keep looking for sandy beaches and only see mud and salt scorched grass.'

'It hasn't settled down yet. Perhaps in a few years we'll get silt piling up here and there,' said Rob, 'but I...' he looked at Lucy and back at Ayisha.

'Of course, I understand. Take your time.'

'Ayisha is lovely,' said Lucy when they were out of earshot.

'Yes, she is. She puts up with me too. Now what's on your mind? I guess Faye's had her baby and you still think it's mine,' said Rob.

'No, I don't. I'm certain Quinn isn't yours.'

'She has had it. Fantastic, and Quinn's such a great name.' Rob went to hug his sister but stopped when he saw her face. 'What's the matter, Lucy, what's happened?'

Lucy ran her sleeve over her face before looking at her brother. 'She's dead, Rob. Faye died when Quinn was born. And it's all my fault.'

'Why do you think it's your fault she died?' said Rob after Lucy had told him about Faye. 'We had a woman die of the same last month. And we have a doctor who could do nothing to help. She said there used to be a drug you could give to prevent it, there isn't any now. This is why we must rebuild. Work together. We shouldn't be isolating like Ben wants.'

Lucy stopped herself telling Rob about her father's murder. Rob would want justice. He had Ayisha and Stefan, but his history with his brother would send him to Cleeve House. She couldn't let it happen, not if she kept her promise to her mother.

'Are you okay? You've gone silent on me again,' said Rob.

'I'm fine, I was thinking. Is that what you're doing? Rebuilding?'

'We're trying to. We've links with a couple of communities within a day's journey, and we do some basic trade with them. Share knowledge too.'

'It sounds like things are really moving for you. I'm glad.'

'I'm going to say this again. You should come to us. You'd like it. Tell Emily she can come with Quinn. And Lottie. What good will it do Lottie staying with Ben?'

'I worry about Lottie; I don't know if I can pull her away from Ben. He keeps her with him a lot now. I hardly see her, and Emily is distraught. I'm failing Lottie, just like I failed Faye.'

'It won't help anyone if you keep blaming yourself. Will you tell Emily she can come?'

'Yes, of course I will. But I don't think she will if it means leaving Lottie.'

'I'm going to have to go and see what I can do. Lottie and I got on before I left.'

'It's pointless. And Ben's still got his rottweiler watching his back.'

'You mean Stuart Reever?'

'Yes. Thankfully, all he's done to me is try and get in my head. He hasn't tried anything physical. But I can tell he thinks about it.'

'I could bring someone with me. Someone with muscle.'

'You want to start a war? Don't do it, Rob. I'll do everything I can to persuade Emily. I'll let you know next week. Now we'd better be getting back to your lovely Ayisha. And Stefan, he's a cute kid.'

'He lost his dad in the flood. I'm desperately trying not to pretend to be his father, only do the best I can for him.'

* * *

They walked back to where Stefan diligently supervised the fire and the roasting fish.

'This looks the nicest piece, so this is for you,' he said, handing Lucy a skewer.

Lucy's face began to crumble, tears forming under the onslaught of this innocent kindness spontaneously displayed. She turned her almost tears into a smile for the ten-year-old's watching face.

'It smells delicious, I bet you caught it as well as cooked it.'

Stefan beamed his answer at her before he spoke. 'I did, it's a bass, you don't get many of them.' His broad smile emphasising the significance of the achievement.

During the afternoon Rob took Stefan adventuring along the cove.

'He's changed,' said Lucy.

'Rob?' said Ayisha. 'How?'

'He seems more centred, more in tune with himself, and others. He was always pretty relaxed, and a bit selfish if I'm honest. Now he seems to take the things which matter more seriously.'

'You mean Stefan.'

Lucy laughed. 'Yes, Stefan, of course, but not just him. The whole Selmouth thing. He's talked a lot about it. He seems really involved, keen for it to succeed, and not just for himself.'

'It would be hard not to be involved and stay at Selmouth.'

'Is it imposed involvement? Does your leader make everyone take part?'

It was Ayisha's turn to laugh. 'We don't have a leader, Lucy. Everyone is involved. If there's something which affects the whole community, everyone is listened to until a solution is found.'

'Surely it can't work, what if someone has to make decisions immediately?'

'What if they do? Everyone makes decisions all the time. If they have the good of the community at heart, they make the right decision. If they don't, they'll have to justify themselves to everyone else. Sometimes it takes a little while for newcomers to understand this, we're patient.'

'It sounds idyllic.'

'It's anything but. There's a ton of hard work and a desperate fight to survive going on every day. It seems obvious the best way to win the fight is to cooperate. I expect Rob's already invited you.'

Lucy opened her mouth to reply but playful screams from Stefan racing towards them and fake whoops and yells from Rob chasing him interrupted them.

Talk flowed, along with laughter and smiles for the rest of the day. Lucy had to explain her missing eye to satisfy ten-year-old curiosity. Cleeve House, and its horrors, were forgotten in the happy dance of people invested in a future that held promise. Inevitably, the tide turned, and Rob, Ayisha and Stefan boarded their boat to sail up the coast to their home in Selmouth, leaving Lucy waving from the shore.

Alone, she trudged the path up from Goff's Cove. In her head half formed schemes to persuade Emily to leave, to steal Lottie away. Only if both were safe would she have fulfilled her promise. The plans in her head were soon demolished by her heart, which knew Ben would never let Lottie go, and even if she did manage, somehow, to steal her away, he would follow and wreak a terrible vengeance.

The lightness, happiness almost, she experienced with Rob gradually dissipated as she walked back to Cleeve House, the place of happy childhood memories and adult horrors. From the top of the path a westering sun sat on the horizon and the house lay in shadows cast by the nearby hills. Darkness descended on Lucy, pressing into her heart. Is this what her life would be forever now? A life of violence, shame, fear. A life devoid of hope, kindness, love.

She carried a bag with enough fish to feed them all for a couple of days, enough to bring gratitude from all who still lived at Cleeve House, but for Lucy the bag carried a host of unrealisable hopes, and it weighed heavy on her shoulders.

Chapter 57

Lucy recognised the smell of cooking meat long before she got to the house. Nobody greeted her as she arrived, offered to carry her bag. No one was in the yard. Voices spilled from an open kitchen window; carried on the now familiar smell of roasting flesh. Lucy's mouth could do nothing about her reflexes as she licked her lips. She knew there would also be potatoes and beans, and strawberries to follow. A proper meal.

When she pushed her way into the candle lit kitchen, they were all sitting there, eating. From Lottie through to Andy and Ben, all had a bowl before them, almost empty.

Ben looked up when the door opened. 'Lucy, there you are, we wondered what had happened to you.'

'But I've brought fish,' she said.

'Everyone was hungry, we couldn't wait any longer. Don't worry, we've saved you some.'

Lucy looked around the room at all the faces. The normality of the abhorrent meal present in everyone. None questioned what they ate, what it meant for their humanity.

There, at the end of the table, Lottie sat gnawing a bone.

Lucy noticed Stuart's absence. Could it be Stuart they were eating? Surely not? She saw Andy enjoying his meal. A father couldn't eat his son, could he?

Only yesterday she'd told herself it had to stop. Despite her hunger, her saliva dripping from her half open mouth, Lucy determined today would be the start of the end.

'I'm going to have some fish. I'll have the potatoes and beans; I don't want any meat.' Her voice was steady, her resolve strong, as she walked through to the stove.

'Are you mad,' said Ben, loud enough to attract the attention of the whole group.

'No, I'm not. But I think I might have been.' Lucy began to unpack fish from her bag.

'You can't let this be wasted,' said Ben, accusation in his voice.

'I'm sure someone will eat it. Why don't you?'

'What's the matter with you, Lucy? You've never been like this before.'

'There's nothing wrong with me, Ben, nothing at all,' she said, and began to prepare the fish, sliding the sharp knife along its belly and discarding the innards before taking off the head with a swift slice of the blade.

'I'm stuffed,' called Ben to the room, 'there's a spare portion of meat going for anyone who wants.'

A chorus of demands met the offer. Lucy saw Ben scan around the room before his eyes lit upon Marcus.

'Here, Marcus, you have it. You look like you could manage another load.' Ben scraped the meat into his bowl.

Ben's voice and the sound of him scraping at the plate of meat with his knife sent a shiver up Lucy's spine.

As they finished eating, they began to drift away. Ben called Lottie to him, and they left hand in hand, Emily's eyes following her daughter's departure.

'Goodnight, Lottie, do you want a kiss?' Emily called.

Lottie ignored her, said something quiet to her father who laughed.

Sue sighed and shook her head as she watched her go. 'Come on, Andy, we're done here.'

Only Emily and Marcus were left. Emily cradling Quinn in her arms. They got up to leave.

'Don't go yet, Em. Can we talk?'

'Sure, Marcus, take Quinn and settle him down. Look after him 'til I get there will you?'

Marcus took the baby leaving the two women alone.

'Are you happy with this, with what's happening here?' said Lucy.

'Come on, Lucy. You know I'm not. What alternative is there?'

Lucy told Emily about Rob, about Selmouth, about the invitation.

'I can't leave,' said Emily, 'you must see that. It would mean leaving Lottie.'

'Take her with you.'

'Ben never lets her out of his sight unless he's hunting. Then she's locked in his room.'

Lucy watched a desperate sadness grip Emily, her hands fidgeted and pulled at her sleeves, her eyes casting about, not settling on anything, least of all Lucy's face. 'If I could get Lottie away, would you go?' Lucy saw a brief flickering of hope in Emily's eyes, soon quenched by her desperate situation.

'Yes, no, I don't know. I can't imagine it happening. You could go, why don't you? No one would blame you for escaping this hellhole.'

Before Lucy could answer the door opened and in came Sue.

'I've got to see to Quinn now,' said Emily, getting up to leave, 'we'll talk again.'

'I thought I'd come and help you clear up, my love. You finished yet?'

'I need to do something, Sue. Can you make a start? I won't be gone long.'

'Of course I will, my love, take as long as you need.'

She knew it would be a body, the smell of blood now a commonplace in her life. She recoiled at the first glimpse of the sight that met her, staggered back a couple of steps. The candle almost fell from her grip as she brought a hand to cover her mouth, suppressed a cry before it was born. Still, she had to look again.

In the wheelbarrow Andy had used for her final journey, lay what remained of Faye. The corpse had been gutted; the entrails left in the bottom of the barrow. Half-submerged in offal and blood were the hands and feet, laying on top of them Faye's head, face up, stared at Lucy from sightless eyes; her hair, matted with stiff blood, stood above the head, gathered and bent into the shape of the hand which had last held it.

She turned to leave, her hand over her mouth, but the door had swung closed. Panicking, Lucy dropped the candle, and plunged the tiny fetid space into blackness. In the darkness she tripped and fell against the door, pushing it open, letting in a draught of fresh night air. She took a breath, stumbled, and fell to her knees. Again, she heard Ben's voice as he gave Marcus the extra portion of meat, and poor unknowing Marcus ate every morsel. Lucy barely had time to duck behind the shed before she lost control of her stomach, spraying the base of the shed and her feet with half-digested fish.

When her stomach had emptied and the shaking had stopped, Lucy stood, wiping her mouth in the crook of her elbow.

Lucy recrossed the yard to the house. In the candlelit kitchen Sue busied herself with the pots and pans. Lucy slipped past the doorway, to the hall. Occasional glints of starlight, sparking through bare windows, relieved the total darkness as Lucy climbed the stairs, the familiarity of the old house making the ascent an easy one.

At the top of the stairs, she paused. The doors to her and Stuart's rooms stood next to each other, darker sentinels in the black night watching her progress. She listened for any sign of occupation in Stuart's room, heard nothing. Now she wished she'd asked about him at the meal. He could be with her brother. The thought put a falter in her step and an extra beat in her pulse. She drew a breath and continued past the dark, mournful doors.

At the back of the house, she came to Ben's room and stopped. Should she knock, or should she just walk in? She wanted to barge the door down and scream at him, but he would only laugh at her. Besides, the door was probably locked. If she tried to open it and failed, he would wonder who it was, what they wanted.

She raised her knuckles to the door and paused while she rehearsed what she would say, then gave a couple of quiet taps. 'Ben, it's Lucy, can I come in?'

Chapter 58

Lucy heard no sound coming from Ben's room, no voices, no footsteps, nothing. She took a couple of measured breaths, calmed her racing heart. Began to count. When she got to twenty, she raised her hand to knock again. Before her knuckles met the door, she heard the turn of a key, the slide of a bolt, and the door swung open.

'Lucy, what are you doing here? Come in.'

'I need to talk to you.'

'You stink of fish. Sit down. Talk to me about what?'

He waved at a large couch, its back against the foot of the unmade double bed. Candles flickered on a dressing table and at the bedside. A velvet curtain covered an alcove to one side of the bed.

'This is nice,' said Ben sitting beside her, 'a bit like old times when you used to come to me with your teenage problems. Remember Jimmy Parker?'

'Yes, I remember Jimmy. You scared him.'

'He was giving you a tough time. What's wrong now? Is it Stuart?'

'I thought you liked Stuart. He's your hunting partner,

isn't he?'

'If he's been pestering you, you don't need to worry about him anymore.'

Lucy frowned a question, 'What do you mean?'

'Exactly what I say. You don't need to worry about him anymore. He was too young for you anyway.'

'He's not dead, is he?' Despite her dislike, hatred even, of Stuart she didn't wish him dead. There had been too much killing, too much grief.

'No, he's not dead. But he won't be coming back. He's done a runner, couldn't stand the pace, got too bolshy and cocky, so he had to go.'

'He's not dead?'

'No, did you want him to be?'

'No, no, I was just making sure.'

'If it's all that's bothering you, little sister, you don't need to worry anymore, it's been dealt with by your big brother.' Ben smiled at her.

Once clean, white, and polished, Ben's teeth were now chipped, yellowing, their boundaries marked with black lines. His beard straggled from a once clean-shaven chin and was now flecked with grease and blood. Ben, who used to be particular in his appearance, had tattered, filthy clothes, one of his shoes had a flapping sole, his hands were spotted with stains, his fingernails chipped and black.

Ben didn't resemble her brother in looks, words or deeds. His thick black leather belt carried a hunting knife, the only aspect of him bearing any semblance of order or organisation.

'Was that all you wanted to say?' he said, into the silence shrouding Lucy.

'There's something else. It's about what we eat. It can't go on like this. There must be some other way. We can't keep eating... people.'

Ben gave an exasperated sigh. 'We've been through all this before. We've been having this conversation for months. Have you any better ideas to keep us alive?'

'The garden's producing now, there's fish. If we could find some more chickens, we could—'

'Get real, Lucy. The garden gives us a few veg. Welcome, yes, but it's not going to feed us all, and come winter it will be empty again. And fish, we get some. It feeds us for a day or two. Some weeks there's none. Let's be generous, say we eat fish once a week on average, what do we eat the other six?'

'We could get a boat, fish out at sea, catch more?'

'And drown in the process. Why, when there's a ready source of meat available not too far away? No, we'll carry on as we are. Besides, it's easier now there's not so many of us.'

Lucy counted the deaths. Her father and mother. Rob chased away. Poor little Adam, and now Faye. The thought of Faye brought visions of what lay in the shed into focus. She let out a sob.

'Come on, little sis, it's no good pulling waterworks on me, is it? You know they won't work. I know you feel bad about it all, but it's the only way to get us through this.'

She'd always hated it when he called her "little sis"; now she hated him for more serious things. She hated him for his cruelty to Rob, for allowing her mother to die, for mutilating Faye's body, for killing her father.

'It's hard, Ben. I don't think I can do this anymore.' She started to cry. She worked hard to produce heavy realistic sobs. They convinced Ben, who stood up and bent to pull her to her feet. She knew what he would do, what he'd always done whenever she was upset, whenever she'd gone to him with her petty adolescent problems.

Ben clasped her left hand to pull her up, the grime on both

their hands disguising the sweat coming from her palm, from both her palms. The fingers of her free hand felt the newly honed sharpness of the small knife in her pocket, gripped its hilt, turned it to conceal it in her hand. Her heart pounding as she rose, she spread her thumb away from the knife, placed it on Ben's chest, feeling for and finding his breastbone and the ribs a little to the right, feeling his heartbeat, much slower and regular than hers. Couldn't he tell? Didn't her heart give her away? She knew her face would if she looked at him and ducked her head into his shoulder. She could still change her mind, if she failed, missed the target, only wounded him, he would surely kill her. What lay before her if she didn't do this now? He would know and never trust her again; she'd never get another chance like this. She felt a sob rising in her, almost suppressed it, but let it out, knowing he would take it as a sign of weakness and hug her all the harder. What choice did she have, what else could she do? His arms went round her, encircling her, as she knew they would. It had to be now. Turning the knife in her hand, the blade beside the sternum, between the third and fourth ribs, she lodged the hilt in the notch of her shoulder. She took a breath; it would be either her last one or Ben's.

Ben pulled her close to give the bear hug he'd given many times before. Too late he felt the knife push against him, into him, his grip slackened.

'What's...' Ben began.

Lucy pulled with the arm around his waist and pushed with her shoulder and hand. The knife slid smoothly through his shirt, his skin, his ribs, and into his heart.

Ben began to push against her, she turned the knife in her hand, heard the blade against the bone of his ribs, felt the wetness of his blood. She let go with the arm around his waist and let him push her away, taking the knife with her.

A crimson bloom spread swiftly from the wound. Ben let out a garbled cry, 'Lucy...'

His right hand felt for his own knife in his belt, his fingers finding the hilt. His eyes full of disbelief. Lucy watched from two paces, careless of her own life. His eyes glazed, his fingers slackened their hold, his knees bent, and he crashed to the floor.

It was done.

Lucy let out a wail as the knife slid from her fingers and fell, but she did not cry. She could shed no tears for her brother. Perhaps, sometime, she may remember him as he used to be, but now her head filled with images of her father, her mother, of poor Faye. No one else could have done this. She would mourn him, like the rest of the dead, when the time came. Now a sense of relief flooded her. She took a breath. It felt like she'd been holding her breath for hours. It's over at last, she thought as she watched her brother die.

A movement in the corner of the room dragged her attention away from the body to the curtained alcove. There, wide-eyed, stood Lottie, watching. How long she'd been there Lucy did not know. There she was, her eyes on Lucy, fixed, staring, accusing. For a moment Lucy couldn't move, couldn't breathe, held by her niece's stare, her eyes so like Ben's.

'Lottie,' she finally said, stepping towards her.

Lottie began to scream. She made no words, only screams. Screams as loud as banshees, screams that filled the room, spilled under the door, out the window, screams bursting into Lucy's head, beating on her eardrums, screams which used all the small girl's breath, then a pause, air sucked in filling her lungs like bellows, and they began again. As Lucy approached, she ran behind the curtain into the dark, still screaming.

'Lottie, it's all right, Lottie,' called Lucy. She picked up a candle from the bedside table. In the flicker of candlelight Lottie knelt on her small bed in the alcove, tight against the corner of the room, back towards her, screaming into the night.

Lucy stepped up to the bed to comfort the girl. She stretched her hand out to stroke her. Lottie recoiled from the touch of Lucy's blood-stained hand, her screaming redoubled.

Chapter 59

Emily, further from the stairs when the screaming started, still reached the first step at the same time as Sue. Shouldering the older woman aside she took the stairs two at a time, the klaxon of her daughter's screams driving her legs.

She threw open the door and rushed into the room. Her eyes took in the scene, Ben on the floor, clearly dead, blood pooling from his chest. In the corner alcove she saw Lucy's back; hidden in the shadow, the source of the screams.

'Lottie, Lottie,' yelled Emily, rushing forward, shoving Lucy aside and reaching for her child. 'It's all right, no one will hurt you, I'm here, hush, hush.' She wrapped her arms around Lottie and pulled her close. Lottie's screams continued. She wriggled, kicked, and twisted at her mother's attempts to hold her.

'I didn't know she was here, I didn't see her,' said Lucy into the screams.

Emily pulled her daughter tighter, ignoring the blows from the young limbs. 'I told you she was always here.' The words spat at Lucy's face.

Emily backed out of the alcove with the squirming child.

The screams paused; Lottie's eyes fixed on the body of her father. 'Daddy,' she yelled, 'she did it, she did it,' and the screaming began again.

Sue arrived in the doorway and took in the scene with a sweep of her eyes. The body, Lucy covered in blood, the squirming shrieking child in Emily's arms.

'Daddy, Daddy, Daddy,' screamed Lottie, squirming in her mother's grip, her arms outstretched towards the body.

'Oh my Lord, you've killed your own brother,' said Sue.

Lucy and Emily both looked at Sue, and the look was enough to chase her from the room.

Lucy turned to Emily. 'I couldn't see her, I thought she was asleep.'

Emily shook her head. 'I need to get her out of here.'

Lottie had stopped screaming, but not stopped fighting her mother.

'I want Daddy, I want Daddy,' she yelled as she struggled against her mother's restraining arms.

Lucy retrieved her knife from the floor, wiped the coagulating blood on Ben's corpse, and slipped it into its sheath. She searched Ben's clothing for the bunch of keys he carried and locked the door behind her, before going to her own room.

The voices of Emily and Lottie still carried up the stairs despite the muffle of a closed door. She was alone on the upper floor of the house once crowded with her family. Now it was empty, drained of the life forces which had made it home.

Lucy lay on her bed, wide awake and exhausted. She would not sleep, could not. She knew the night would bring self-recrimination aplenty, she would play the scene over in her head a thousand times and it would never change. She would remember everything about her brother, all his generosity and kindness in her youth; and she would think about the recent past, the time at Cleeve House, trying to see what happened to him, why he changed, what drove him down that terrible path. She would think about all this in the short darkness of the summer night, and she knew there would be no answers to the biggest of questions, why? The past is done, it cannot alter. The knowledge brought no solace to her, only a resolve. Tomorrow will be different, tomorrow there will be changes.

Chapter 60

Lucy still lay wide-awake on her bed when the birds began singing as if nothing had happened during the night. The grey of early dawn broke into the gold of a summer day. Not a moment's sleep had divided the long-short night for her. Resolve settled within her like cooling lava, heavy and solid. Her parents were dead. One brother had been chased away by the cruelty of the other she had killed. They had all lost. It was time for her to make a sacrifice and begin anew. She rose with sunlight beaming through the gap in the curtains.

Beneath her bed lay a small trunk holding the few items which belonged to her parents. She rummaged inside, pulling aside a decorative box made by her father, a small watercolour painted by her mother, until she found her mother's shears, and her father's cut-throat razor, wrapped in the strop he used.

She saw no one in the yard when filling the bowl from the water butt. She saw no one in the house when climbing the stairs back to her room. The only person she saw was herself reflected in the mirror. She applied the shears to her hair, first trimming the long hair around the back and sides, following the dome of her skull, taking off all the shears would allow.

The last tiny sliver of soap and the cold water from the butt made little lather, but still she applied the cut-throat to her head, ignoring the occasional nick and drips of blood. What does a little more count for after all that had been shed? Finally, she shaved the brow from above her single seeing eye.

When she was done, she stood for a moment in front of the mirror, holding the blade of the razor to her neck. It would only take a second.

She honed the razor against the strop before wrapping one in the other and returning it, and the shears, to the trunk. There were sounds in the house now. Others were rising, their new day beginning. They would all congregate in the kitchen. Sitting around the table before the day began had become a ritual, instituted by Ben so he could hand out orders.

Lucy again looked at herself in the mirror. She had missed a few small tufts. They would not be noticed, hidden amongst the browning scabs. The loss of hair made her eye deeply piercing, other-worldly, as if she had only recently stepped onto Earth, an alien cyclops. She nodded at recognising this. In a way it was true.

She left her room and went to Ben's. His body, now attracting flies, lay untouched, the blood around him now a coagulated mass. She knelt and unfastened the leather belt he wore, pulling it and his knife, from his body. She used the knife to scrape what she could of his blood from the belt and fastened it around her own waist.

Lucy pushed open the door of the kitchen. They all turned, their eyes meeting her singular glare, swiftly sliding away, cutting to look elsewhere, at each other, at the floor. She watched them avoid her gaze. Their faces told the gruesome tale of the day before. Sue sat beside Marcus, trying to comfort him, Marcus's face tear-stained and downcast. Andy's ashen face said he'd been to the shed and seen what remained of Faye. Emily, harassed by a hungry infant and Lottie's histrionics, seemed on the edge of hysteria herself.

Lucy scanned the room for a moment. 'Quiet.' The word delivered with authority, not a request, a demand.

Lottie, about to scream at Lucy, shrank from the challenge and hid behind her mother, sneaking fearful looks.

'We have much to do. First Andy and I will bury Faye while everyone else goes to the hovel and cleans it. Then we will gather to remember her.'

'What about Ben?' ventured Emily.

'After we have remembered Faye, Marcus and I will dig a grave for Ben while Andy and Sue remove the body from the house. Then we will bury Ben and gather to remember him.'

Lucy glared around the room. No one spoke. 'Now all of you except Andy must go to the hovel and not return until I come and get you. Understand?'

Silent nods came from around the room.

'Now go.'

The chairs clattered and the people left.

When only Andy remained Lucy said, 'I'm sorry, Andy. I couldn't ask Marcus to help, not after...'

'No, of course not. I understand. Let's dig the grave first and do this as quickly as we can.'

'You're a good man, Andy Reever.'

Andy replied with a wan smile as they left to find spades and shovels.

After burying the bodies and saying words meaning nothing

to the dead and little to those left alive, they returned to Cleeve House to eat.

'Andy and Emily will take from the garden and Sue and Marcus will cook dinner. Call me when it's ready. I'll be in my room. I don't want to be disturbed until then.' Lucy delivered the words as commands while she scanned the people before her with a steely eye, enforcing a new distance between them.

'What will we eat?' said Sue.

'We'll be eating whatever is available in the garden.' She spoke as if to children, stating the obvious in measured words.

'What about meat?'

'There is no meat, there will be no meat. Never again in this house will anyone eat that meat.' She looked around them all. Only Emily met her eye. 'Does anyone have a problem with that?' The words, delivered through taught lips, met with a silent response.

Lucy closed her door. Is this how Ben felt? Alone, responsible, uncertain yet determined. She allowed herself a moment to believe her brother might have felt all those things before she acknowledged the truth, he'd become utterly evil. She'd done what she had to do to rid the community of the monster. Now they all looked at her the same way they had looked at Ben. With awe and with fear. They would do anything she demanded of them; this was Ben's legacy to her. She didn't want fear and awe, she wanted friendship, family, love.

Chapter 61

Lucy took Emily and Marcus with her to Goff's Cove. Emily carried Quinn while Marcus by turns chased, carried, and was chased by, Lottie.

'You remember Uncle Rob, don't you?' said Marcus to Lottie during one of the "carrying" phases.

'I think so. Is he nice?'

'Yes, he is, he's great, and look, there he is.' They had run ahead of Lucy and Emily and now waved frantically down at Rob.

Rob had Stefan and Ayisha with him; they all waved back.

'Who's that?' said Stefan.

Rob named everyone as they came into view and gave a small explanation of who they were. 'You know Lucy of course, and that's Marcus with my niece, Lottie.' Rob saw a flash of anxiety cross Stefan's face. 'She doesn't know much about the sea. I think you should show her what you know. Would you do that?'

'Oh yes,' said Stefan, grinning his relief.

'And there's Emily, my brother's wife, and she's carrying

baby Quinn,' he finished.

'You have a brother! Is he coming?'

'I don't think so. Look, there's no one else.'

'I don't know if we have enough fish for them all,' said Stefan, a frown creasing his brow.

'Don't worry, we'll manage.'

'What happened to your hair?' asked Rob when he and Lucy engineered a few minutes alone.

'You'd better know now. Ben's dead. I killed him.'

Rob didn't speak for a minute. He stuffed his hands into his pockets, stared at the sandy earth and his feet. Held his mouth tight as if keeping words in. He drew a breath through his nostrils.

'Christ, Lucy, when will it end, hasn't there been enough —'

'You weren't there,' cut in Lucy, 'you don't know anything about it.'

'But he was your brother.'

'And so are you. He would have killed you, wouldn't he?'

'That's not the point —'

'Point? You think there's a point to all this?' She waved her arm around. 'I had no choice. You don't have to see me. I'll go now.'

'No wait, Lucy. I'm sorry. I want to see you, I've been looking forward to today, and so has Stefan. Please stay. I was just shocked. Not now, some other time, will you tell me about it?'

'I don't know, Rob. It's all been horrible.'

'Is that why you...' Rob waved a hand at Lucy's head.

'Cut my hair? Hah. Yes, no, I suppose. It doesn't matter.'

'What doesn't matter, your hair?'

'What matters is Emily is here, with Lottie. And they'll go

to Selmouth if the invite is still there. Is it?'

'Of course it is, but why are you angry with me?'

'I'm not. She has to take Quinn, of course, and Marcus wants to go. Will you have him?'

'Yes, he'll be welcome. He may have to wait until next week. There won't be room in the boat. I didn't know. I wouldn't have brought Ayisha and Stefan if I'd known there would be passengers.'

'Emily and Lottie aren't getting on, but she's hit it off with Marcus. I'd be worried about them being separated.'

'I get on with Lottie. I don't think you need worry, look.' Rob nodded at where Lottie and Stefan were crouched, heads together, investigating a rockpool. Lottie listened to whatever Stefan said with rapt attention. 'If it will help, she can stay with Ayisha and me until Marcus comes.'

'Emily will be relieved. She's got her hands full with Quinn.'

'Okay, when will you be coming? Next week with Marcus?'

Lucy paused a beat before she spoke. She looked at Rob, but her eye didn't see him, just stared through him into the distance. 'I'm not coming.'

'Why not? You'll enjoy it. There are people you'd get on with, people you'd like.'

'I'm not coming.' Company was the last thing she wanted. Today, Emily, Lottie and Quinn. Next week Marcus would leave. Just the rest of the Reevers and she would be alone.

'Don't decide now. Think about it. Let me know next week when I come for Marcus,' said Rob.

'I don't need to think about it.'

Rob looked at her. Her bald head gave her a raw look, almost savage. 'You've changed. Is it about Ben?'

'Like I said, Ben's dead. I killed him. He's gone. It can't be about him. It's about me. I won't be going to Selmouth.'

'I can tell you're hurting, Lucy. How can I help you?'

She made the mistake of looking at his eyes, full of concern for her. She flicked her glance away, over his shoulder into the distance, and drew a salty breath through her nose, her lips tight shut. She had decided her path and would tread it alone.

'Won't you need to be going soon?' she said, her voice flat, monotonic, her eye glazed, unfocused.

'Yes, we will. I'll see you next week. Won't I?'

She didn't answer.

'If you don't come to the cove, I'll come to the house,' he said. The determination in his voice jemmied its way into her brain.

Lucy shrugged her shoulders as if none of it mattered. 'Okay, I'll be here.'

Rob tried to hug her, but she turned away and walked over to the others. She didn't join the enthusiasm for change which Emily and Marcus shared, but remained silent, waiting for them to leave.

Lottie tried hard to be miserable as she boarded the little boat. Rob giving her the tiller and Marcus splashing from the shore brought a rare smile to her lips. Emily's sigh of relief as she stepped aboard, carrying Quinn, helped shrug the weight she'd been carrying from her shoulders.

'Wait,' called Marcus at Lottie, who stopped her splashing while Marcus leaned on the boat and gave Quinn a kiss on his forehead.

'You will come next week, Marky?' said Lottie.

'I'll come even if I have to swim,' he called, 'and you look after Quinn for me.'

Rob sculled the boat away from the shore before raising

the sail.

Marcus waved frantically from the shoreline, calling and shouting until the boat rounded a headland.

'It's exciting, isn't it?' he said, turning to Lucy.

Lucy gave him a wan smile. 'I suppose it is. I need to get back.' She stood and began the climb up to the path to Cleeve House.

Marcus followed her. During the walk back he asked occasional questions about Selmouth or Rob or sometimes Ben. Lucy gave single word answers, or said she didn't know, until Marcus too fell silent.

Chapter 62

At the end of The Lane Andy and Sue stared at Dunster Cottage. The walls still stood, but the windows and roof were gone.

'I don't think it's as bad as we expected,' said Andy.

'It looks a mess to me,' said Sue.

'I don't know. Some of the roofing timbers have survived, look.' Andy pointed at where the roof of the cottage once sheltered them.

'They look charred, they'll not be safe, surely.'

'They may not be up to Building Control standards, but they'll support some sort of shelter, corrugated iron or marine ply, say.'

'We only need to lay our hands on some and magic it over here.'

Sue's sarcasm went unnoticed by Andy. 'We could get some stuff from other abandoned houses. I think we can make this work.'

'You're serious, aren't you?'

'Yes, course I am. I don't want to stay at Cleeve House, it's a nightmare. Isn't that how you feel?'

'Of course I want to get out of there, it's horrible. I just —'

'There we are then. We could get the east end weatherproof in no time; then get started on the rest. We have most of the summer to get things ship shape.'

Sue said nothing. Andy took in her despondent face. 'What's wrong? I thought this is what you wanted.'

'I thought we might go to Selmouth, where Marcus is going. And baby Quinn will be there.'

'I hoped Stuart might come back. If we're not here, what will he do?' It was Andy's turn to look despondent.

'Andy, you've searched all over and found no trace of him.'

'It doesn't mean he isn't out there somewhere. We don't know what happened to him, all we know is he went missing. It's less than two weeks ago. He could be on his way here right now.'

'I wouldn't be surprised if Ben hadn't killed him. I never did trust him.'

'Don't say that, Sue. It's my son were talking about, not an animal.'

'It wouldn't have worried Ben though would it.'

'He might be dead, but I can't give up hoping, can I? You wouldn't if it were Marcus.'

'You may be right, Andy, but I don't want to stay here, on our own. There'll be other people at Selmouth, other families.'

'I should abandon my son and go off where he'll have no idea where to find me?'

'You think I should send both my son, and my grandson, away and maybe never see them again, just so I can keep you company in this ruin on the off-chance Stuart might do us the honour of a visit. Is that what you think?' Her eyes flashed anger, her mouth sprayed saliva.

For a few moments they glared at each other. 'It's been a while since we've had a serious falling out,' said Andy, a tentative smile turning the corners of his mouth and creasing his eyes.

'I guess we've been too busy keeping out of the way of... you know who.'

'I don't want to split you up from Marcus, of course I don't. And I know how fond you are of Quinn. I'm worried, that's all.'

'I understand, love. There's no hurry. But let's be serious about this. Is there really any chance of us finding the materials we need, transporting them back here, and making this place habitable? There's only two of us.'

'It would take a long time. But it could be done.'

'Here's another question. Do you want to live near the road again? Where any survivors might come past, might decide they like the look of the place?'

'You're thinking back to the night we left, aren't you?'

'Course I am, Andy. You haven't forgotten, have you?'

The vision of their last night at Dunster Cottage came back to Andy. Again, he saw his son standing at the window, crossbow in his hand, calmly killing the driver of the truck. The more he remembered of Stuart over the last nine months the more he realised how he'd changed. How once he'd fallen under Ben's sway those changes magnified. If Stuart did return, would he have any feelings for his father? Or just treat him with the barely hidden contempt he had of late?

'You might be right, Sue. Maybe we should go to Selmouth. Start over completely. Let's go to the cove to say goodbye to Marcus and we could talk to Rob about it, see if they'll have us.'

'You don't want to try and repair this place again?'

'No, I don't think I do. Let's make a fresh start. We've done it before.'

'Are you sure?'

'It's a couple of days' walk away. I could, maybe, come over now and then to see if there's any sign of Stuart. Even if I found him, I don't think he'd want to come and live with me again. Not after all we've been through.'

'It was a good place to live, but I think we need to move on,' said Sue.

'We'd better tell Lucy. You don't suppose she'll object, will she?'

'No, she encouraged Marcus. She can't say no to his mother.'

'Of course I think it's a good idea,' said Lucy, when Sue asked her about Selmouth. 'Marcus will be glad you're going too.'

'Do you think Rob will be okay with it, and all those other folks there?' asked Sue.

'Yes, and if he has room in the boat, he'll probably take you straight away.'

'D'you hear, Andy? We might be gone tomorrow.'

'Most likely, I should say,' said Lucy.

'Yes, I hear,' said Andy, 'I was thinking about Stuart. If he turns up will you tell him where we've gone?'

'Of course I will,' said Lucy. 'It's not too far, and I expect Rob will still sail his boat to the cove sometimes.'

'Are you sure?' asked Andy. 'I know you and him didn't get on.'

'That's in the past. Things have changed now. If I see him, I'll tell him you're at Selmouth. You know I keep my word.'

'That seems reasonable doesn't it?' said Sue.

Andy paused before speaking. 'I guess you're right,' he said, avoiding Sue's eye.

'What about you, Lucy, won't you be going?'

'I'm staying here. It's what I want. There's enough growing in the garden now, thanks to all your efforts, and

I'm looking forward to the quiet.' The Reevers didn't look convinced, but Lucy didn't care. 'Now I'm going to my room. I'll see you all tomorrow.'

'She's become a strange one,' said Andy, after Lucy had left.

'And her hair! Why did she do that to herself?'

'I might have done something similar myself if what's happened to her had happened to me,' said Andy.

'Hasn't it? If they won't have us at Selmouth we'll have to go elsewhere. I don't think I can stand it here any longer than I must. We've been through a terrible time here.'

'Yes, we have,' said Marcus, coming into the kitchen.

'We have what?' said Sue.

'Been through a lot. I can't wait to get away from here, I hate it.'

'Tomorrow you'll be off to see Quinn. You'll be glad of that,' said Sue.

'Yeah, I'm looking forward to it and to seeing...' he caught himself.

'You mean Emily?' said Sue.

Despite his mumbled denial Marcus's face gave him away. 'I'm too tired to talk anymore, I'm going to bed,' he said, getting up to go and sleep in the lounge.

Chapter 63

Lucy slipped from her room and out of the door while the Reevers talked at the kitchen table. She wandered past the empty and neglected chicken coop and up past the orchard until she came to the hovel. She stood silently outside for a few minutes before retracing her steps. Already Cleeve House felt changed. She passed by the house and walked up to the cairn and the five-bar gate, unopened in months. In the spring her father would have oiled the hinges and latch, treated the timbers, as he had every year; now neglect allowed nettles and brambles to grow around the gate posts and interlace the bars. She paused by the five graves and thought about the people buried there. Her father, gentle and forgiving to the last; her mother dead for sticking to the principles she believed. She took a breath standing before the empty grave of infant Adam, dead before he could experience life. Then Faye, so full of life, so young, dead through no one's fault, yet still Lucy felt responsible for her dying, even more responsible than for the death of her brother, Ben, lying in the last grave and killed by her own hand.

In the quiet moments she spent at these graves Lucy cried

silently. The tears rolled down her cheek and fell to her shirt, unnoticed. Here, alone, she allowed her grief to express itself, released the iron hold she kept on herself when before the others at Cleeve House. Soon they would all be gone, and she could allow her grief freedom.

An animal noise in the thickening night disturbed her reverie. She couldn't place the sound, too deep for a fox's bark. Lucy shook herself. Darkness had fallen and only starlight and a thin crescent moon lit her return to the now silent house.

Lucy took a candle stick from the kitchen to light her way to her room, standing it on the bedside table. She knew she wouldn't sleep but blew out the candle in a pretence of preparation. Laying on her bed, she replayed, again, the events of the last nine months. Again, she found places where a change in her actions would have made a difference. Again, she berated herself for her incompetence, her thoughtlessness, her self-indulgence. Again, she told herself it was all her fault. Again, as the night drew around her, she lay without sleep, her single eye wide open, her head spinning thought trails of what might have been.

Through the open window Lucy could hear a breeze whiffling through trees, nothing else. Apart from Marcus in the lounge below, the house was empty. She closed her eyes and slowed her breathing in her attempt at sleep. Then she was wide awake, eye open. Had she heard the creak of a floorboard? It couldn't be, why would Marcus come up here? The muffled rattle of the door handle sprang her upright and to intense concentration, her eye focused upon where she knew the door to be. The blackness of the door swung to a dim grey as it opened, and a figure stood briefly outlined in grey before stepping into the room.

'Marcus? Is it you, what do you want?' Her confidence undermined by the quaver in her voice.

A hand grabbed the clothes on her chest and gripped them tight, pulling her towards the intruder.

'Where's your fucking brother?' The voice was coarse and unmistakable.

'Stuart!'

The hand gripped her tighter, another slapped her face. 'Where's your fucking brother?'

'He's not here, he's…'

Another slap, harder, knocking Lucy's head to one side. 'Where the fuck is he? I've a score to settle.'

'He's dead.'

Another slap. 'You're lying, where is he?'

'I'm not, there's a grave, at the cairn, go and see.' Urgent desperation added believability to her plea. In the grey she saw him pause; arm raised. She readied herself for another blow.

'How?'

'I killed him.'

The blow was hard and heavy, she tasted blood in her mouth.

'You're lying again. He's your brother.'

'I had to after Faye.' Lucy spat blood from her mouth. 'She died but he ate her.'

'And you killed him for that?' She heard the sneer in his voice. 'You've saved me killing him myself. But it wasn't just him brought me here.'

Stuart pushed her down onto the bed and she heard the clink of a belt buckle. 'It's about time I had this, I've waited long enough.'

Lucy stretched her arm out, groping for the hockey stick, finding it. The swing at Stuart's head bounced off his shoulder. She pulled it back to swing again.

'You bitch,' said Stuart, blocking the blow with his arm and grabbing the stick. He gave it a twist and yanked it from her arm and tossed it behind him.

Lucy heard the stick clatter on the floor, then a fist thumped her head.

'Don't piss about with me. This time you're really going to get it.'

Lucy tried to scramble away across the bed, but he grabbed her, hitting her again, hard. The darkness swam about her, swirling around her head, sucking her down into the pitch black of unconsciousness.

As she came round someone was shaking her, shouting at her. She swung her arm and clenched fist, feeling it connect.

'Ow, Lucy, it's me. Are you all right?'

She shook her head a little, it hurt. 'Marcus? What... I don't... where's...'

'Are you okay? I thought you were dead.'

'No, I'm not dead, I'm not okay either. Where's...'

'I think I've killed him.'

Lucy's eye began to clear. In the dim light she forced herself to focus and looked at Marcus. The dawn would be arriving soon, the grey of early morning, winning over the grey of late night, spilled into the room. Still laying on the bed, she watched Marcus look at her, turn away, embarrassed. She pushed herself up, fighting the dizziness threatening to reclaim her, until she was sitting up on the bed, and pulled a sheet over herself. There was Stuart, on the floor, blood leaking from a wound in his head.

'What happened?'

'I heard a crash and thought something had happened to you. I came to look. The door was open, and I saw Stuart. He was... I saw the hockey stick, and you looked dead, I knew we'd never get to Selmouth if Stuart was here. I hit him. As hard as I could. I think he's dead. Andy will kill me.'

Lucy began to recover. She tried to stand but wobbled. 'Pass me that coat. Now help me stand, I need to get my bearings.'

'What am I going to do? I've killed Stuart, what's going to happen to me?'

'Sit down here next to me, no, the other side so we don't have to look at him. Now listen to me, Marcus. Nobody knows he's here.'

'How do you know?'

'I know, he told me. Nobody knows he's here and tomorrow you are leaving, and so is Andy and your mum. If you don't tell them neither will I.' She waited.

'You mean, don't tell them ever?'

'That's right don't ever tell them. Leave the body here, they'll never know, they never come to my room. Tomorrow, after you've all gone, I'll see to it.'

'You'll do that? For me?'

'Yes, Marcus. I'll do it for you, but you must promise me never to tell.'

'I'm useless at keeping secrets, Lucy, useless.'

'This time you can't be useless. This time you must keep it secret. Think of Quinn, he's going to need you.'

The enormity of the secret and the possibility of losing Quinn battled over Marcus's face.

'If anyone asks,' said Lucy, 'say you heard a bump in the night and found I had fallen over in the dark. It will explain my bruises. Can you do that?'

Marcus gulped. 'I'll try, yes I will.'

'The sun will be up soon. You go back to your room. I'll see you at breakfast and I'll thank you for looking after me in the night. Everyone will be fine with that. You'll go off to Selmouth and can forget all about this.'

Lucy closed the door behind Marcus and leaned against it, getting her breath. She looked over at Stuart laying on the floor. His head still bleeding. Then she heard him groan. She'd never checked, never felt for a pulse. How stupid she was, taking the word of Marcus. He was beginning to come round, a flicker of the eyelids. His eyes would be open in a minute, she cast around and there was the hockey stick, on the floor where Marcus had dropped it.

Keeping an arm's length away, she skirted the semi-conscious Stuart, and picked up the hockey stick. As she swung, his eyes opened and looked at her, his arm came up to protect him from the blow. The hook crushed into his fingers and into his head. It was the first of many blows rained down on Stuart until his head was a bloody pulp and Lucy was exhausted.

Chapter 64

When Lucy rounded the corner of the path to Goff's Cove and saw Rob landing his boat the tension fell away from her. She rolled her shoulders, stretched, and relaxed. She led the small, smiling, procession down the path, all of them waving at Rob. A slight breeze rippled the surface of the tranquil sea. The sun shone in a clear blue sky; a sky that would have brought Lucy joy a year ago, but now only relief at the prospect of finally being alone.

That morning she had done as she promised; thanking Marcus in front of Sue and Andy before they had chance to comment on the bruises on her face. No one questioned the cause of the bruises. Except Rob.

'What's happened to you?'

'I fell over in the dark, bashed myself.'

'Come on, Lucy, you don't...'

Lucy stretched out a hand and put it on his arm. 'Hush, don't ask. Not here,' she whispered.

'Hmm,' Rob grimaced. 'I have a gift for you. From Ayisha and everyone at Selmouth.' From the boat he lifted a small cage made from hazel twigs bound with baler twine. Inside were two small hens. 'Only bantams I'm afraid. The eggs won't be big or plentiful like the Welsummers, but they may help.'

'But you must need them. There are lots of mouths to feed at Selmouth.'

'These are for you; it was decided last night. We have plenty. We hatched lots this spring, and we can't feed them all. We want you to have these.'

'I don't have anything to give you.'

'We don't need anything, you've...' Rob stopped as he watched tears fall from his sister's cheek. She still held the chickens, and each sob shook the cage. Rob disentangled her fingers from the makeshift handle and set the cage down before enveloping her in his arms.

'I'm sorry, Rob,' she said, composing herself. 'It's just this is the first good thing that's happened for so long. I feel I need to give you something.'

'You've given Selmouth the best thing you ever could by sending Emily there. And now Marcus.'

'And I have yet another favour to ask,' she said.

'Ask away, there's nothing can shock me these days.'

'Can you take Andy and Sue as well?'

'All of them? You'll be alone.'

'Yes.'

'Suppose Stuart Reever returns?'

'He won't.'

She watched Rob absorb the certainty in her words, deciding not to challenge her.

'Are you sure it's what you want, to be alone?'

'It's what I need.'

Lucy watched Rob do some calculations in his head.

'You really do want to be alone. Okay, if they want to go, let's ask them.'

* * *

When the tide turned Marcus's growing excitement became infectious. Even Lucy smiled at him when he realised they would finally be leaving. Before they left Lucy responded to Rob's nodded request for a private chat.

'What's going on, Lucy? You're going to become a hermit, are you sure it's what you want?'

'I am, at least for a while.'

'I can't give up on you so easily. There's only you and me left from the family now. All we've got is each other. I'm still going to pitch up here every week. And if you're not here I'll come and find you.'

'You've forgotten Emily and Lottie. Besides, you've got Ayisha and Stefan to think about. I'll be fine.'

'I'm still going to come. And I'll bring Stefan sometimes and you don't want to make him walk all the way to Cleeve House, do you?'

'Okay, I'll be here.'

Lucy did her best to join the almost happy atmosphere which preceded setting sail for Selmouth. She shared a hurried whisper with a concerned Marcus and relieved him of responsibility for Stuart's demise. Then, with splashes and waves, shouts and blown kisses, they were gone. Sculled out of the cove into the sea and swept up the coast by the tide.

She watched them out of sight, then picked up the cage with the two bantams. 'Just the three of us now. Come on, girls, I'll show you your new home.' She set off on the slow walk back to Cleeve House.

Acknowledgements

This work would be a shadow of what it is without the insightful and freely shared thoughts of many people. I would like to thank some of them personally here. In no particular order I owe great thanks to: Penny Mountain, Paul Saville, Liz Wheeler, Bob Rowley, Katherine Stokes, Marianne Thomas, and Joanna Briffa. My sincere apologies to all the people I've missed who deserve to be here.

In addition, I would also like to thank members, past and present, of Cygneture Writers. Their feedback from early concept through to finished book has been invaluable.

My greatest thanks go to my wife, Jane, without whose forbearance and tolerance this book could never have been written.

Rik Lonsdale - January 2023

About the author

Rik Lonsdale's lifelong desire to write had been held in check through three previous careers and the raising of children. Eventually he was able to turn his energies to learning the art and craft of writing. Water and Blood, his first novel, was inspired by his concern for the future of civilisation and humanity.

Rik lives in Dorset, UK. When he isn't writing you can probably find him at the bottom of his garden tending his vegetable plot.

If you would like to know more about Rik and his writing journey you can find him at www.riklonsdale.com or on social media.

If you enjoyed 'Water and Blood' you can let the author know through his website, via social media, or by writing a review.